MEGA ROBO BROS

by NEILL CAMERON

ADDITIONAL COLORING by LISA MURPHY

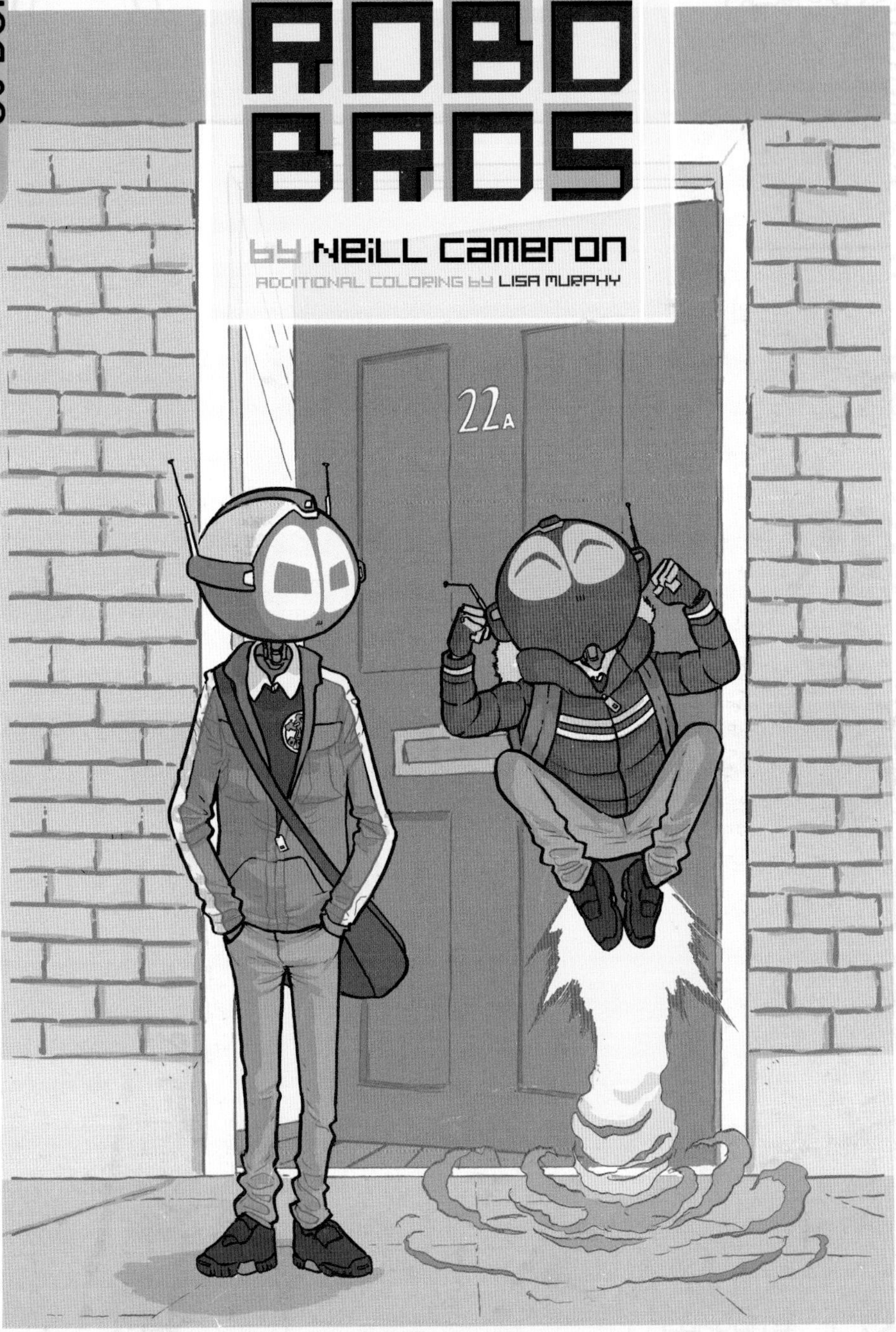
22A

FICKLING
dfb
David Fickling Books
the PHOENIX
SCHOLASTIC

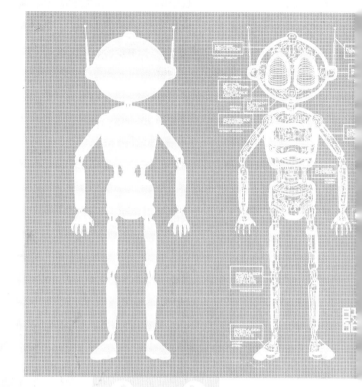

" to attend

For Logan. Obviously.

Text copyright © 2018 and illustrations copyright © 2016 by Neill Cameron

All rights reserved. Published by Scholastic Inc., *Publishers since 1920*, by
arrangement with David Fickling Books, Oxford, England. SCHOLASTIC and associated
logos are trademarks and/or registered trademarks of Scholastic Inc.
DAVID FICKLING BOOKS, THE PHOENIX, and associated logos are trademarks and/or
registered trademarks of David Fickling Books.

First published in the United Kingdom in 2016 by
David Fickling Books, 31 Beaumont Street, Oxford OX1 2NP.
www.davidficklingbooks.com

The publisher does not have any control over and does not assume any
responsibility for author or third-party websites or their content.

No part of this publication may be reproduced, stored in a retrieval system,
or transmitted in any form or by any means, electronic, mechanical, photocopying,
recording, or otherwise, without written permission of the publisher.
For information regarding permission, write to Scholastic Inc., Attention:
Permissions Department, 557 Broadway, New York, NY 10012.

This book is a work of fiction. Names, characters, places, and incidents
are either the product of the author's imagination or are used fictitiously, and
any resemblance to actual persons, living or dead, business establishments,
events, or locales is entirely coincidental.

Library of Congress Cataloging-in-Publication Data available

ISBN 978-1-338-18595-9

10 9 8 7 6 5 4 3 2 1   18 19 20 21 22

Printed in China   38
First edition, April 2018

on of their
empts at

CONTENTS

Meet the "Mega Robo Bros"

News // UK // Technology // Robotics

13 August
by V. Chandra, staff writer

On a quiet residential street near
Stepney Green in East London,
something extraordinary is happening.
Because one of these unassuming
terraced houses is home to Alex and
Freddy Sharma – two young brothers
who argue over all the usual brother stuff,
who play video games and love ice cream
and hanging out with their friends. And who
also happen to be the most sophisticated
robots in the country, or indeed
possibly the world.

No one's quite sure on that last point –
in part because so few reporters have
been given access to the boys. Their adopted
mother is the world-renowned cyberneticist
Doctor Nita Sharma, Chief Scientific Officer
of R.A.I.D., and she guards their privacy
fiercely. I've been granted a rare interview
today, but when I arrive at their door I can't
help but feel Dr. Sharma is eyeing me
suspiciously; her manner is very quiet
and reserved.

Freddy is, on the other hand, is less so.
I enter the living room to find him charging
around with a pair of bright purple
underpants on his head, yelling "EAT YOUR

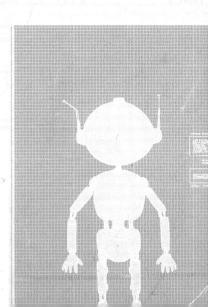

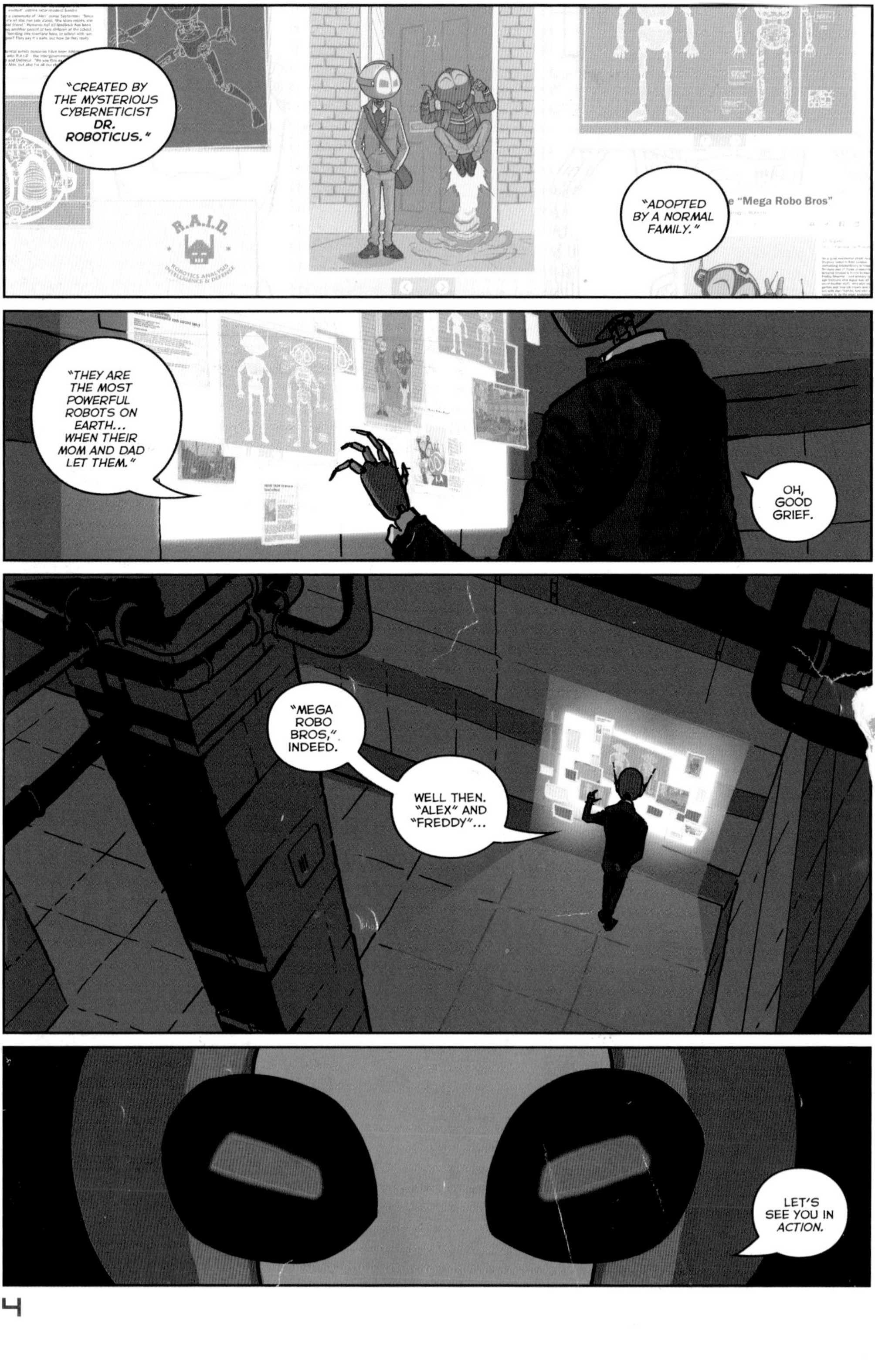
"CREATED BY THE MYSTERIOUS CYBERNETICIST DR. ROBOTICUS."
R.A.I.D.
ROBOTICS ANALYSIS INTELLIGENCE & DEFENSE
"ADOPTED BY A NORMAL FAMILY."
"Mega Robo Bros"
"THEY ARE THE MOST POWERFUL ROBOTS ON EARTH... WHEN THEIR MOM AND DAD LET THEM."
OH, GOOD GRIEF.
"MEGA ROBO BROS," INDEED.
WELL THEN. "ALEX" AND "FREDDY"...
LET'S SEE YOU IN *ACTION.*

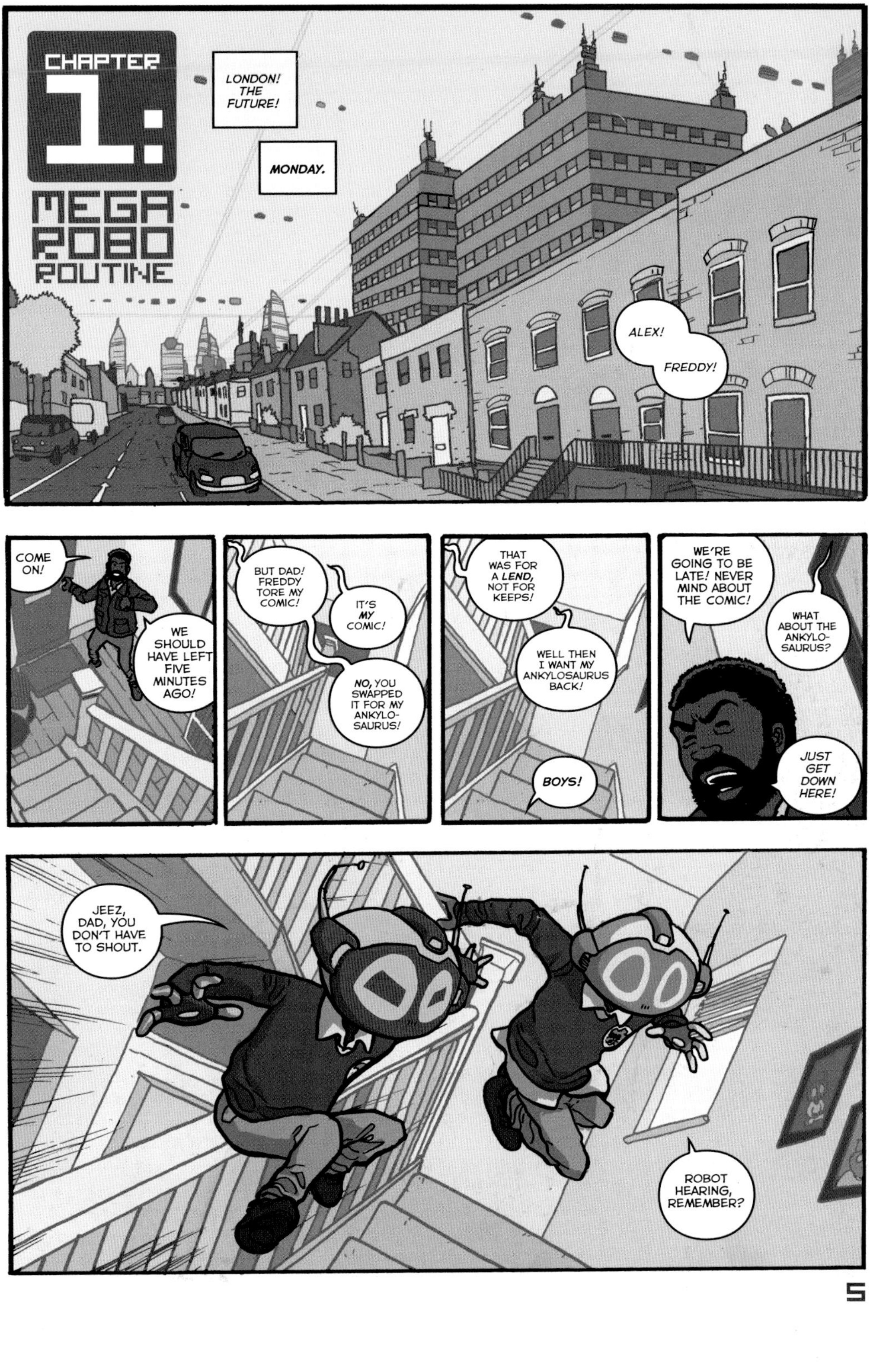
CHAPTER 1:
MEGA ROBO ROUTINE
LONDON! THE FUTURE!
MONDAY.
ALEX!
FREDDY!
COME ON!
WE SHOULD HAVE LEFT FIVE MINUTES AGO!
BUT DAD! FREDDY TORE MY COMIC!
IT'S MY COMIC!
NO, YOU SWAPPED IT FOR MY ANKYLOSAURUS!
THAT WAS FOR A LEND, NOT FOR KEEPS!
WELL THEN I WANT MY ANKYLOSAURUS BACK!
BOYS!
WE'RE GOING TO BE LATE! NEVER MIND ABOUT THE COMIC!
WHAT ABOUT THE ANKYLOSAURUS?
JUST GET DOWN HERE!
JEEZ, DAD, YOU DON'T HAVE TO SHOUT.
ROBOT HEARING, REMEMBER?

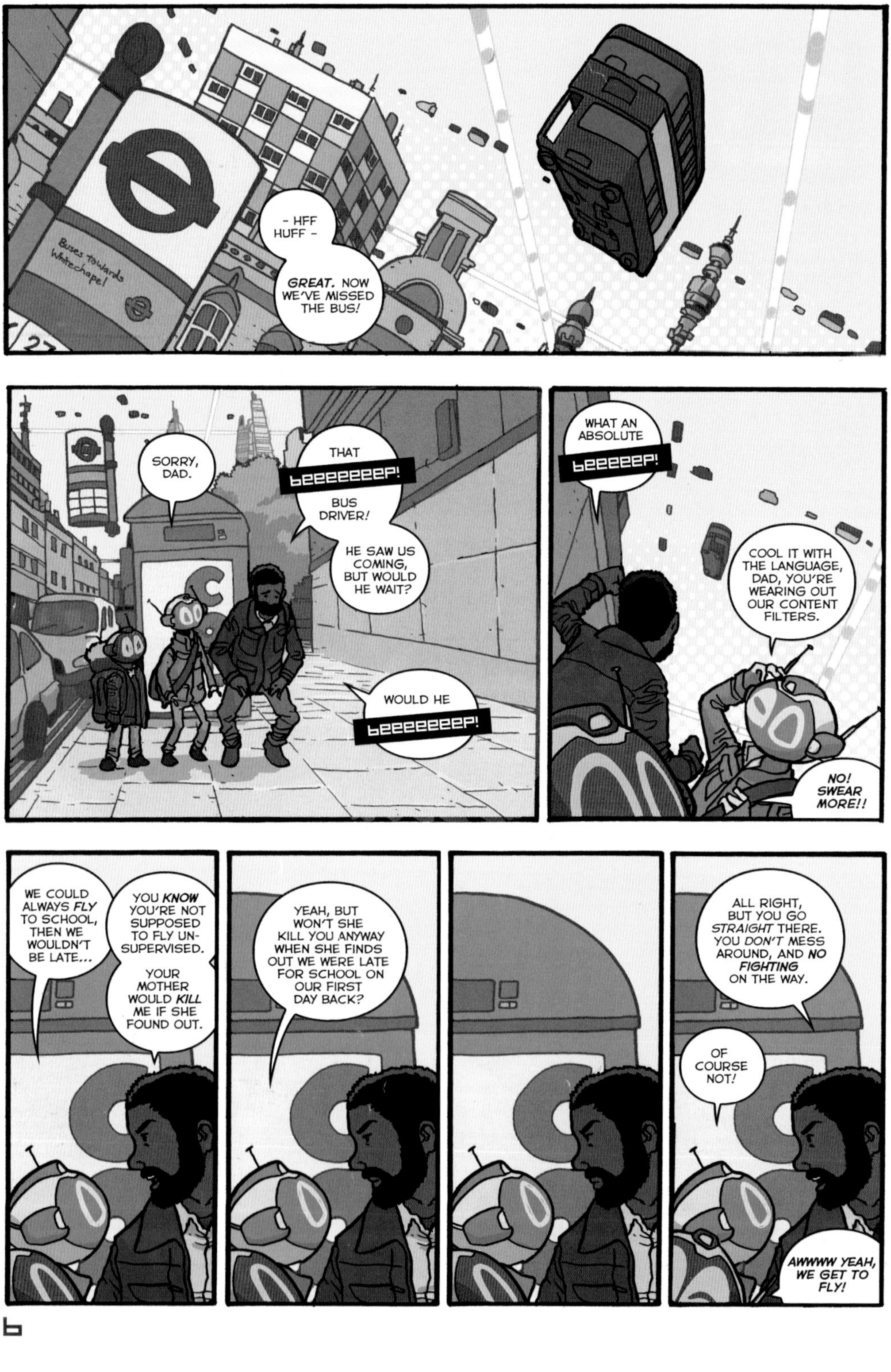
Buses towards Whitechapel
- HFF HUFF -
GREAT. NOW WE'VE MISSED THE BUS!
SORRY, DAD.
THAT
beeeeeeep!
BUS DRIVER!
HE SAW US COMING, BUT WOULD HE WAIT?
WOULD HE
beeeeeeep!
WHAT AN ABSOLUTE
beeeeep!
COOL IT WITH THE LANGUAGE, DAD, YOU'RE WEARING OUT OUR CONTENT FILTERS.
NO! SWEAR MORE!!
WE COULD ALWAYS FLY TO SCHOOL, THEN WE WOULDN'T BE LATE...
YOU KNOW YOU'RE NOT SUPPOSED TO FLY UN-SUPERVISED.
YOUR MOTHER WOULD KILL ME IF SHE FOUND OUT.
YEAH, BUT WON'T SHE KILL YOU ANYWAY WHEN SHE FINDS OUT WE WERE LATE FOR SCHOOL ON OUR FIRST DAY BACK?
ALL RIGHT, BUT YOU GO STRAIGHT THERE. YOU DON'T MESS AROUND, AND NO FIGHTING ON THE WAY.
OF COURSE NOT!
AWWWW YEAH, WE GET TO FLY!

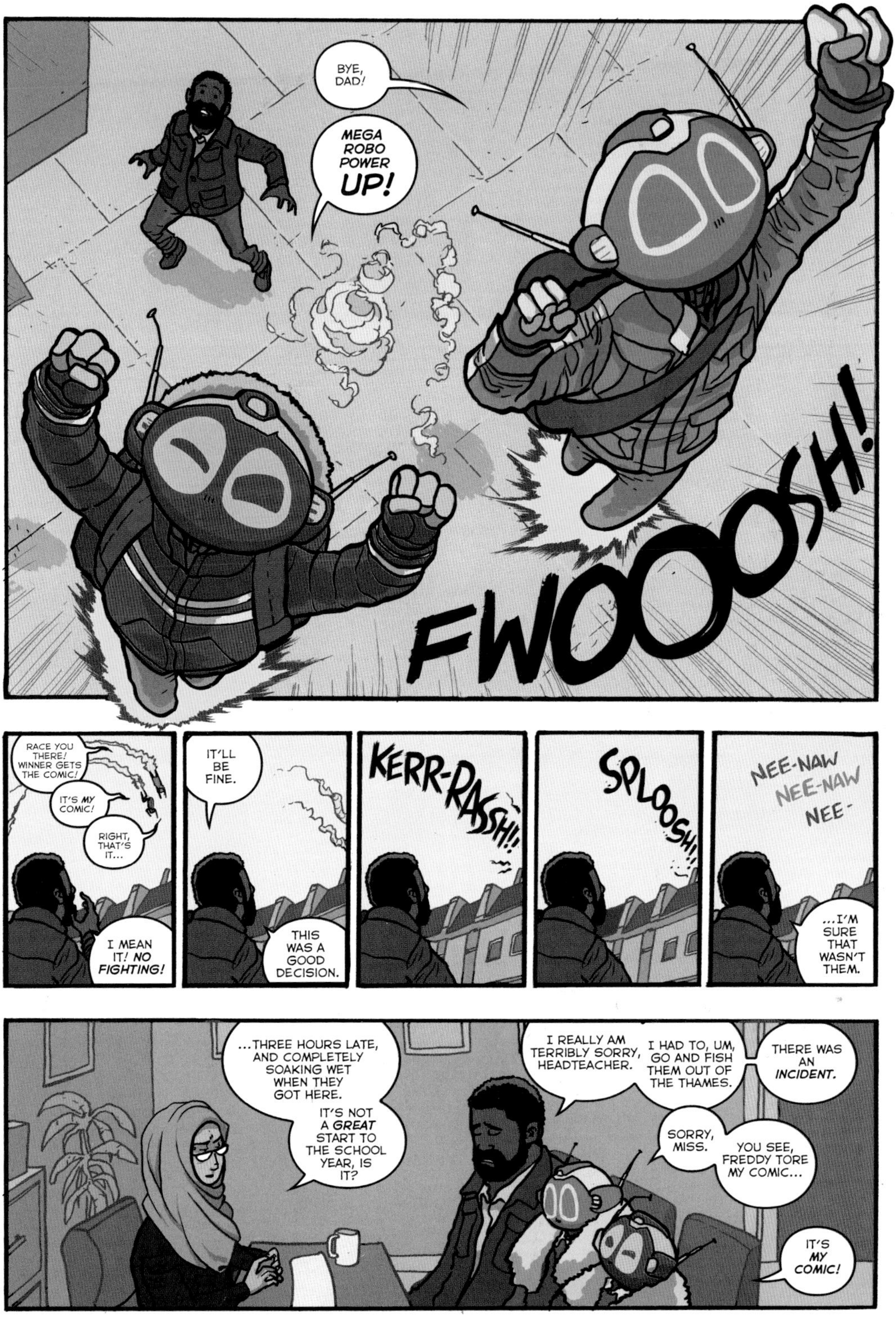
BYE, DAD!
MEGA ROBO POWER UP!
FWOOOOSH!
RACE YOU THERE! WINNER GETS THE COMIC!
IT'S MY COMIC!
RIGHT, THAT'S IT...
I MEAN IT! NO FIGHTING!
IT'LL BE FINE.
THIS WAS A GOOD DECISION.
KERR-RASSH!!
SPLOOSH!!
NEE-NAW NEE-NAW NEE-
...I'M SURE THAT WASN'T THEM.
...THREE HOURS LATE, AND COMPLETELY SOAKING WET WHEN THEY GOT HERE.
IT'S NOT A GREAT START TO THE SCHOOL YEAR, IS IT?
I REALLY AM TERRIBLY SORRY, HEADTEACHER.
I HAD TO, UM, GO AND FISH THEM OUT OF THE THAMES.
THERE WAS AN INCIDENT.
SORRY, MISS.
YOU SEE, FREDDY TORE MY COMIC...
IT'S MY COMIC!

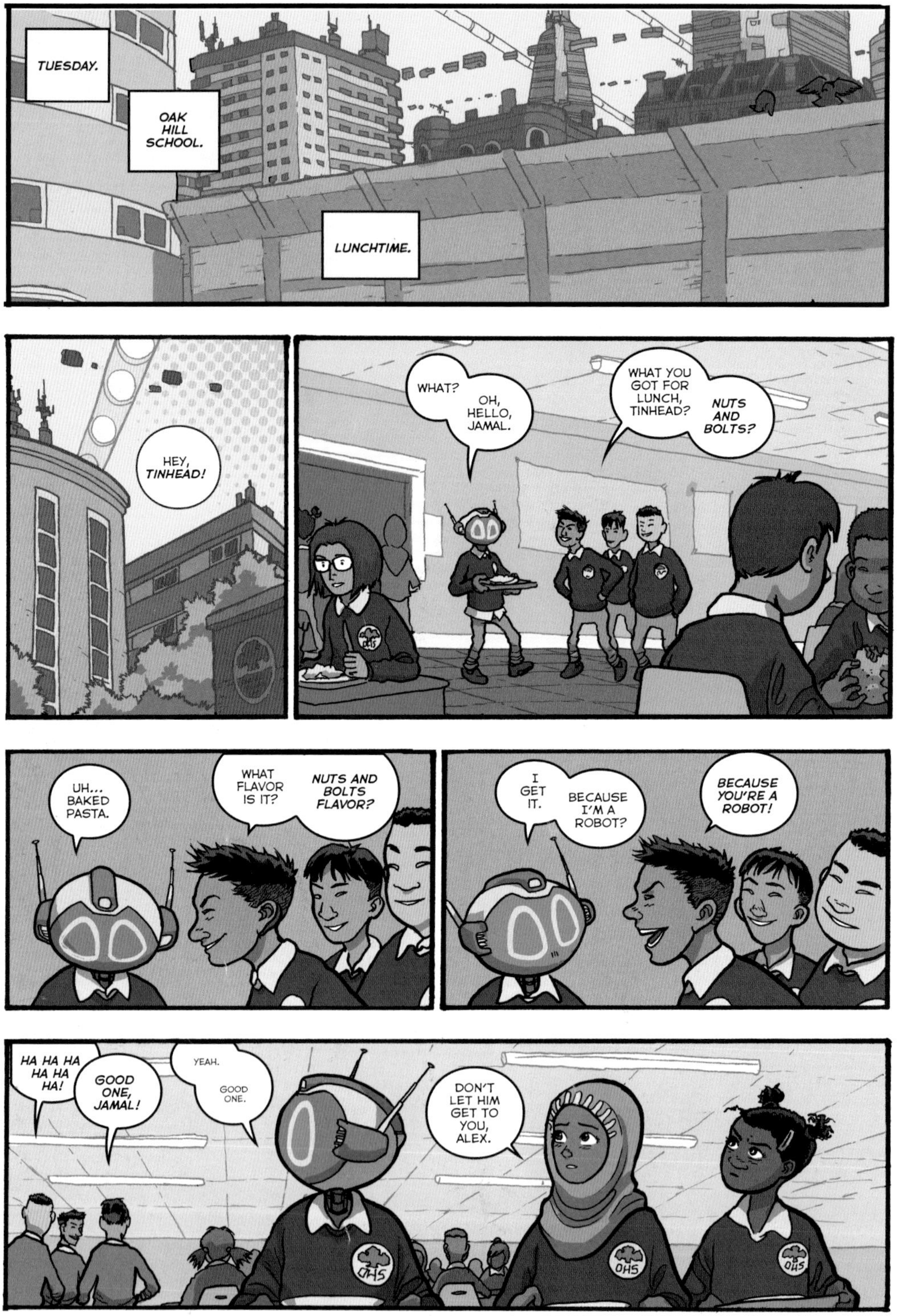
TUESDAY.
OAK HILL SCHOOL.
LUNCHTIME.
HEY, TINHEAD!
WHAT?
OH, HELLO, JAMAL.
WHAT YOU GOT FOR LUNCH, TINHEAD?
NUTS AND BOLTS?
UH... BAKED PASTA.
WHAT FLAVOR IS IT?
NUTS AND BOLTS FLAVOR?
I GET IT.
BECAUSE I'M A ROBOT?
BECAUSE YOU'RE A ROBOT!
HA HA HA HA HA HA!
GOOD ONE, JAMAL!
YEAH.
GOOD ONE.
DON'T LET HIM GET TO YOU, ALEX.

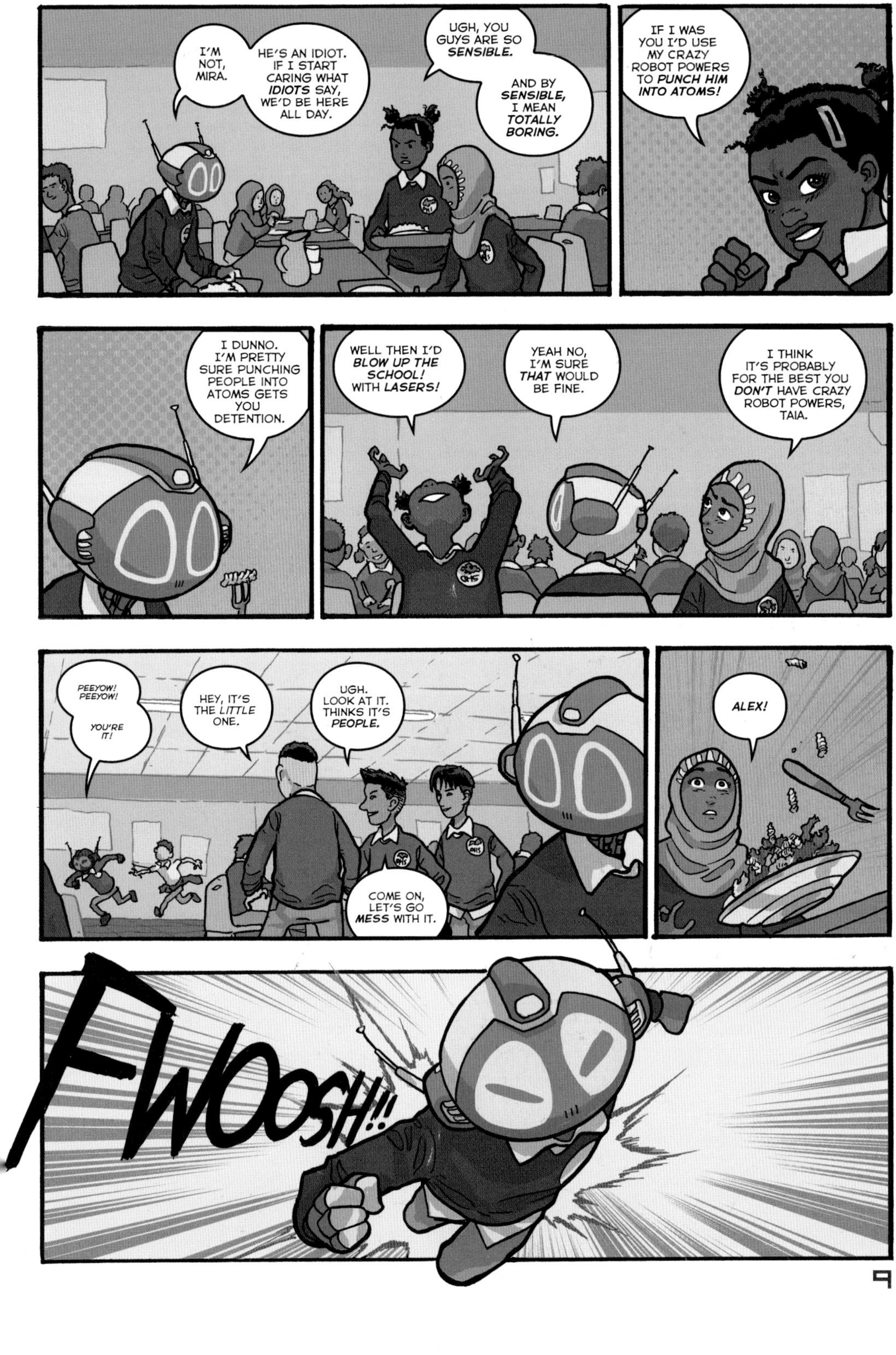
I'M NOT, MIRA.
HE'S AN IDIOT. IF I START CARING WHAT IDIOTS SAY, WE'D BE HERE ALL DAY.
UGH, YOU GUYS ARE SO SENSIBLE.
AND BY SENSIBLE, I MEAN TOTALLY BORING.
IF I WAS YOU I'D USE MY CRAZY ROBOT POWERS TO PUNCH HIM INTO ATOMS!
I DUNNO. I'M PRETTY SURE PUNCHING PEOPLE INTO ATOMS GETS YOU DETENTION.
WELL THEN I'D BLOW UP THE SCHOOL! WITH LASERS!
YEAH NO, I'M SURE THAT WOULD BE FINE.
I THINK IT'S PROBABLY FOR THE BEST YOU DON'T HAVE CRAZY ROBOT POWERS, TAIA.
PEEYOW! PEEYOW!
YOU'RE IT!
HEY, IT'S THE LITTLE ONE.
UGH. LOOK AT IT. THINKS IT'S PEOPLE.
COME ON, LET'S GO MESS WITH IT.
ALEX!
FWOOSH!!

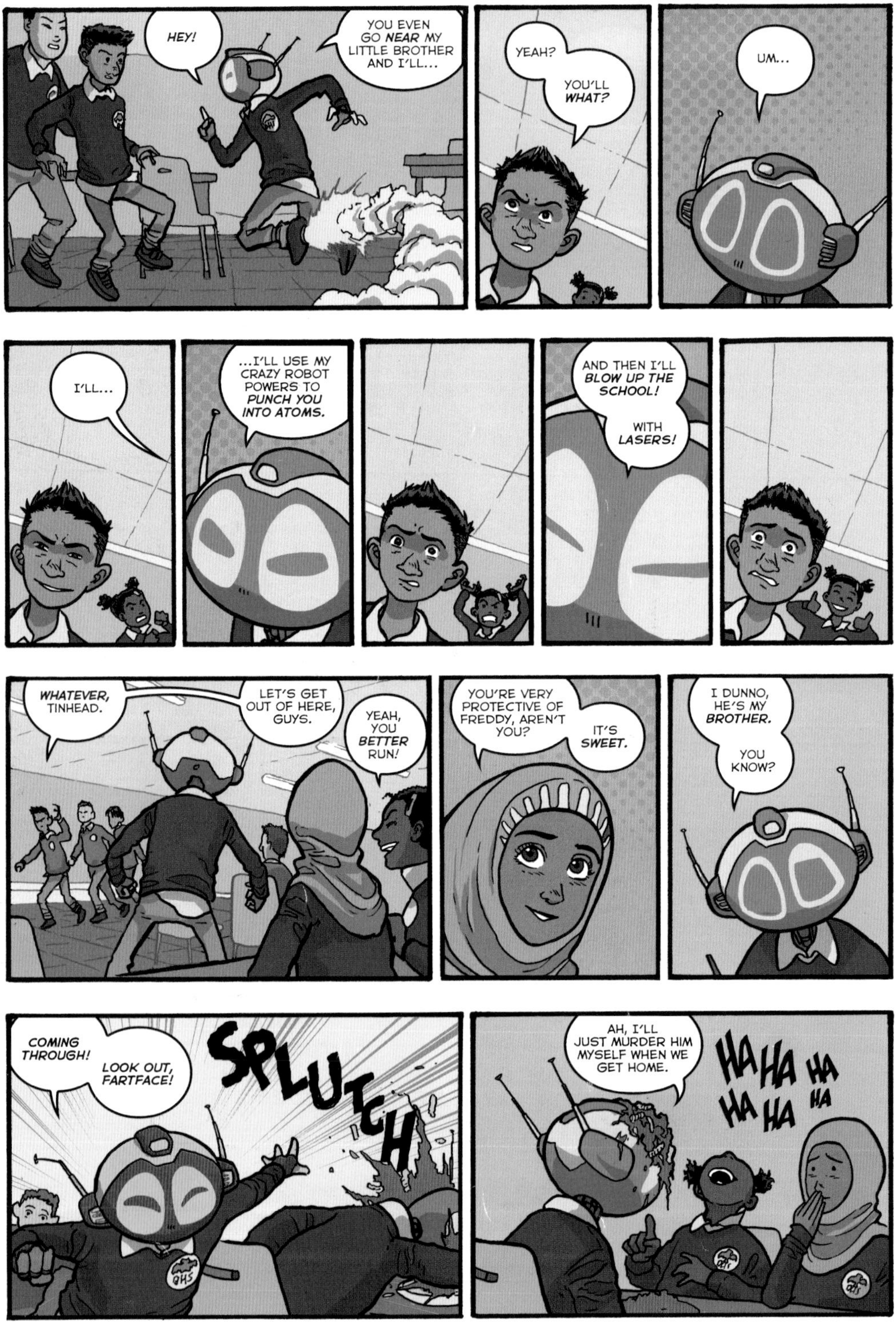
HEY!
YOU EVEN GO NEAR MY LITTLE BROTHER AND I'LL...
YEAH?
YOU'LL WHAT?
UM...
I'LL...
...I'LL USE MY CRAZY ROBOT POWERS TO PUNCH YOU INTO ATOMS.
AND THEN I'LL BLOW UP THE SCHOOL!
WITH LASERS!
WHATEVER, TINHEAD.
LET'S GET OUT OF HERE, GUYS.
YEAH, YOU BETTER RUN!
YOU'RE VERY PROTECTIVE OF FREDDY, AREN'T YOU?
IT'S SWEET.
I DUNNO, HE'S MY BROTHER.
YOU KNOW?
COMING THROUGH!
LOOK OUT, FARTFACE!
SPLUTCH
AH, I'LL JUST MURDER HIM MYSELF WHEN WE GET HOME.
HA HA HA HA HA HA

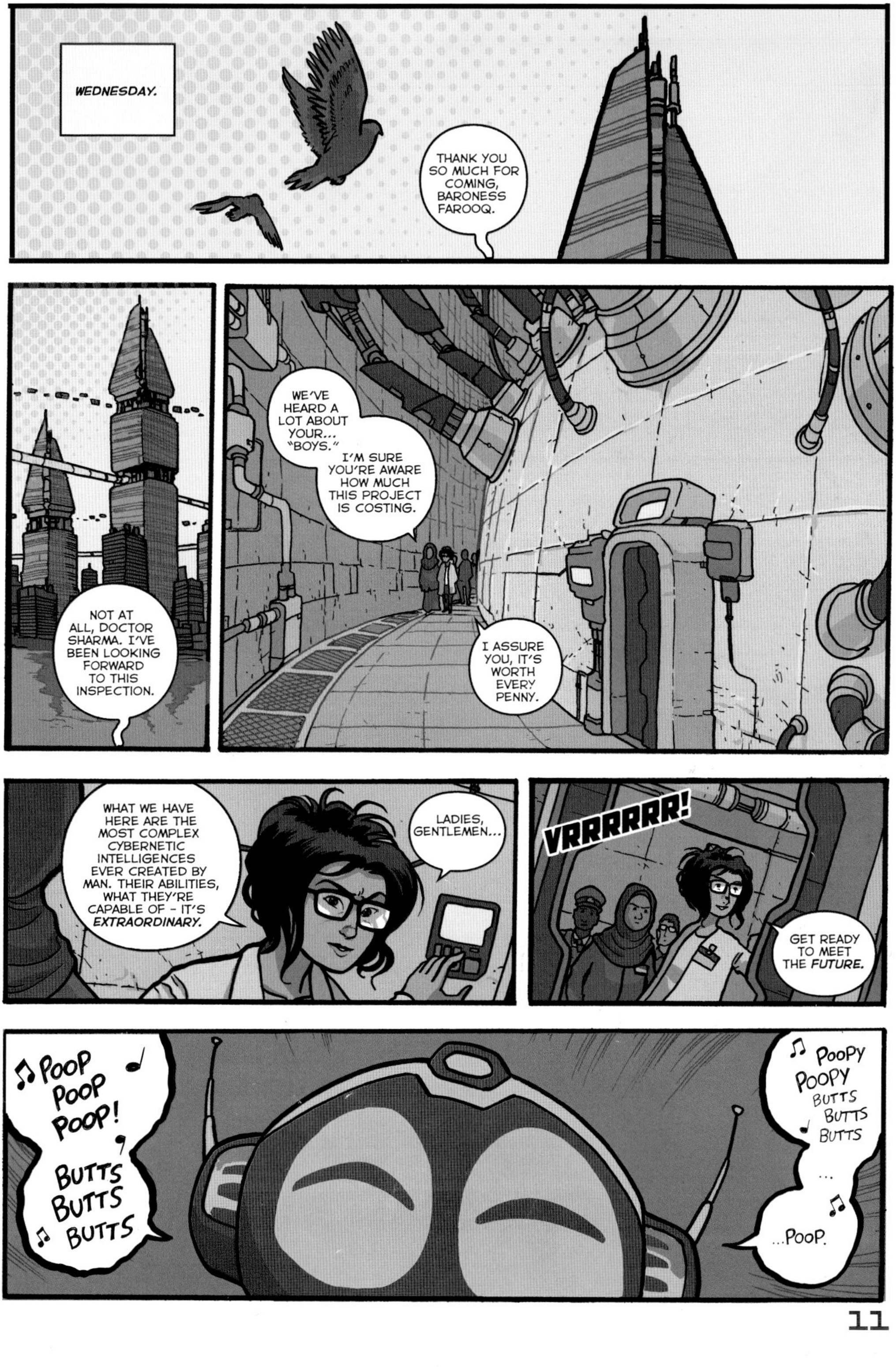

WEDNESDAY.
THANK YOU SO MUCH FOR COMING, BARONESS FAROOQ.
NOT AT ALL, DOCTOR SHARMA. I'VE BEEN LOOKING FORWARD TO THIS INSPECTION.
WE'VE HEARD A LOT ABOUT YOUR... "BOYS."
I'M SURE YOU'RE AWARE HOW MUCH THIS PROJECT IS COSTING.
I ASSURE YOU, IT'S WORTH EVERY PENNY.
WHAT WE HAVE HERE ARE THE MOST COMPLEX CYBERNETIC INTELLIGENCES EVER CREATED BY MAN. THEIR ABILITIES, WHAT THEY'RE CAPABLE OF - IT'S *EXTRAORDINARY.*
LADIES, GENTLEMEN...
VRRRRRR!
GET READY TO MEET THE *FUTURE.*
POOP POOP POOP! BUTTS BUTTS BUTTS
POOPY POOPY BUTTS BUTTS BUTTS
...
...POOP.

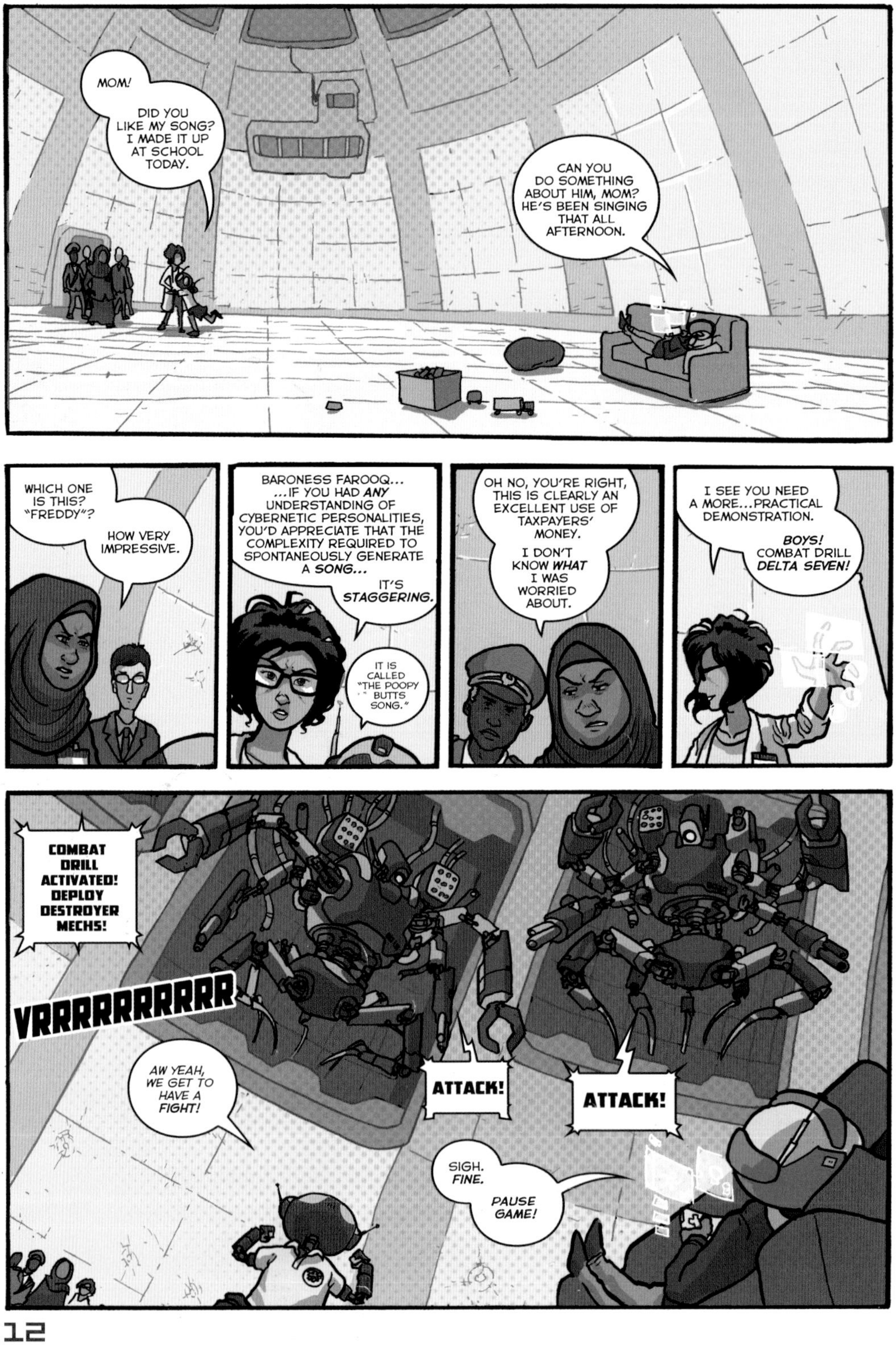

MOM!
DID YOU LIKE MY SONG? I MADE IT UP AT SCHOOL TODAY.
CAN YOU DO SOMETHING ABOUT HIM, MOM? HE'S BEEN SINGING THAT ALL AFTERNOON.
WHICH ONE IS THIS? "FREDDY"?
HOW VERY IMPRESSIVE.
BARONESS FAROOQ... ...IF YOU HAD ANY UNDERSTANDING OF CYBERNETIC PERSONALITIES, YOU'D APPRECIATE THAT THE COMPLEXITY REQUIRED TO SPONTANEOUSLY GENERATE A SONG...
IT'S STAGGERING.
IT IS CALLED "THE POOPY BUTTS SONG."
OH NO, YOU'RE RIGHT, THIS IS CLEARLY AN EXCELLENT USE OF TAXPAYERS' MONEY.
I DON'T KNOW WHAT I WAS WORRIED ABOUT.
I SEE YOU NEED A MORE...PRACTICAL DEMONSTRATION.
BOYS! COMBAT DRILL DELTA SEVEN!
COMBAT DRILL ACTIVATED! DEPLOY DESTROYER MECHS!
VRRRRRRRRRR
AW YEAH, WE GET TO HAVE A FIGHT!
ATTACK!
ATTACK!
SIGH. FINE.
PAUSE GAME!

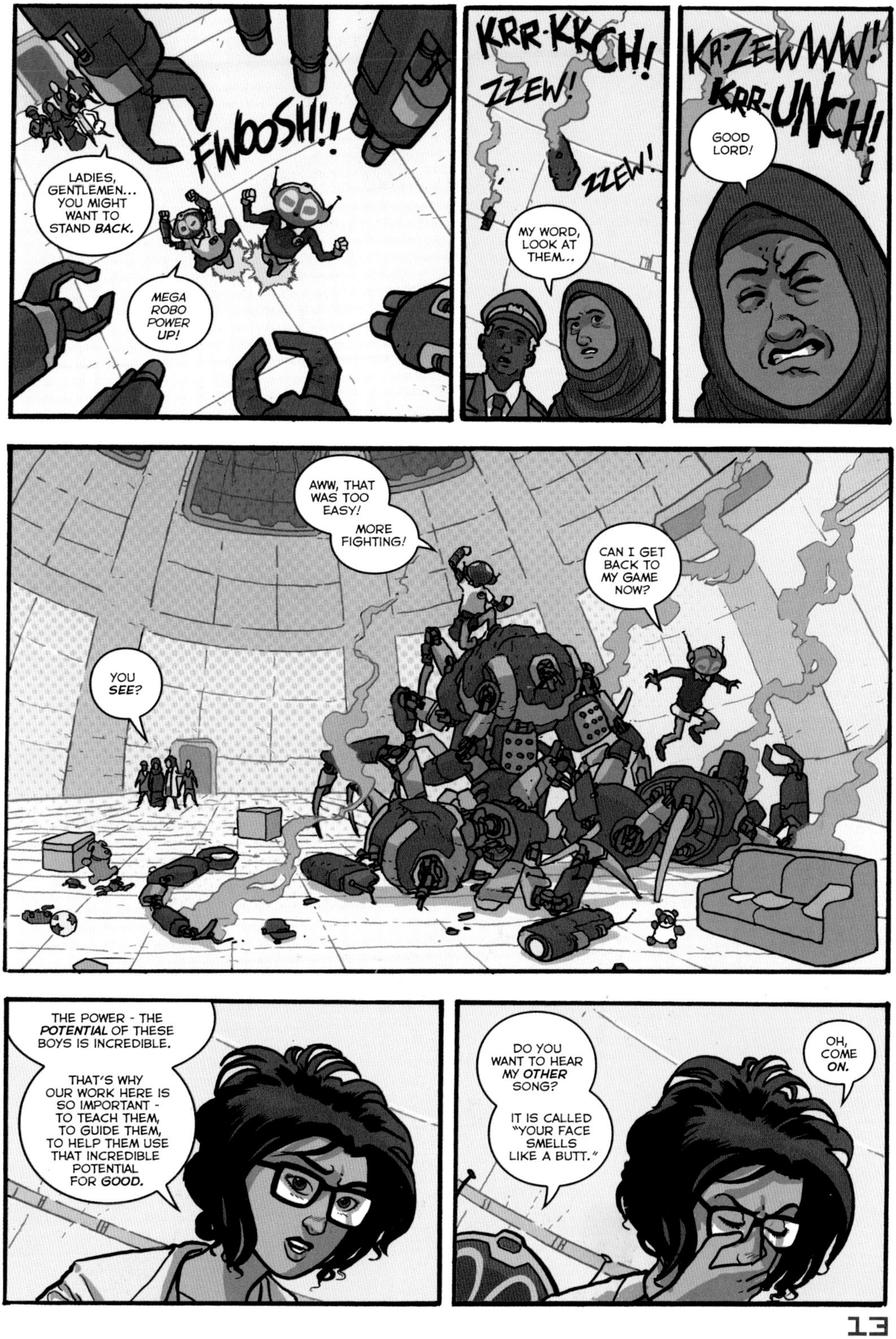
FWOOSH!!
LADIES, GENTLEMEN... YOU MIGHT WANT TO STAND BACK.
MEGA ROBO POWER UP!
KRR-KKCH!
ZZEW!
ZZEW!
MY WORD, LOOK AT THEM...
KR-ZEWWW!
KRR-UNCH!
GOOD LORD!
AWW, THAT WAS TOO EASY!
MORE FIGHTING!
CAN I GET BACK TO MY GAME NOW?
YOU SEE?
THE POWER - THE POTENTIAL OF THESE BOYS IS INCREDIBLE.
THAT'S WHY OUR WORK HERE IS SO IMPORTANT - TO TEACH THEM, TO GUIDE THEM, TO HELP THEM USE THAT INCREDIBLE POTENTIAL FOR GOOD.
DO YOU WANT TO HEAR MY OTHER SONG?
IT IS CALLED "YOUR FACE SMELLS LIKE A BUTT."
OH, COME ON.

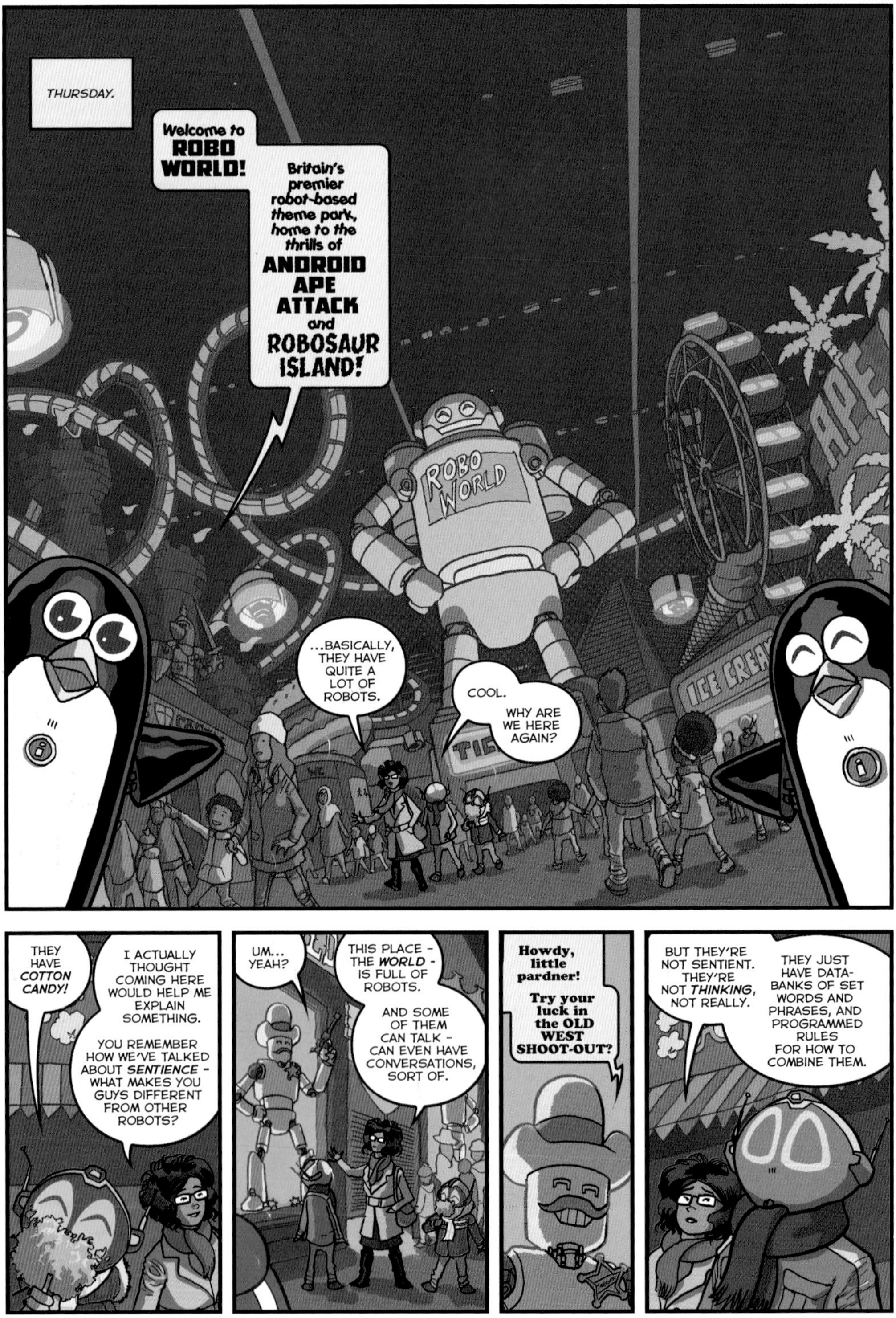
THURSDAY.
Welcome to ROBO WORLD!
Britain's premier robot-based theme park, home to the thrills of ANDROID APE ATTACK and ROBOSAUR ISLAND!
ROBO WORLD
...BASICALLY, THEY HAVE QUITE A LOT OF ROBOTS.
COOL.
WHY ARE WE HERE AGAIN?
ICE CREA
THEY HAVE COTTON CANDY!
I ACTUALLY THOUGHT COMING HERE WOULD HELP ME EXPLAIN SOMETHING.
YOU REMEMBER HOW WE'VE TALKED ABOUT SENTIENCE - WHAT MAKES YOU GUYS DIFFERENT FROM OTHER ROBOTS?
UM... YEAH?
THIS PLACE - THE WORLD - IS FULL OF ROBOTS.
AND SOME OF THEM CAN TALK - CAN EVEN HAVE CONVERSATIONS, SORT OF.
Howdy, little pardner!
Try your luck in the OLD WEST SHOOT-OUT?
BUT THEY'RE NOT SENTIENT. THEY'RE NOT THINKING, NOT REALLY.
THEY JUST HAVE DATA-BANKS OF SET WORDS AND PHRASES, AND PROGRAMMED RULES FOR HOW TO COMBINE THEM.

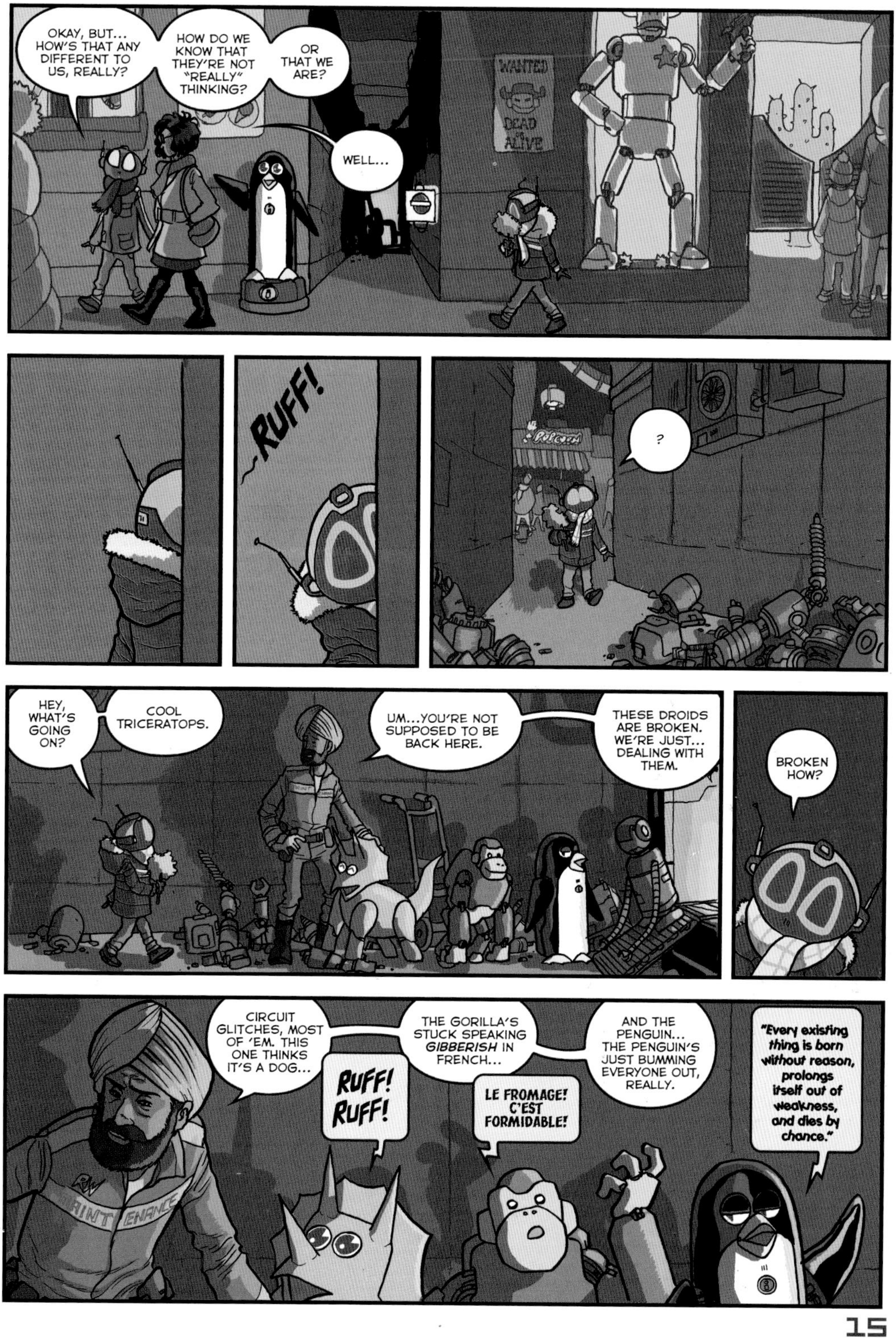
OKAY, BUT... HOW'S THAT ANY DIFFERENT TO US, REALLY?
HOW DO WE KNOW THAT THEY'RE NOT "REALLY" THINKING?
OR THAT WE ARE?
WANTED DEAD OR ALIVE
WELL...
RUFF!
?
HEY, WHAT'S GOING ON?
COOL TRICERATOPS.
UM...YOU'RE NOT SUPPOSED TO BE BACK HERE.
THESE DROIDS ARE BROKEN. WE'RE JUST... DEALING WITH THEM.
BROKEN HOW?
CIRCUIT GLITCHES, MOST OF 'EM. THIS ONE THINKS IT'S A DOG...
RUFF! RUFF!
THE GORILLA'S STUCK SPEAKING *GIBBERISH* IN FRENCH...
LE FROMAGE! C'EST FORMIDABLE!
AND THE PENGUIN... THE PENGUIN'S JUST BUMMING EVERYONE OUT, REALLY.
"Every existing thing is born without reason, prolongs itself out of weakness, and dies by chance."
MAINTENANCE

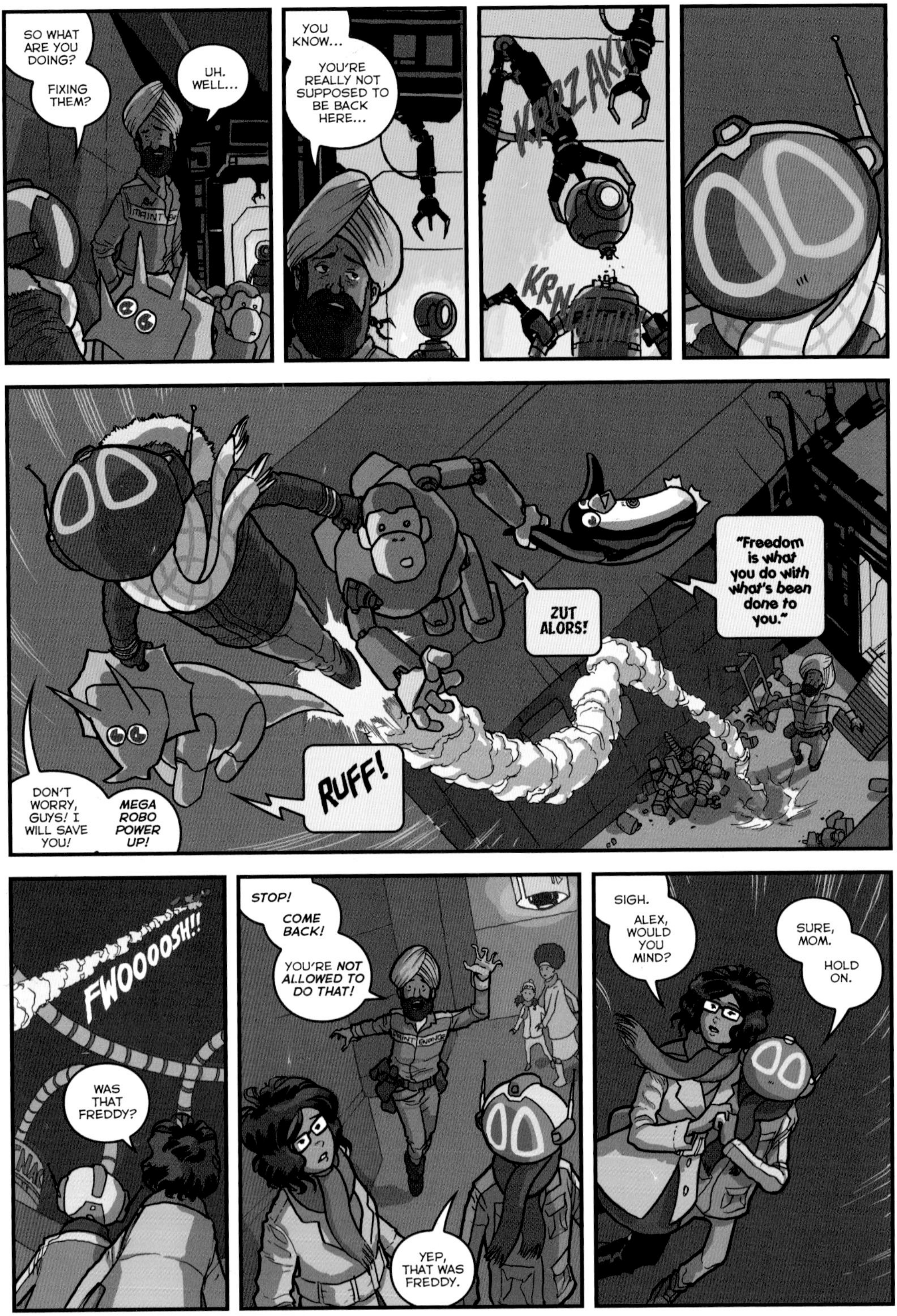
SO WHAT ARE YOU DOING?
FIXING THEM?
UH. WELL...
YOU KNOW...
YOU'RE REALLY NOT SUPPOSED TO BE BACK HERE...
KRRZAK!
KRN
"Freedom is what you do with what's been done to you."
ZUT ALORS!
DON'T WORRY, GUYS! I WILL SAVE YOU!
MEGA ROBO POWER UP!
RUFF!
FWOOOOSH!!
WAS THAT FREDDY?
STOP!
COME BACK!
YOU'RE NOT ALLOWED TO DO THAT!
YEP, THAT WAS FREDDY.
SIGH.
ALEX, WOULD YOU MIND?
SURE, MOM.
HOLD ON.

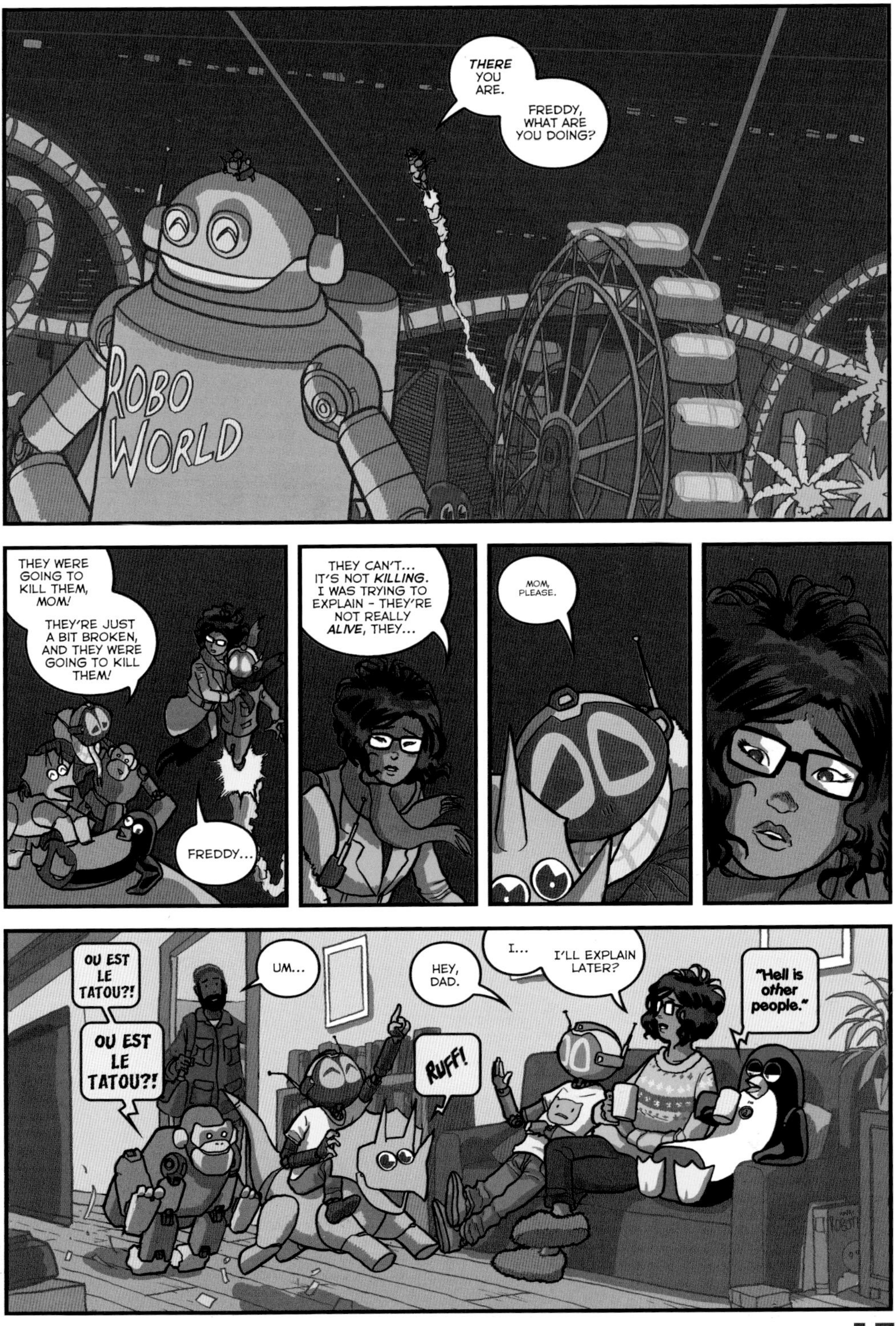
THERE YOU ARE.
FREDDY, WHAT ARE YOU DOING?
ROBO WORLD
THEY WERE GOING TO KILL THEM, MOM!
THEY'RE JUST A BIT BROKEN, AND THEY WERE GOING TO KILL THEM!
FREDDY...
THEY CAN'T... IT'S NOT KILLING. I WAS TRYING TO EXPLAIN - THEY'RE NOT REALLY ALIVE, THEY...
MOM, PLEASE.
OU EST LE TATOU?!
OU EST LE TATOU?!
UM...
HEY, DAD.
I...
I'LL EXPLAIN LATER?
"Hell is other people."
RUFF!

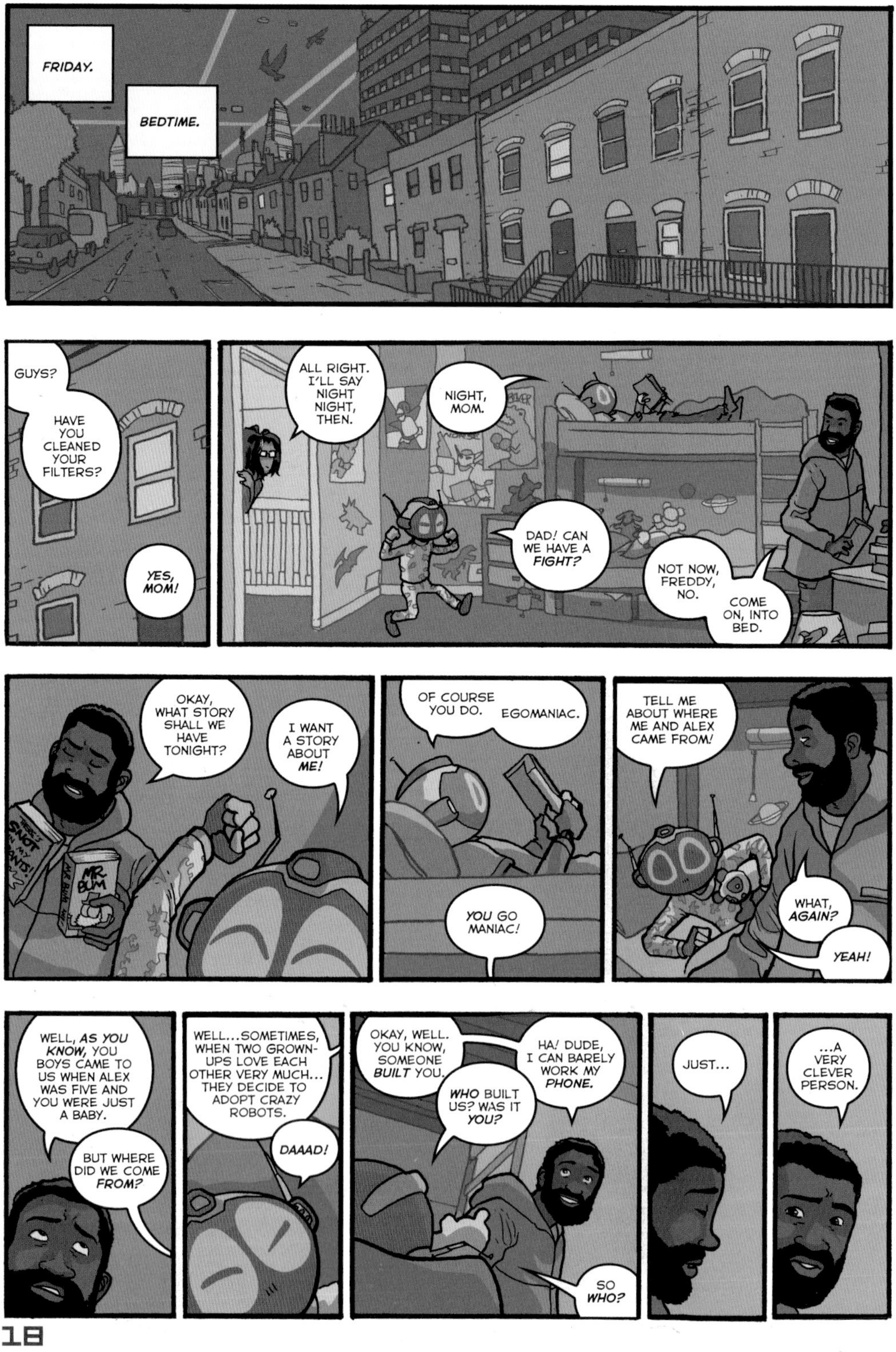
FRIDAY.
BEDTIME.
GUYS?
HAVE YOU CLEANED YOUR FILTERS?
YES, MOM!
ALL RIGHT. I'LL SAY NIGHT NIGHT, THEN.
NIGHT, MOM.
DAD! CAN WE HAVE A FIGHT?
NOT NOW, FREDDY, NO.
COME ON, INTO BED.
OKAY, WHAT STORY SHALL WE HAVE TONIGHT?
I WANT A STORY ABOUT ME!
OF COURSE YOU DO.
EGOMANIAC.
YOU GO MANIAC!
TELL ME ABOUT WHERE ME AND ALEX CAME FROM!
WHAT, AGAIN?
YEAH!
WELL, AS YOU KNOW, YOU BOYS CAME TO US WHEN ALEX WAS FIVE AND YOU WERE JUST A BABY.
BUT WHERE DID WE COME FROM?
WELL...SOMETIMES, WHEN TWO GROWN-UPS LOVE EACH OTHER VERY MUCH... THEY DECIDE TO ADOPT CRAZY ROBOTS.
DAAAD!
OKAY, WELL. YOU KNOW, SOMEONE BUILT YOU.
WHO BUILT US? WAS IT YOU?
HA! DUDE, I CAN BARELY WORK MY PHONE.
SO WHO?
JUST...
...A VERY CLEVER PERSON.

SO WHAT HAPPENED TO HIM? THE CLEVER PERSON?

FREDDY...

IT'S A REALLY LONG STORY. I'LL TELL YOU ALL ABOUT IT WHEN YOU'RE OLDER, I PROMISE.

OKAY, TIME FOR BED.

SLEEP TIGHT, GUYS.

NIGHT, DAD.

THAT STORY WAS...

UNSATISFACTORY.

ALEX?

DO YOU REMEMBER WHAT IT WAS LIKE, BEFORE?

YOU WERE OLDER.

I DON'T REMEMBER *ANYTHING.*

NNN

NNOoO

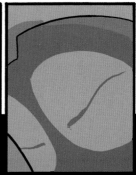

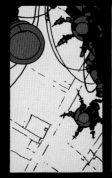

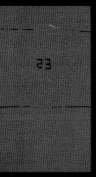

23

NO.

19

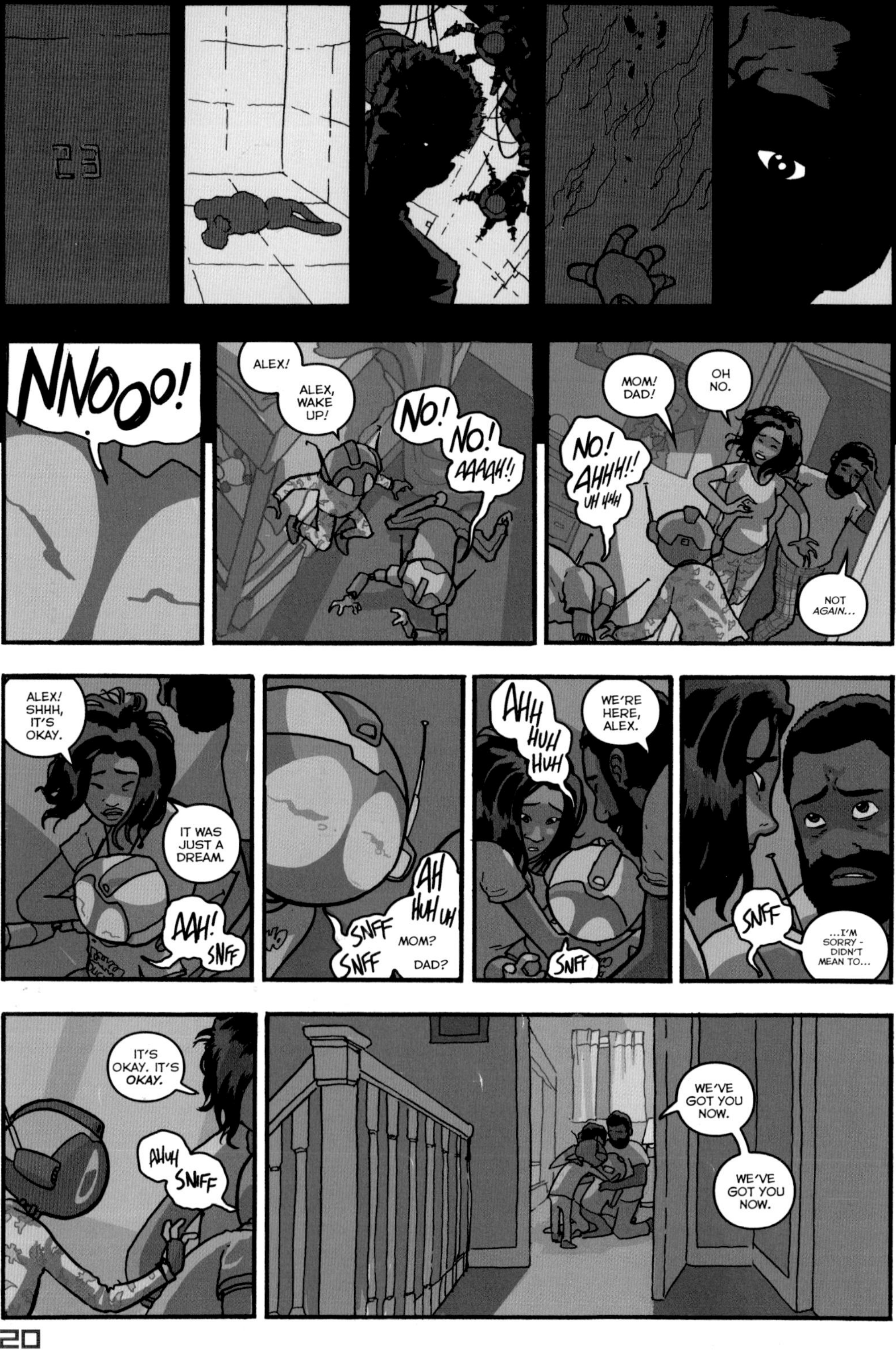

23
NNOOO!
ALEX!
ALEX, WAKE UP!
NO! NO! AAAAH!!
MOM! DAD!
OH NO.
NO! AHHH!! UH UHH
NOT AGAIN...
ALEX! SHHH, IT'S OKAY.
IT WAS JUST A DREAM.
AAH! SNFF
AH HUH UH
SNFF SNFF
MOM? DAD?
AHH HUH HUH
WE'RE HERE, ALEX.
SNFF
SNFF
...I'M SORRY - DIDN'T MEAN TO...
IT'S OKAY. IT'S OKAY.
AHUH SNIFF
WE'VE GOT YOU NOW.
WE'VE GOT YOU NOW.

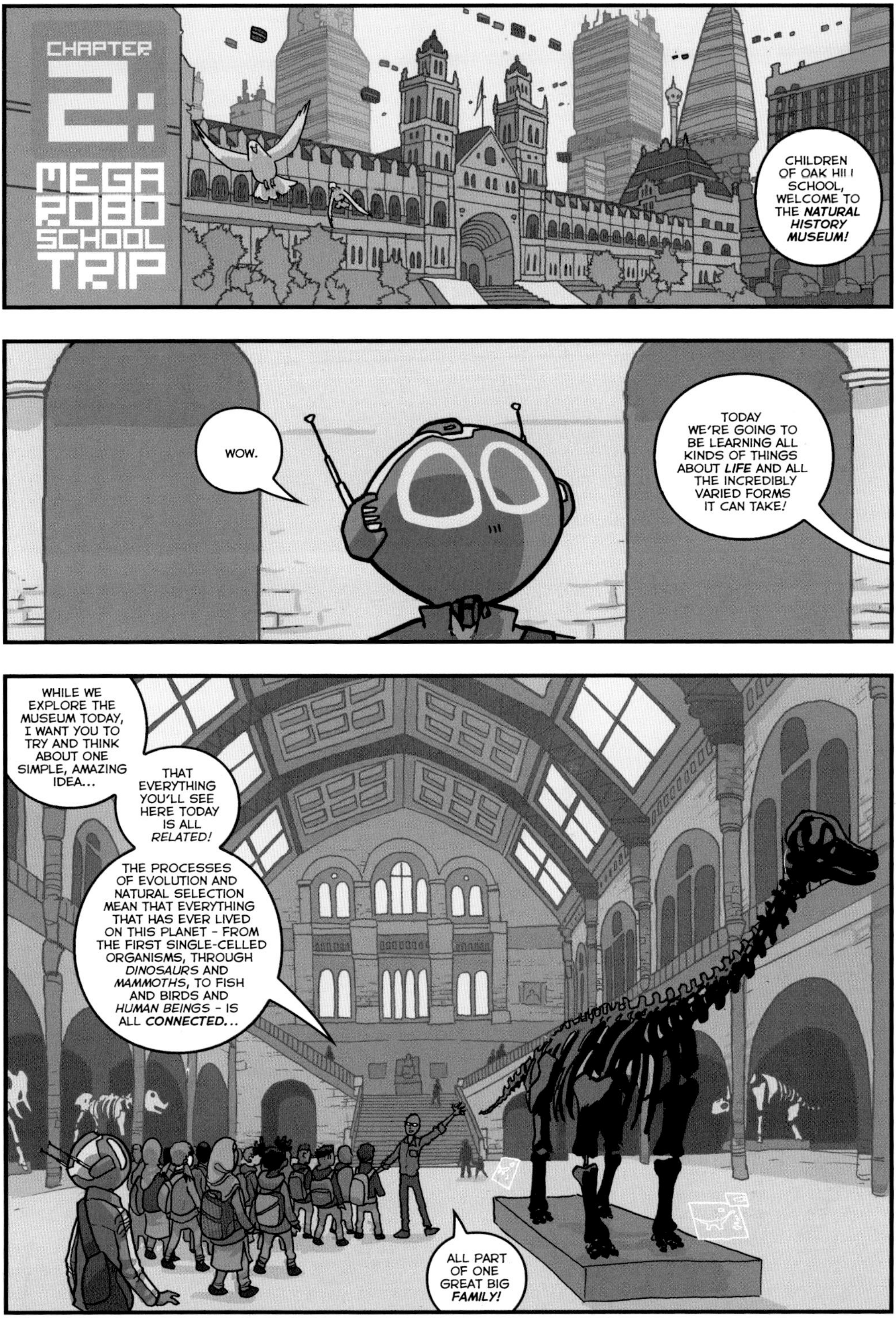
CHAPTER 2: MEGA ROBO SCHOOL TRIP
CHILDREN OF OAK HILL SCHOOL, WELCOME TO THE *NATURAL HISTORY MUSEUM!*
WOW.
TODAY WE'RE GOING TO BE LEARNING ALL KINDS OF THINGS ABOUT *LIFE* AND ALL THE INCREDIBLY VARIED FORMS IT CAN TAKE!
WHILE WE EXPLORE THE MUSEUM TODAY, I WANT YOU TO TRY AND THINK ABOUT ONE SIMPLE, AMAZING IDEA...
THAT EVERYTHING YOU'LL SEE HERE TODAY IS ALL *RELATED!*
THE PROCESSES OF EVOLUTION AND NATURAL SELECTION MEAN THAT EVERYTHING THAT HAS EVER LIVED ON THIS PLANET - FROM THE FIRST SINGLE-CELLED ORGANISMS, THROUGH *DINOSAURS* AND *MAMMOTHS*, TO FISH AND BIRDS AND *HUMAN BEINGS* - IS ALL **CONNECTED...**
ALL PART OF ONE GREAT BIG *FAMILY!*

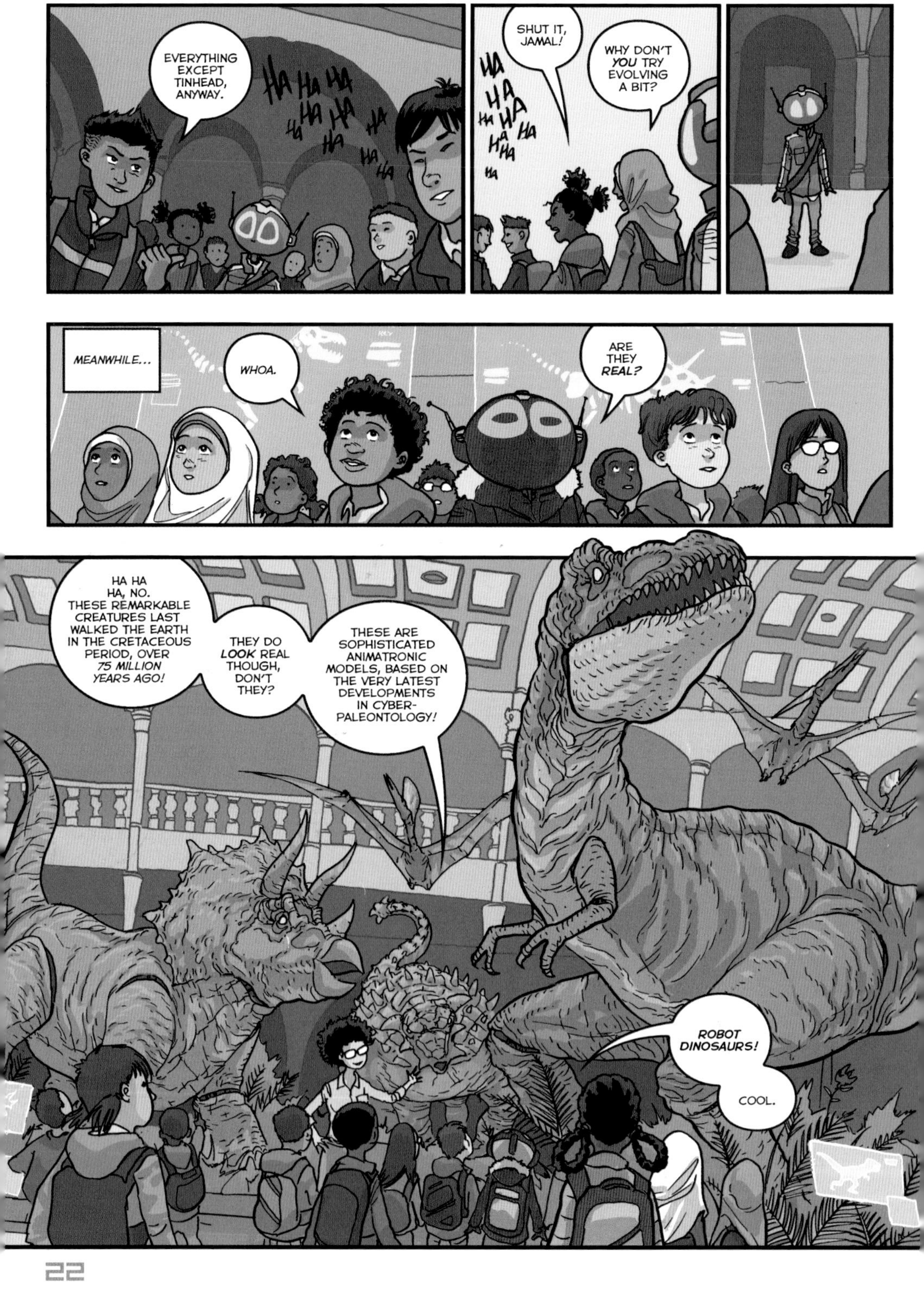
EVERYTHING EXCEPT TINHEAD, ANYWAY.
HA HA HA HA HA HA HA HA HA HA HA
HA HA HA HA HA HA HA HA
SHUT IT, JAMAL!
WHY DON'T *YOU* TRY EVOLVING A BIT?
MEANWHILE...
WHOA.
ARE THEY *REAL?*
HA HA HA, NO. THESE REMARKABLE CREATURES LAST WALKED THE EARTH IN THE CRETACEOUS PERIOD, OVER *75 MILLION YEARS AGO!*
THEY DO *LOOK* REAL THOUGH, DON'T THEY?
THESE ARE SOPHISTICATED ANIMATRONIC MODELS, BASED ON THE VERY LATEST DEVELOPMENTS IN CYBER-PALEONTOLOGY!
ROBOT DINOSAURS!
COOL.

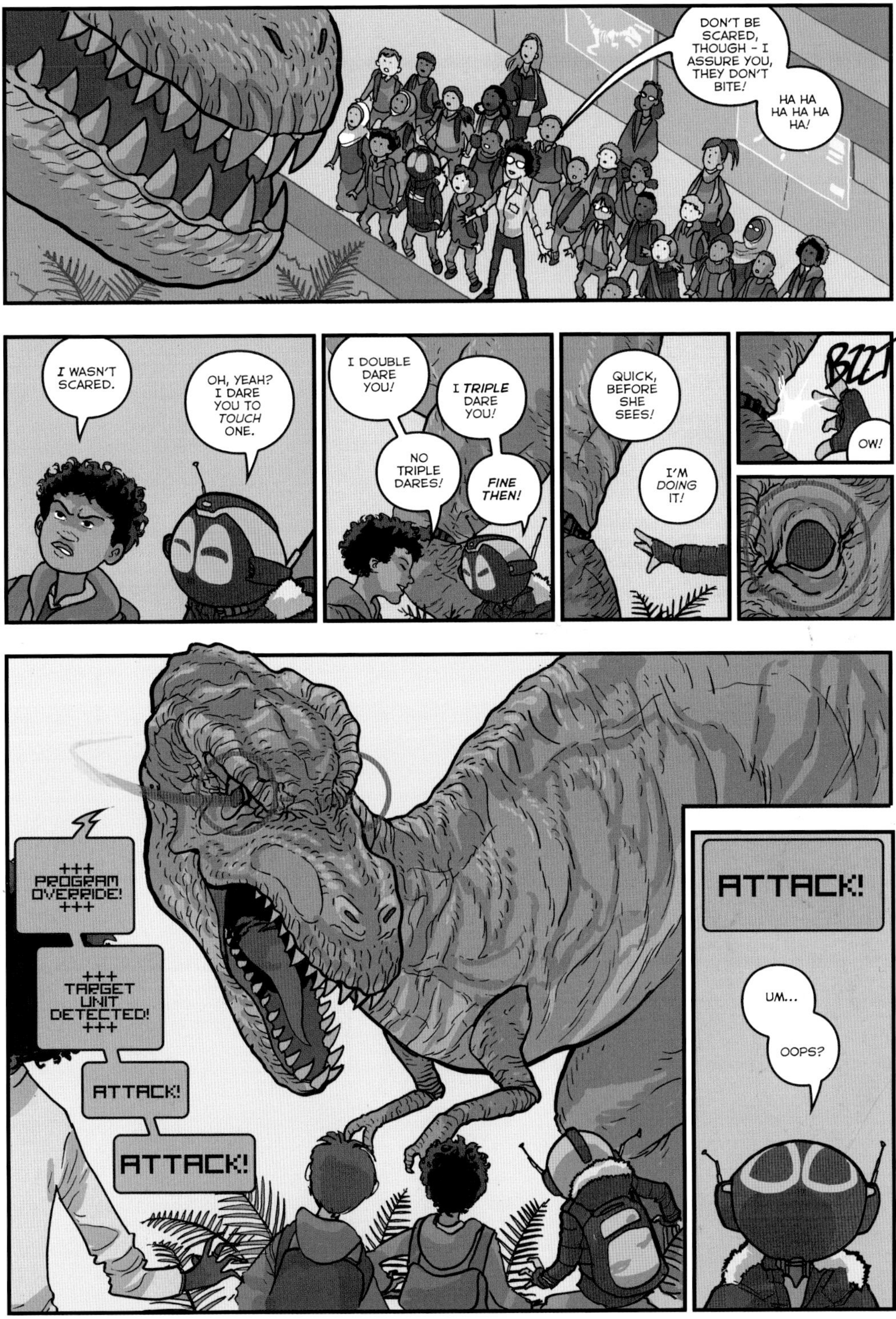
DON'T BE SCARED, THOUGH - I ASSURE YOU, THEY DON'T BITE!
HA HA HA HA HA HA!
I WASN'T SCARED.
OH, YEAH? I DARE YOU TO TOUCH ONE.
I DOUBLE DARE YOU!
NO TRIPLE DARES!
I TRIPLE DARE YOU!
FINE THEN!
QUICK, BEFORE SHE SEES!
I'M DOING IT!
BZZT!
OW!
+++ PROGRAM OVERRIDE! +++
+++ TARGET UNIT DETECTED! +++
ATTACK!
ATTACK!
ATTACK!
UM...
OOPS?

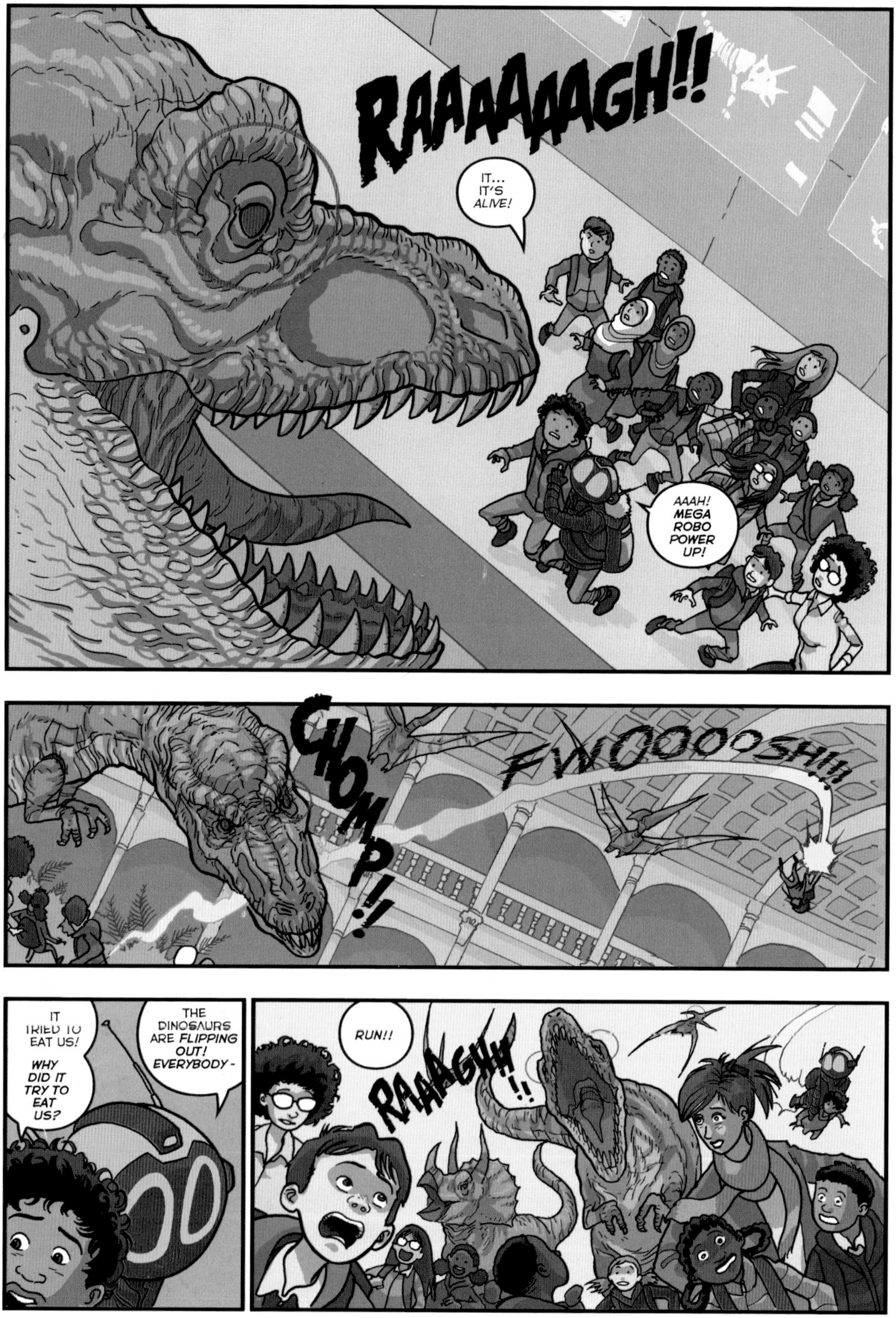
RAAAAAAGH!!
IT... IT'S ALIVE!
AAAH! MEGA ROBO POWER UP!
CHOMP!!
FWOOOOOSH!!!
IT TRIED TO EAT US!
WHY DID IT TRY TO EAT US?
THE DINOSAURS ARE FLIPPING OUT! EVERYBODY -
RUN!!
RAAGHH!!

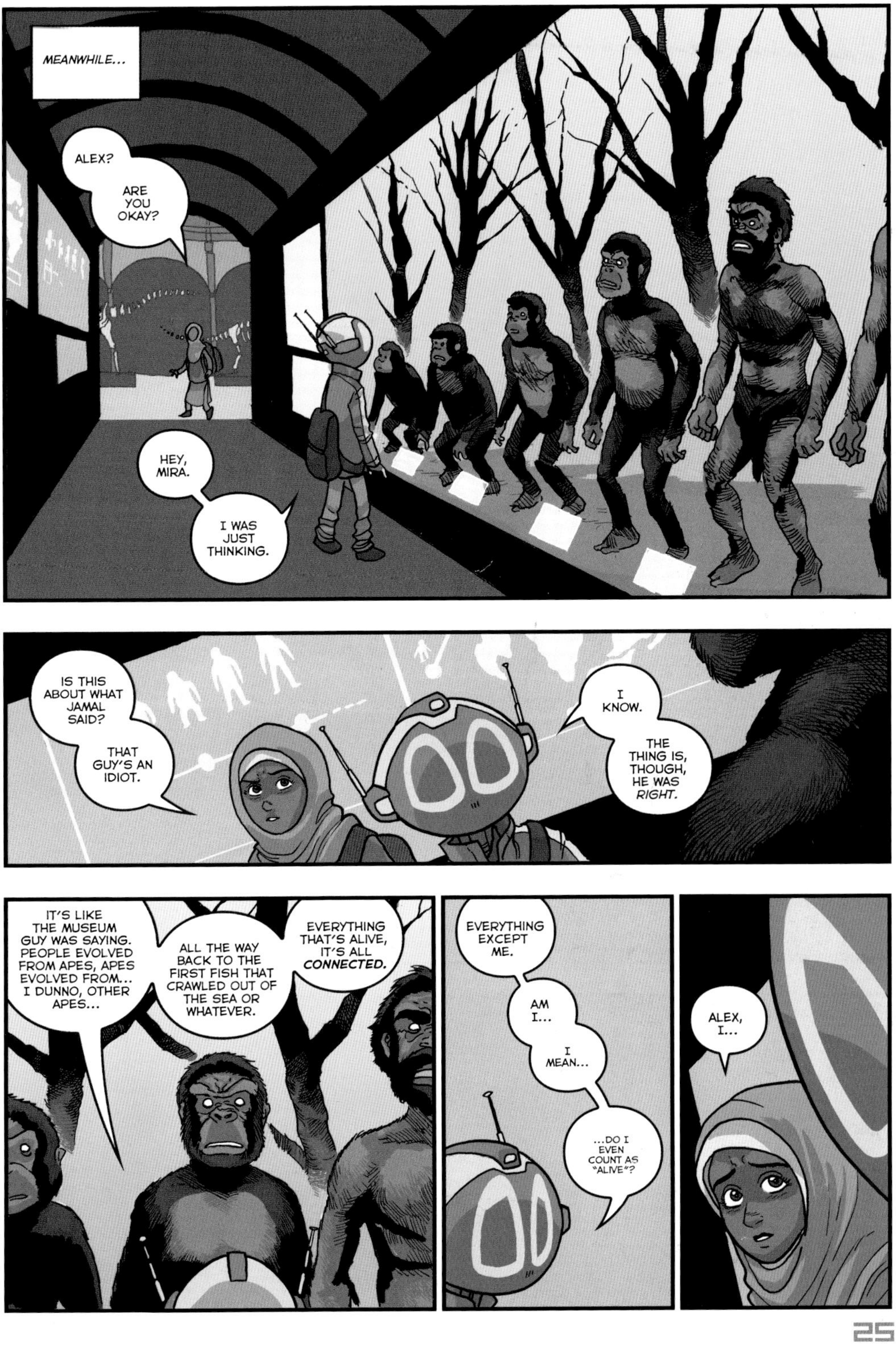
MEANWHILE...
ALEX?
ARE YOU OKAY?
HEY, MIRA.
I WAS JUST THINKING.
IS THIS ABOUT WHAT JAMAL SAID?
THAT GUY'S AN IDIOT.
I KNOW.
THE THING IS, THOUGH, HE WAS *RIGHT.*
IT'S LIKE THE MUSEUM GUY WAS SAYING. PEOPLE EVOLVED FROM APES, APES EVOLVED FROM... I DUNNO, OTHER APES...
ALL THE WAY BACK TO THE FIRST FISH THAT CRAWLED OUT OF THE SEA OR WHATEVER.
EVERYTHING THAT'S ALIVE, IT'S ALL **CONNECTED.**
EVERYTHING EXCEPT ME.
AM I...
I MEAN...
...DO I EVEN COUNT AS "ALIVE"?
ALEX, I...

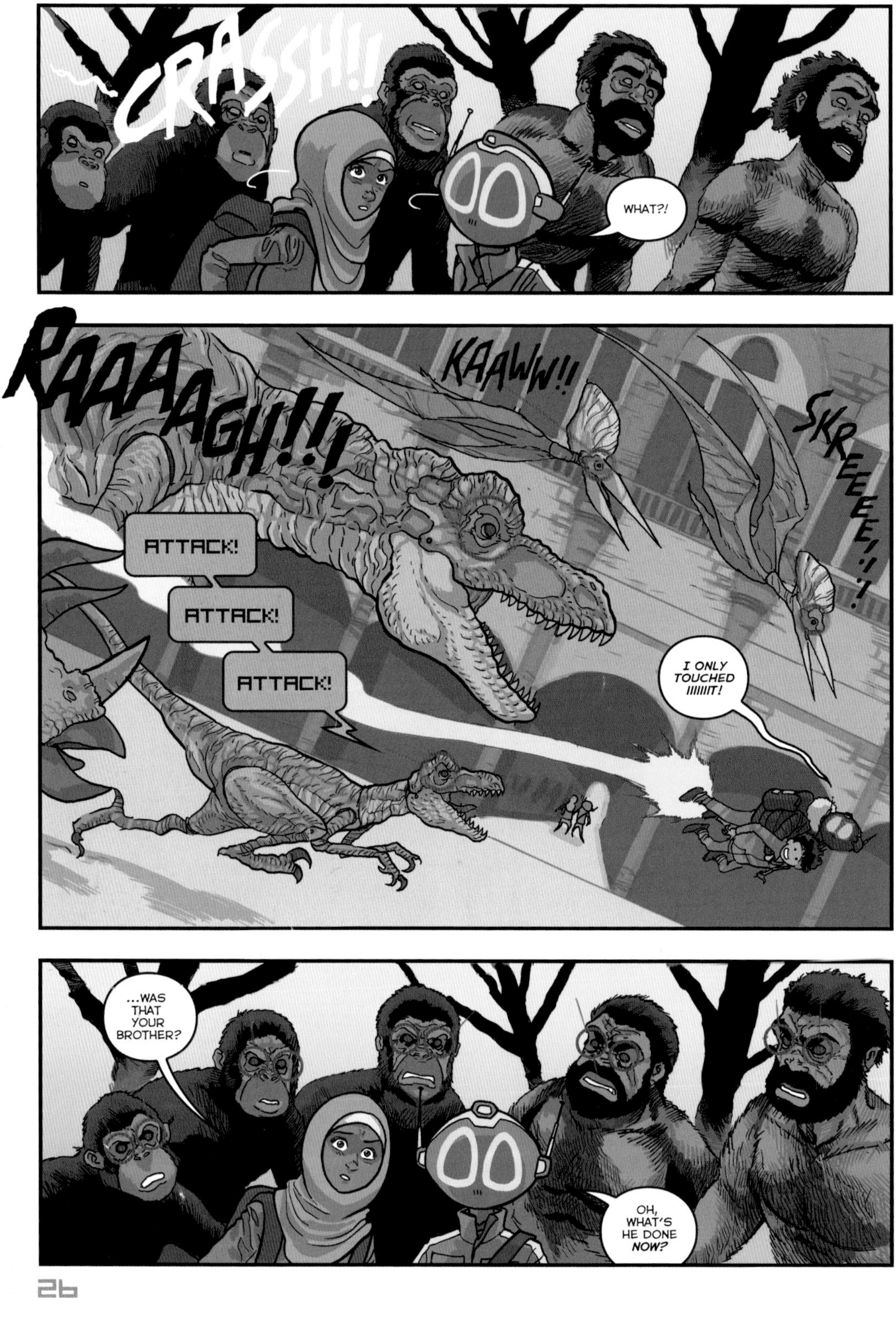
CRASSH!!
WHAT?!
RAAAAGH!!!
KAAWW!!
SKREEEE!!
ATTACK!
ATTACK!
ATTACK!
I ONLY TOUCHED IIIIIIIT!
...WAS THAT YOUR BROTHER?
OH, WHAT'S HE DONE *NOW?*

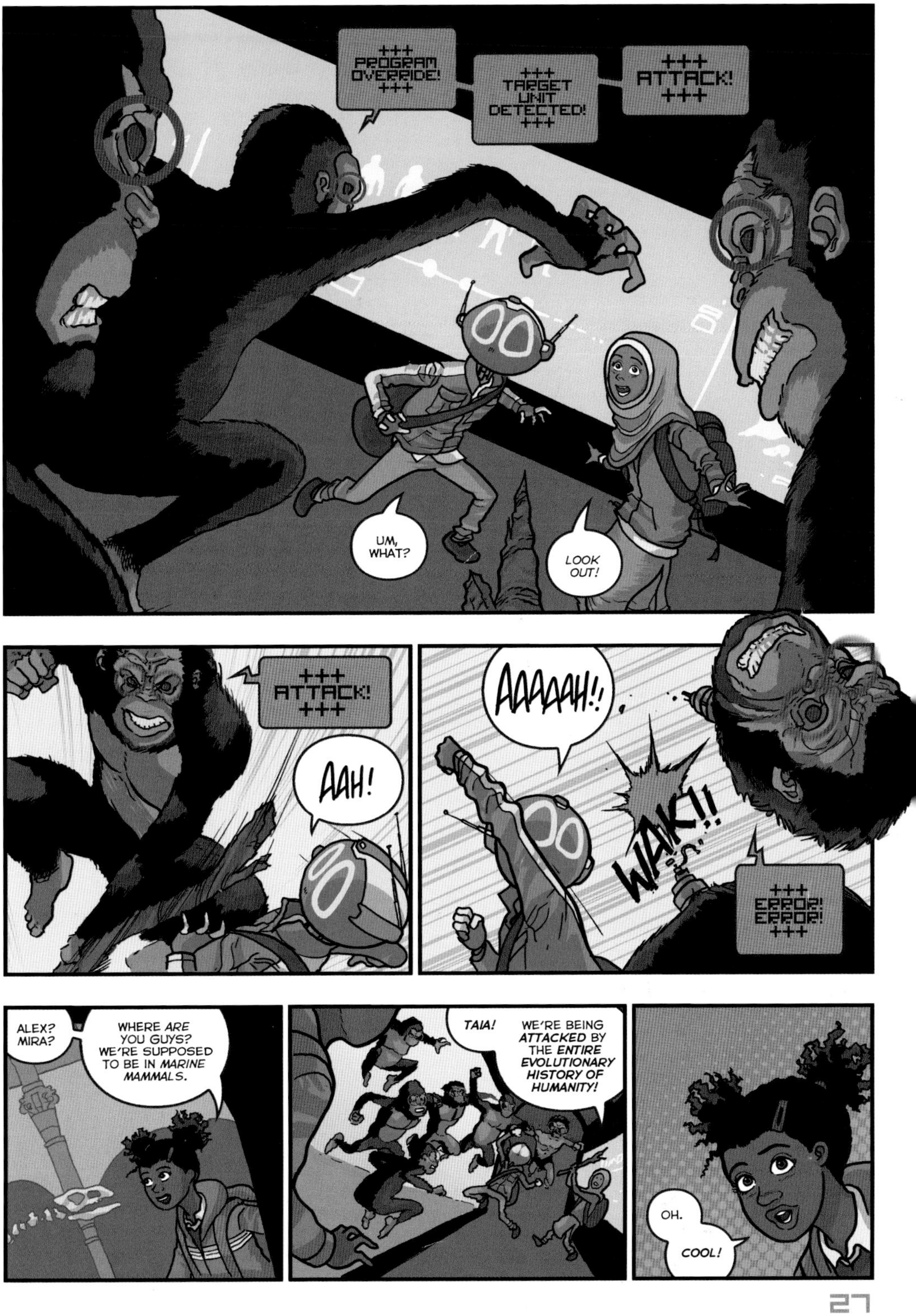
+++ PROGRAM OVERRIDE! +++
+++ TARGET UNIT DETECTED! +++
+++ ATTACK! +++
UM, WHAT?
LOOK OUT!
+++ ATTACK! +++
AAH!
AAAAAH!!
WAK!!
+++ ERROR! ERROR! +++
ALEX? MIRA?
WHERE ARE YOU GUYS? WE'RE SUPPOSED TO BE IN MARINE MAMMALS.
TAIA!
WE'RE BEING ATTACKED BY THE ENTIRE EVOLUTIONARY HISTORY OF HUMANITY!
OH.
COOL!

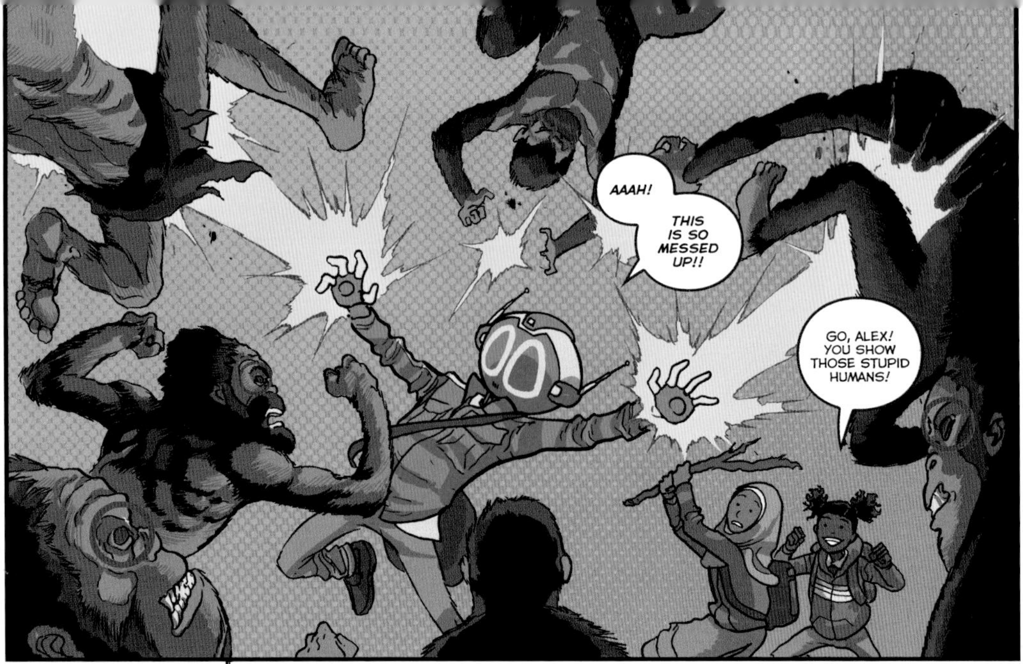
AAAH!
THIS IS SO MESSED UP!!
GO, ALEX! YOU SHOW THOSE STUPID HUMANS!

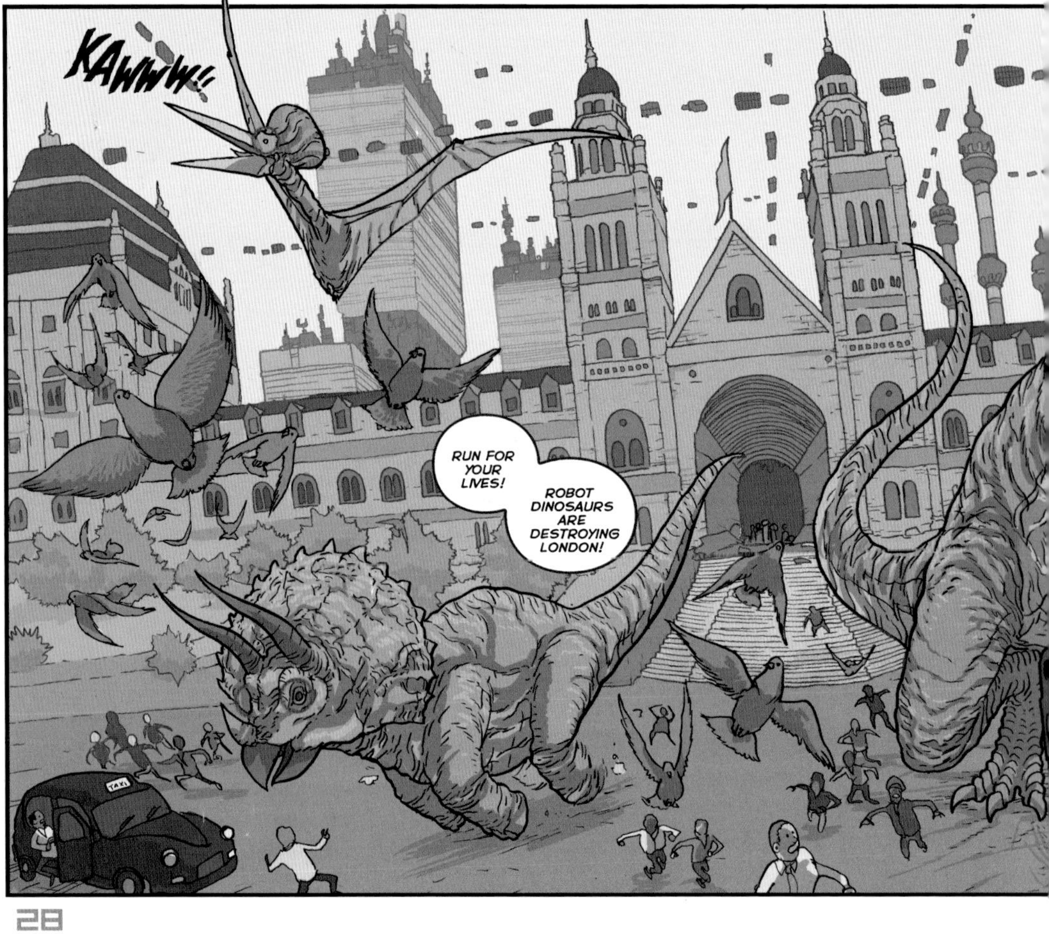
KAWWW!!
RUN FOR YOUR LIVES!
ROBOT DINOSAURS ARE DESTROYING LONDON!
TAXI

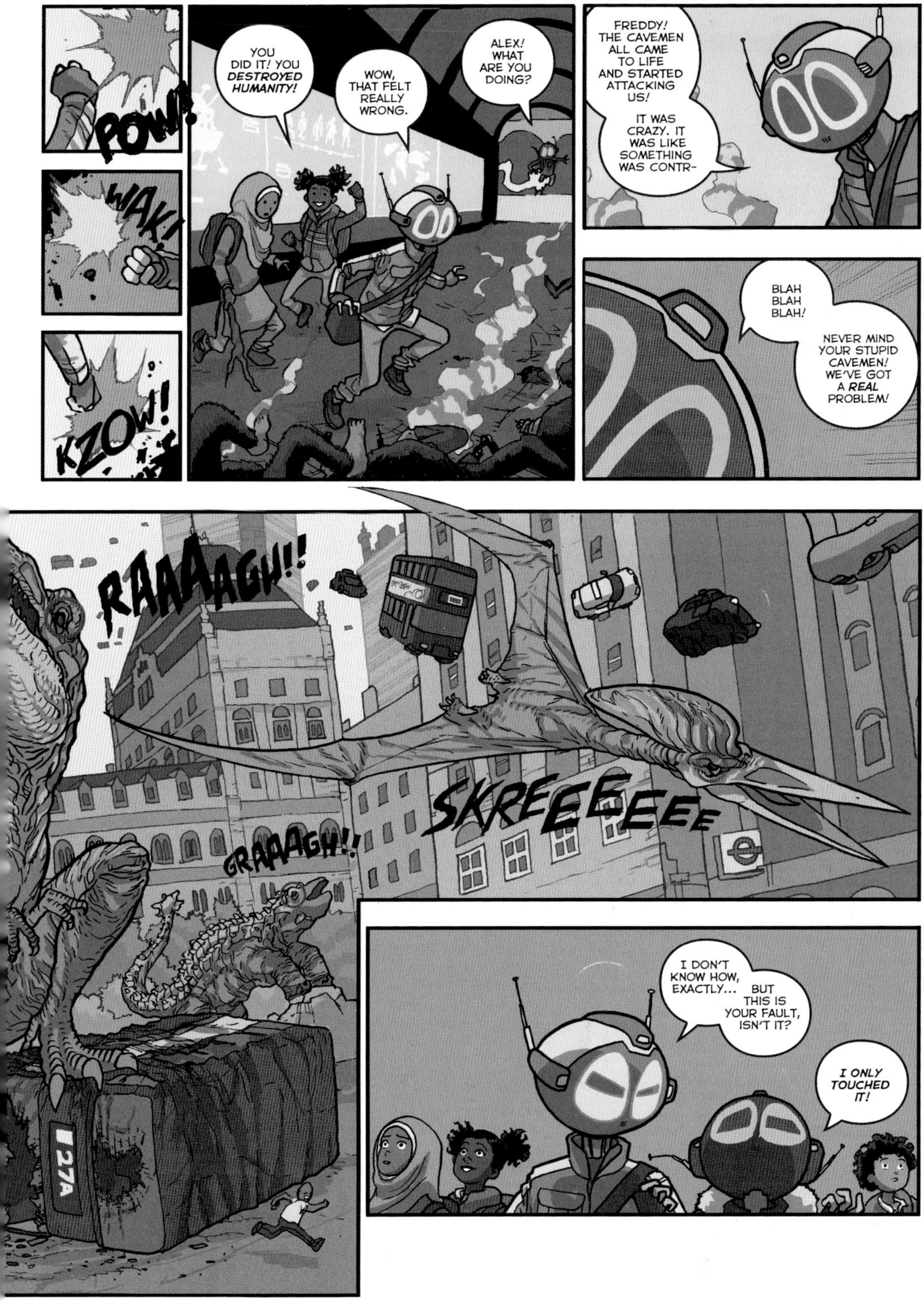
POW!
WAK!
KZOW!
YOU DID IT! YOU *DESTROYED HUMANITY!*
WOW, THAT FELT REALLY WRONG.
ALEX! WHAT ARE YOU DOING?
FREDDY! THE CAVEMEN ALL CAME TO LIFE AND STARTED ATTACKING US!
IT WAS CRAZY. IT WAS LIKE SOMETHING WAS CONTR-
BLAH BLAH BLAH!
NEVER MIND YOUR STUPID CAVEMEN! WE'VE GOT A *REAL* PROBLEM!
RAAAAGH!!
SKREEEEEEEE
GRAAAGH!!
27A
I DON'T KNOW HOW, EXACTLY... BUT THIS IS YOUR FAULT, ISN'T IT?
I ONLY TOUCHED IT!

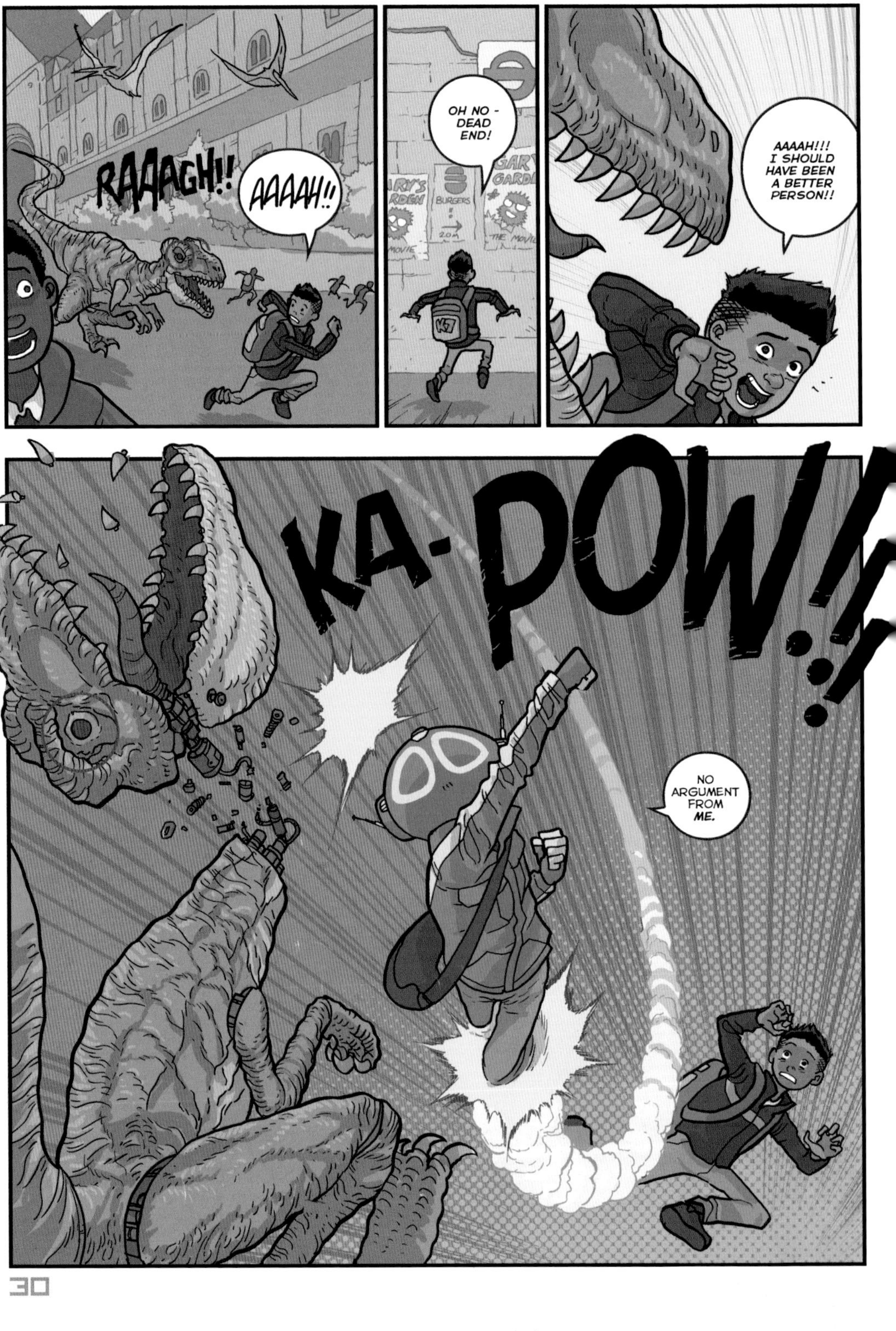
RAAAGH!!
AAAAH!!
OH NO - DEAD END!
GARY'S GARDEN
BURGERS
2.0M
THE MOVIE
AAAAH!!! I SHOULD HAVE BEEN A BETTER PERSON!!
KA-POW!!!
NO ARGUMENT FROM *ME.*

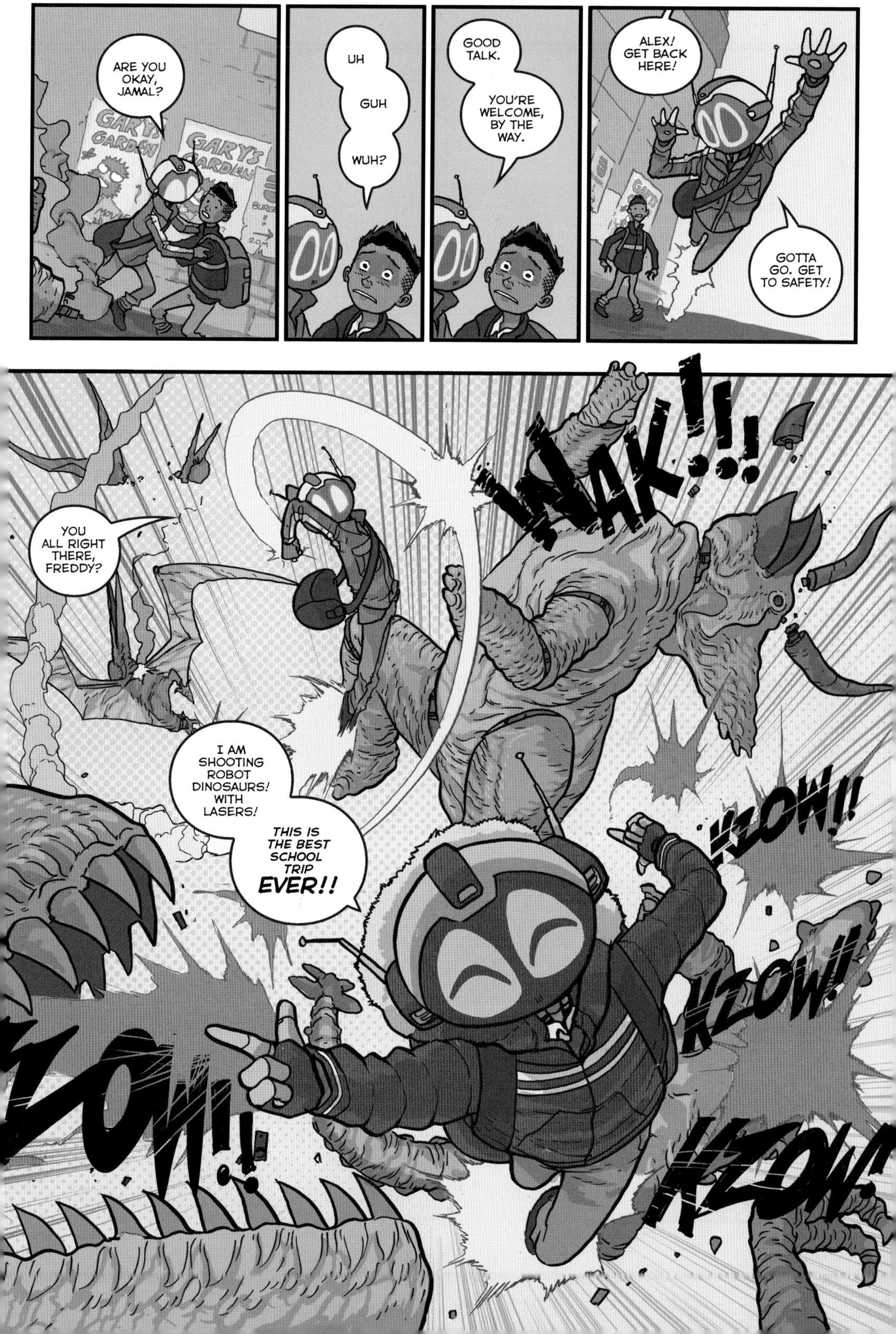

ARE YOU OKAY, JAMAL?
UH
GUH
WUH?
GOOD TALK.
YOU'RE WELCOME, BY THE WAY.
ALEX! GET BACK HERE!
GOTTA GO. GET TO SAFETY!
WAK!!!
YOU ALL RIGHT THERE, FREDDY?
I AM SHOOTING ROBOT DINOSAURS! WITH LASERS!
THIS IS THE BEST SCHOOL TRIP EVER!!
KZOW!!
KZOW!!
ZOW!!
KZOW!

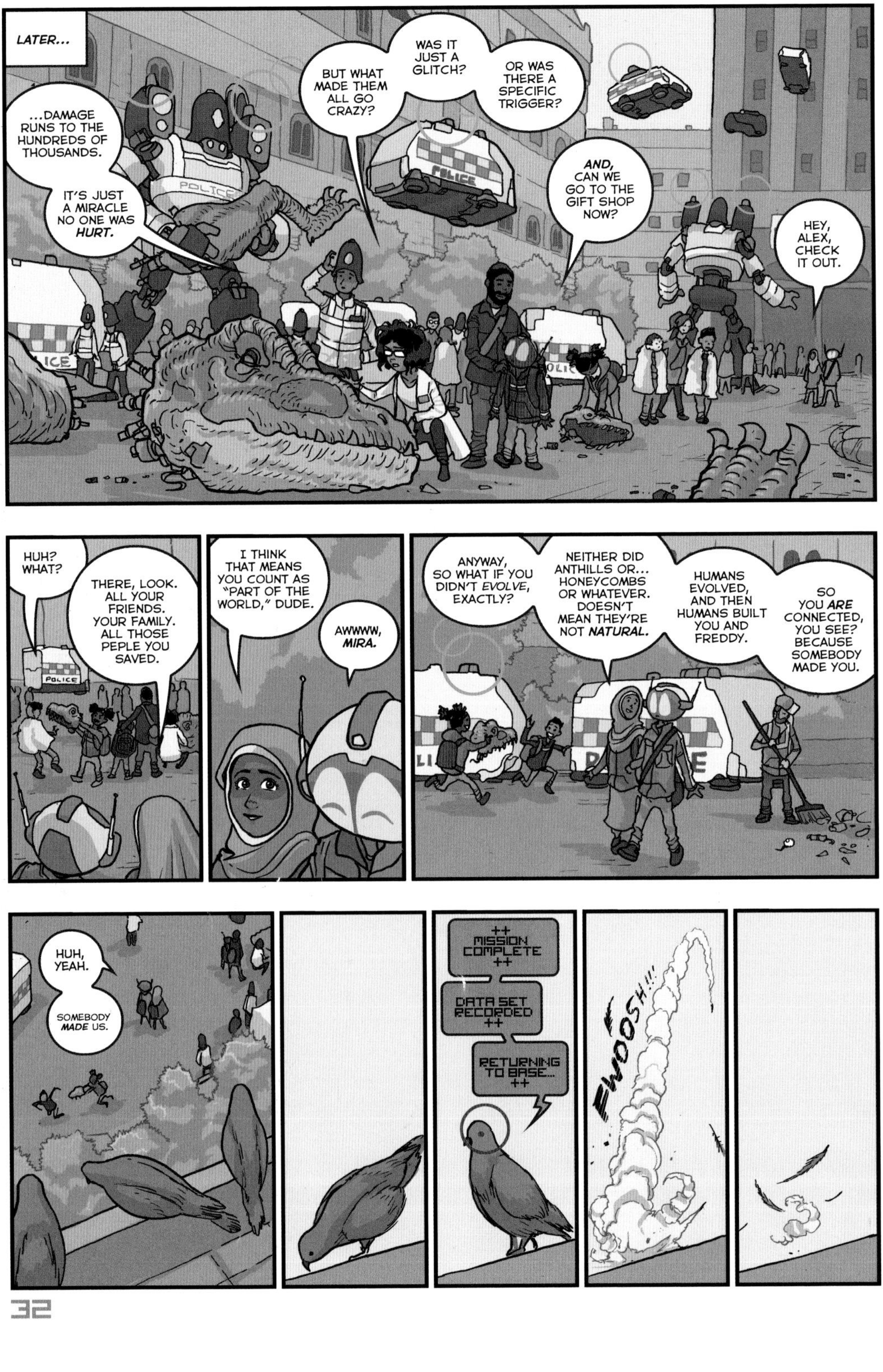
LATER...
...DAMAGE RUNS TO THE HUNDREDS OF THOUSANDS.
IT'S JUST A MIRACLE NO ONE WAS HURT.
BUT WHAT MADE THEM ALL GO CRAZY?
WAS IT JUST A GLITCH?
OR WAS THERE A SPECIFIC TRIGGER?
AND, CAN WE GO TO THE GIFT SHOP NOW?
HEY, ALEX, CHECK IT OUT.
HUH? WHAT?
THERE, LOOK. ALL YOUR FRIENDS. YOUR FAMILY. ALL THOSE PEPLE YOU SAVED.
I THINK THAT MEANS YOU COUNT AS "PART OF THE WORLD," DUDE.
AWWWW, MIRA.
ANYWAY, SO WHAT IF YOU DIDN'T EVOLVE, EXACTLY?
NEITHER DID ANTHILLS OR... HONEYCOMBS OR WHATEVER. DOESN'T MEAN THEY'RE NOT NATURAL.
HUMANS EVOLVED, AND THEN HUMANS BUILT YOU AND FREDDY.
SO YOU ARE CONNECTED, YOU SEE? BECAUSE SOMEBODY MADE YOU.
HUH, YEAH.
SOMEBODY MADE US.
++ MISSION COMPLETE ++
DATA SET RECORDED ++
RETURNING TO BASE... ++
FWOOSH!!!

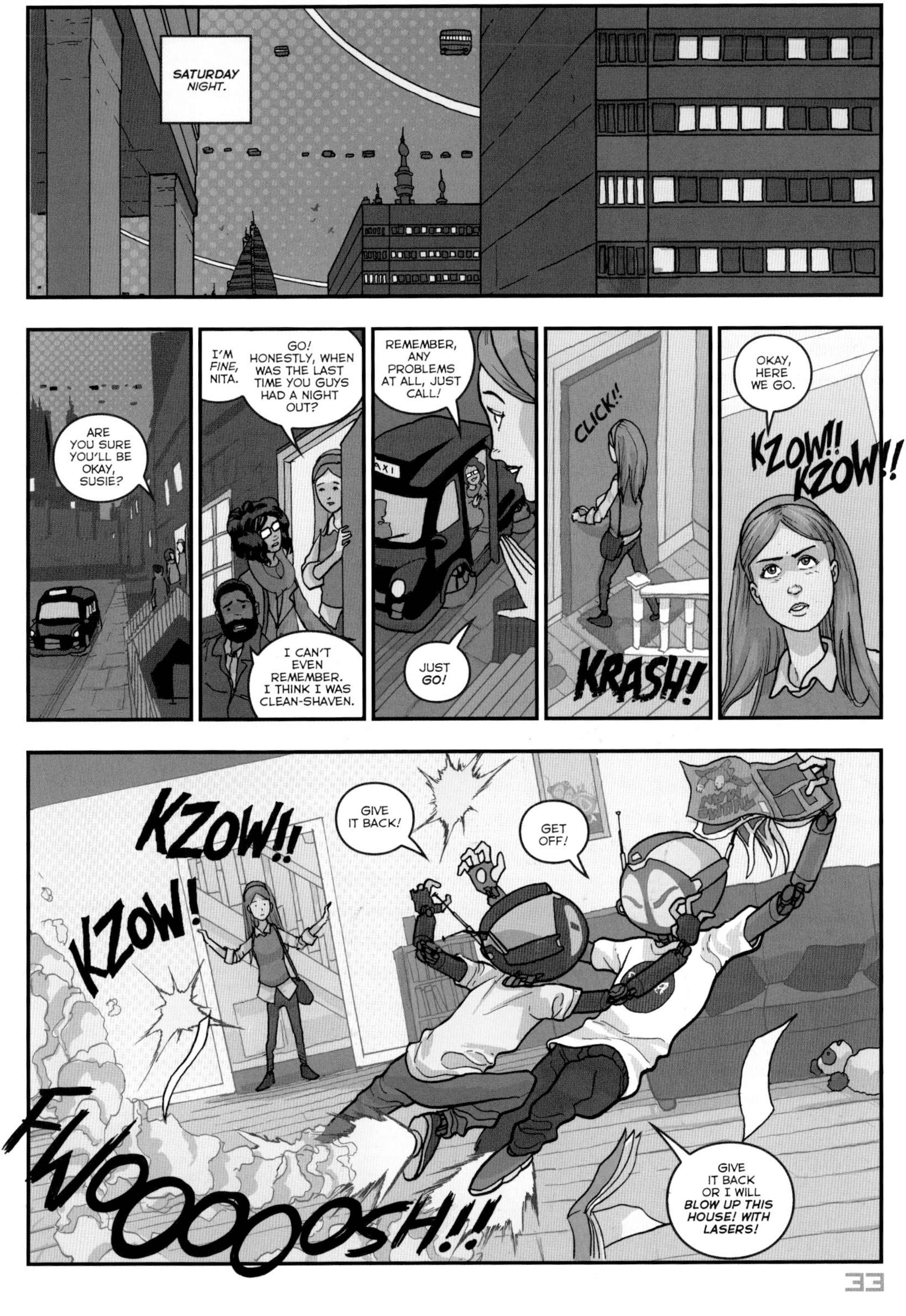

SATURDAY NIGHT.
ARE YOU SURE YOU'LL BE OKAY, SUSIE?
I'M FINE, NITA.
GO! HONESTLY, WHEN WAS THE LAST TIME YOU GUYS HAD A NIGHT OUT?
I CAN'T EVEN REMEMBER. I THINK I WAS CLEAN-SHAVEN.
REMEMBER, ANY PROBLEMS AT ALL, JUST CALL!
TAXI
JUST GO!
CLICK!!
KRASH!
OKAY, HERE WE GO.
KZOW!! KZOW!!
KZOW!!
KZOW!
GIVE IT BACK!
GET OFF!
GIVE IT BACK OR I WILL BLOW UP THIS HOUSE! WITH LASERS!
FWOOOOOOSH!!

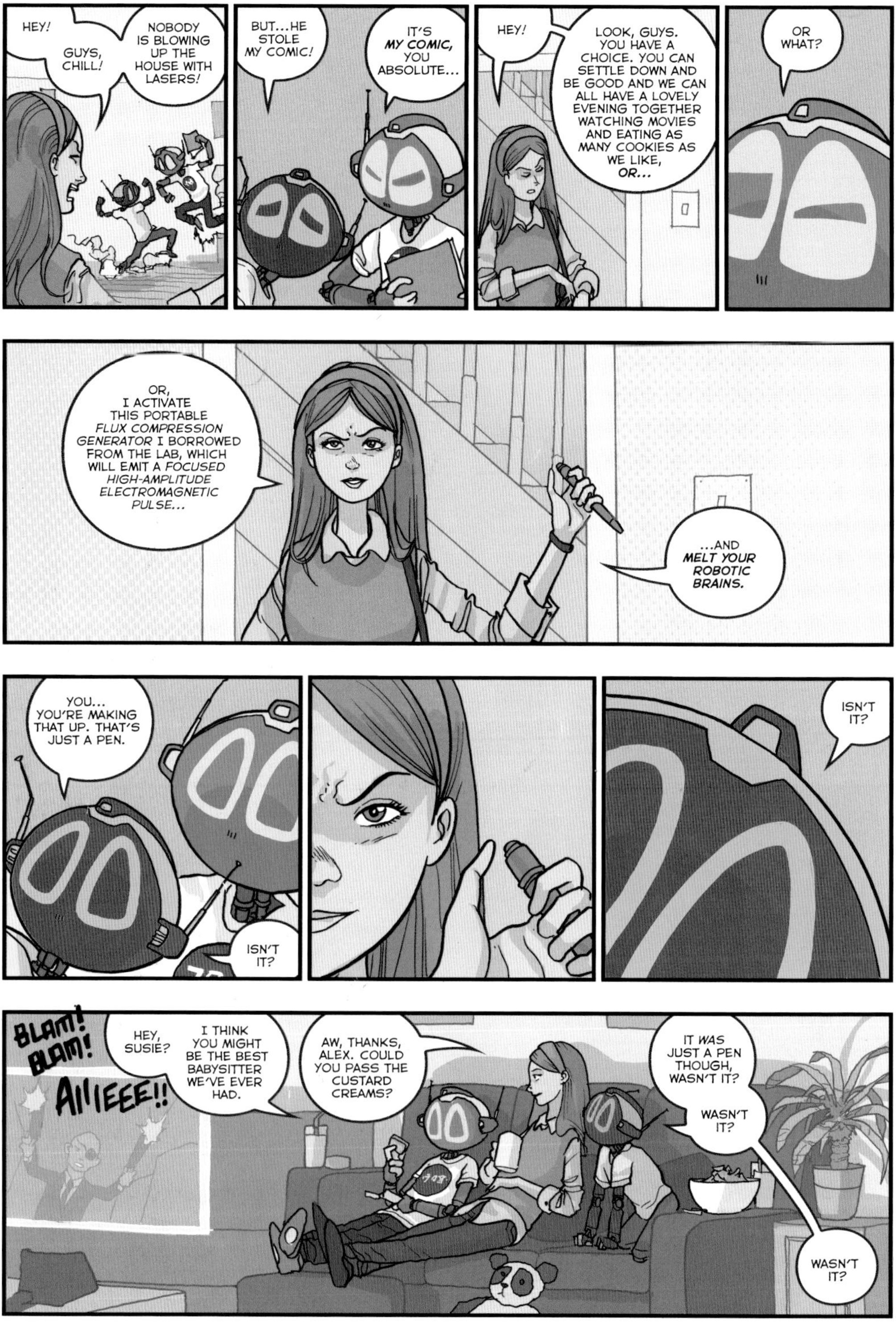
HEY!
GUYS, CHILL!
NOBODY IS BLOWING UP THE HOUSE WITH LASERS!
BUT...HE STOLE MY COMIC!
IT'S MY COMIC, YOU ABSOLUTE...
HEY!
LOOK, GUYS. YOU HAVE A CHOICE. YOU CAN SETTLE DOWN AND BE GOOD AND WE CAN ALL HAVE A LOVELY EVENING TOGETHER WATCHING MOVIES AND EATING AS MANY COOKIES AS WE LIKE, OR...
OR WHAT?
OR, I ACTIVATE THIS PORTABLE FLUX COMPRESSION GENERATOR I BORROWED FROM THE LAB, WHICH WILL EMIT A FOCUSED HIGH-AMPLITUDE ELECTROMAGNETIC PULSE...
...AND MELT YOUR ROBOTIC BRAINS.
YOU... YOU'RE MAKING THAT UP. THAT'S JUST A PEN.
ISN'T IT?
ISN'T IT?
BLAM! BLAM!
AIIIEEE!!
HEY, SUSIE?
I THINK YOU MIGHT BE THE BEST BABYSITTER WE'VE EVER HAD.
AW, THANKS, ALEX. COULD YOU PASS THE CUSTARD CREAMS?
IT WAS JUST A PEN THOUGH, WASN'T IT?
WASN'T IT?
WASN'T IT?

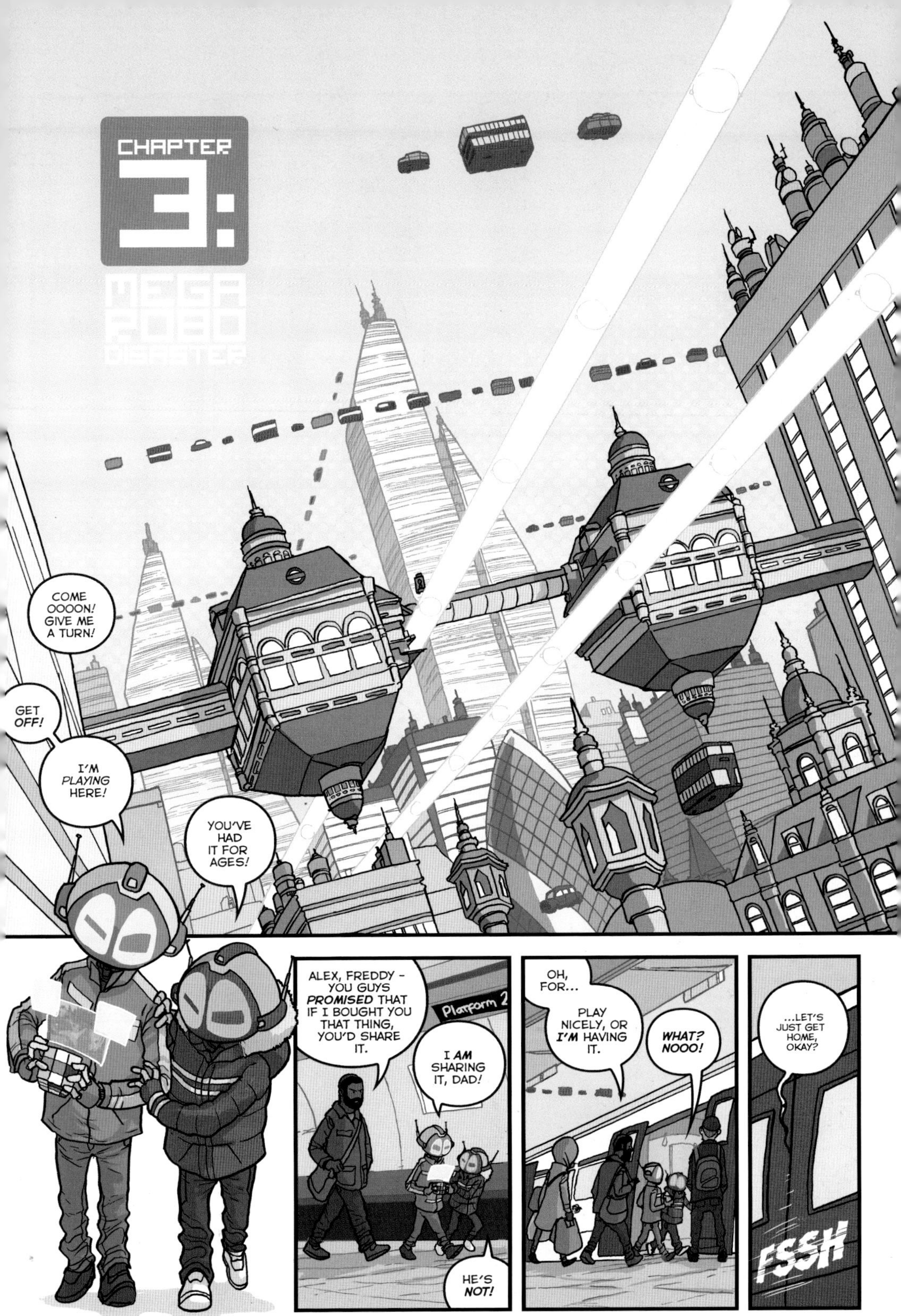
CHAPTER
3:
MEGA ROBO DISASTER
COME OOOON! GIVE ME A TURN!
GET OFF!
I'M PLAYING HERE!
YOU'VE HAD IT FOR AGES!
Platform 2
ALEX, FREDDY - YOU GUYS PROMISED THAT IF I BOUGHT YOU THAT THING, YOU'D SHARE IT.
I AM SHARING IT, DAD!
HE'S NOT!
OH, FOR...
PLAY NICELY, OR I'M HAVING IT.
WHAT? NOOO!
...LET'S JUST GET HOME, OKAY?
FSSH

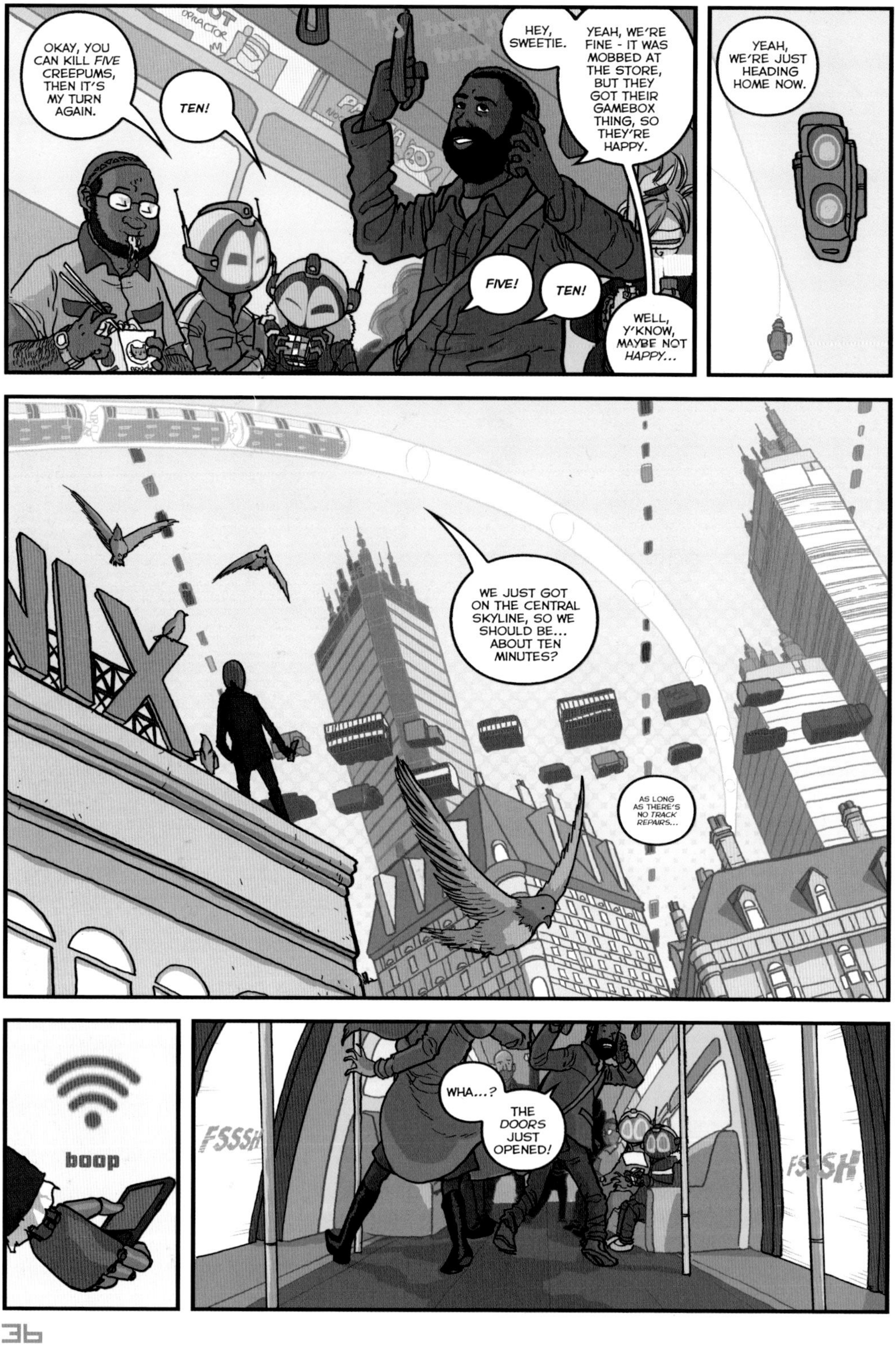
OKAY, YOU CAN KILL *FIVE* CREEPUMS, THEN IT'S MY TURN AGAIN.
TEN!
HEY, SWEETIE.
YEAH, WE'RE FINE - IT WAS MOBBED AT THE STORE, BUT THEY GOT THEIR GAMEBOX THING, SO THEY'RE HAPPY.
FIVE!
TEN!
WELL, Y'KNOW, MAYBE NOT *HAPPY*...
YEAH, WE'RE JUST HEADING HOME NOW.
WE JUST GOT ON THE CENTRAL SKYLINE, SO WE SHOULD BE... ABOUT TEN MINUTES?
AS LONG AS THERE'S NO *TRACK* REPAIRS...
boop
FSSSH
WHA...?
THE *DOORS* JUST OPENED!
FSSSH

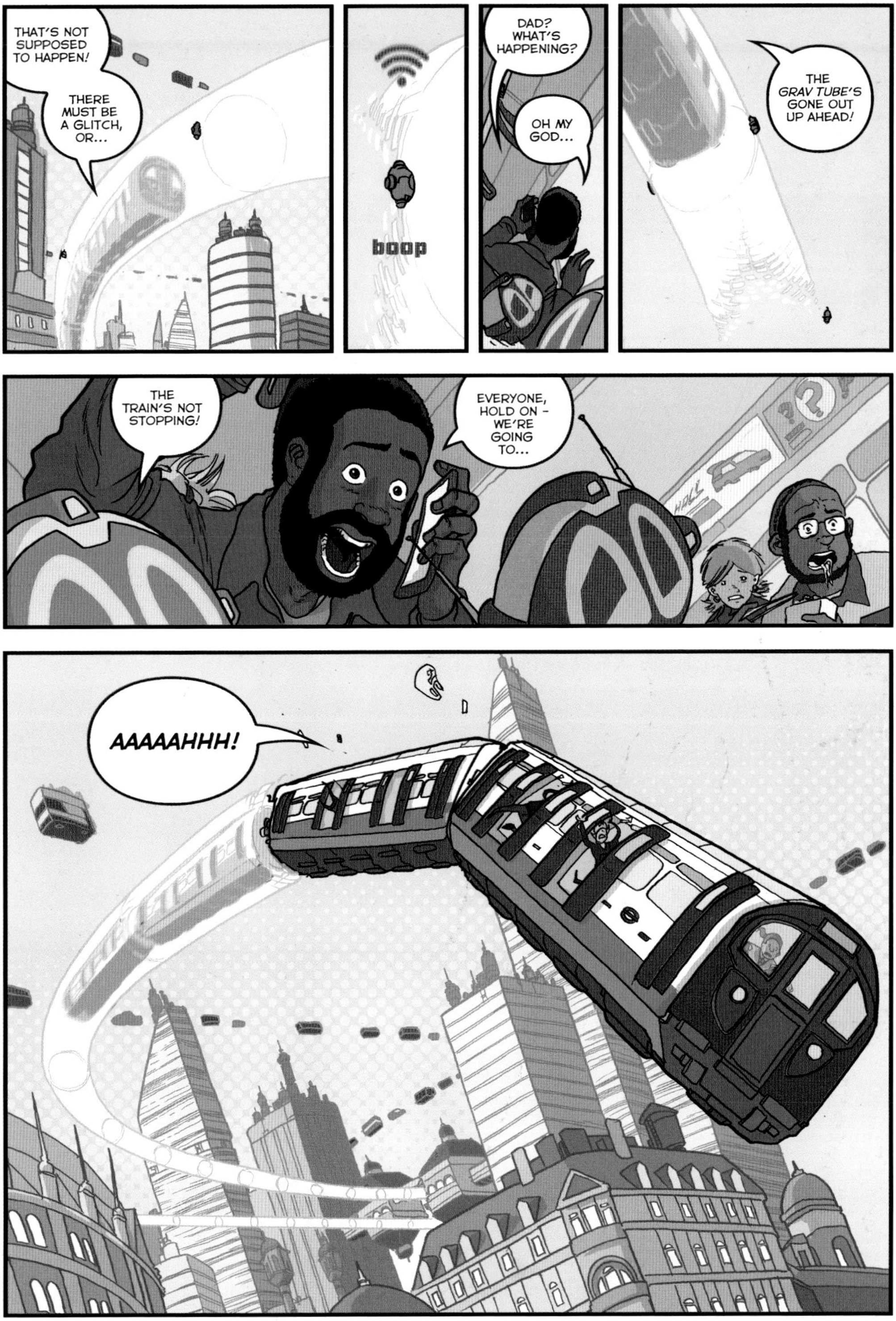
THAT'S NOT SUPPOSED TO HAPPEN!
THERE MUST BE A GLITCH, OR...
boop
DAD? WHAT'S HAPPENING?
OH MY GOD...
THE *GRAV TUBE'S* GONE OUT UP AHEAD!
THE TRAIN'S NOT STOPPING!
EVERYONE, HOLD ON - WE'RE GOING TO...
AAAAAHHH!

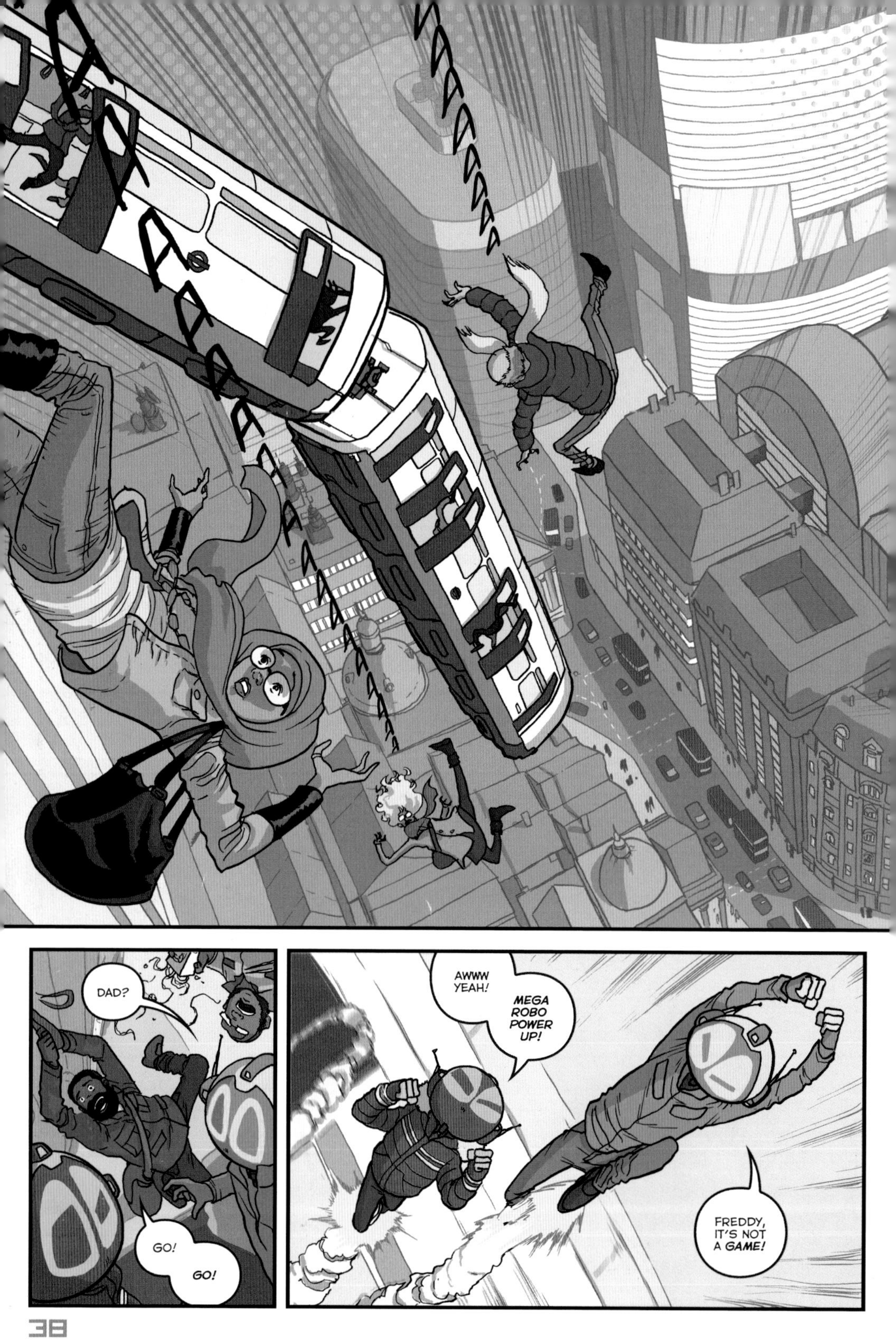
DAD?
GO!
GO!
AWWW YEAH!
MEGA ROBO POWER UP!
FREDDY, IT'S NOT A GAME!

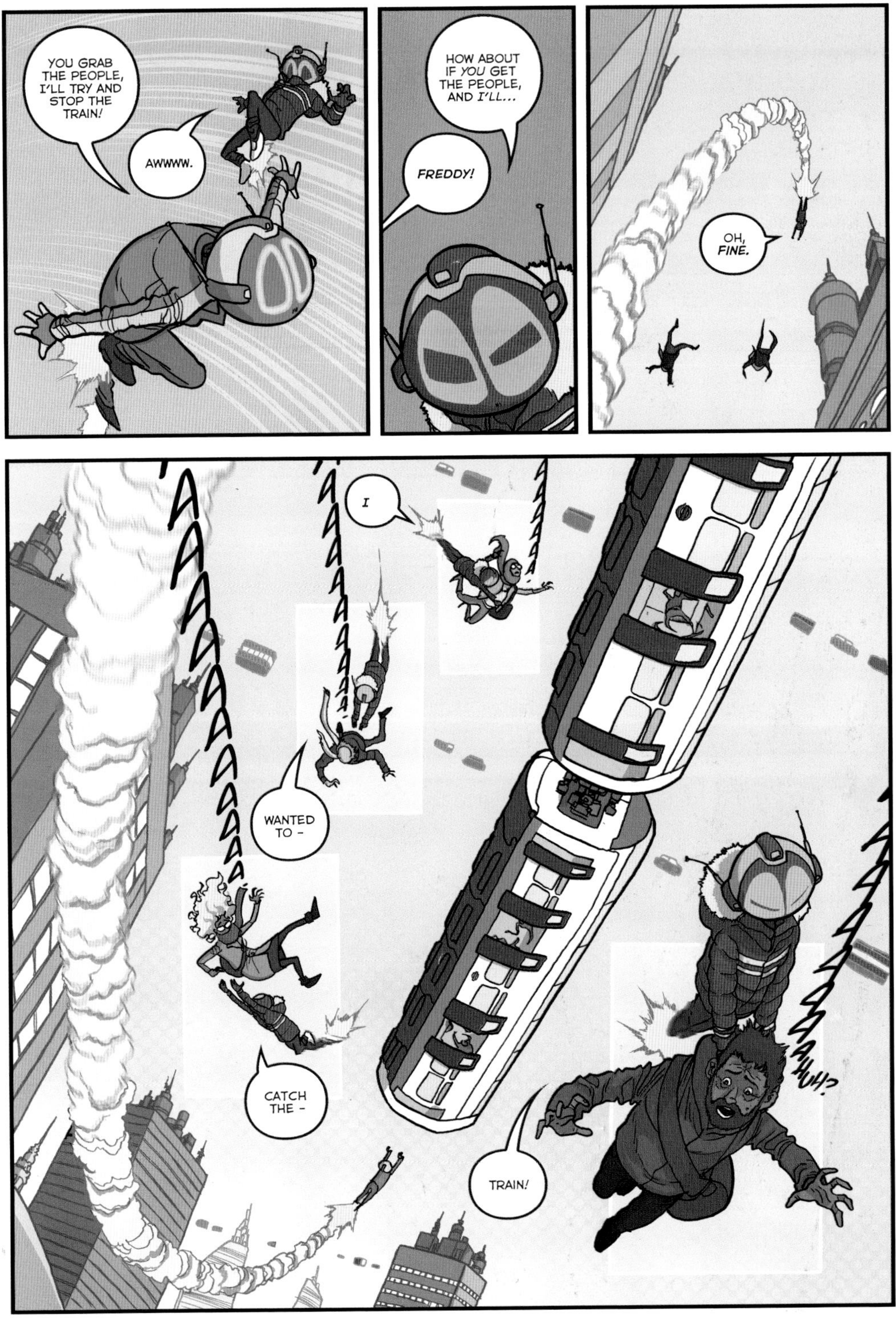
YOU GRAB THE PEOPLE, I'LL TRY AND STOP THE TRAIN!
AWWWW.
HOW ABOUT IF *YOU* GET THE PEOPLE, AND *I'LL*...
FREDDY!
OH, *FINE.*
I
WANTED TO -
CATCH THE -
TRAIN!

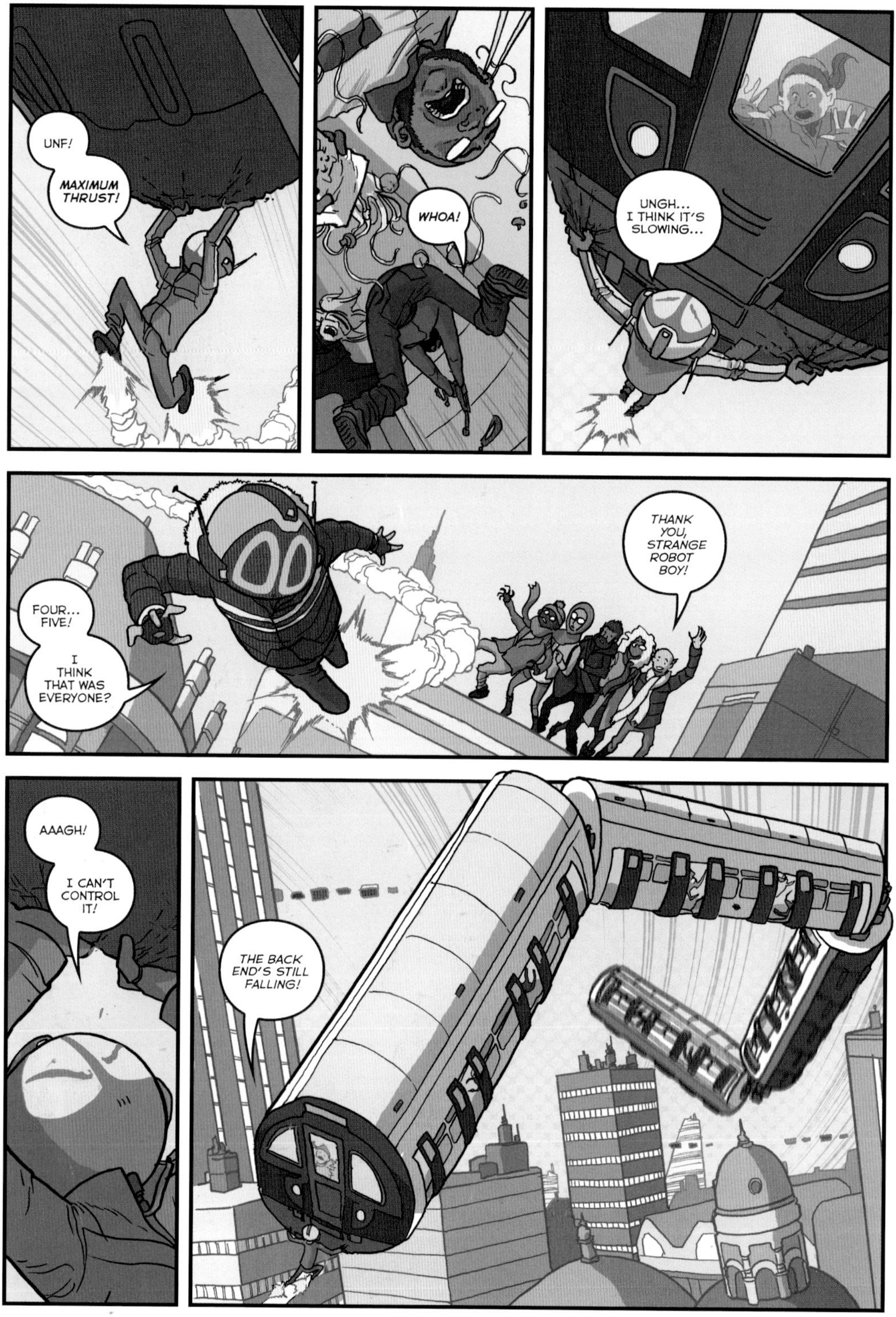
UNF!
MAXIMUM THRUST!
WHOA!
UNGH... I THINK IT'S SLOWING...
FOUR... FIVE!
I THINK THAT WAS EVERYONE?
THANK YOU, STRANGE ROBOT BOY!
AAAGH!
I CAN'T CONTROL IT!
THE BACK END'S STILL FALLING!

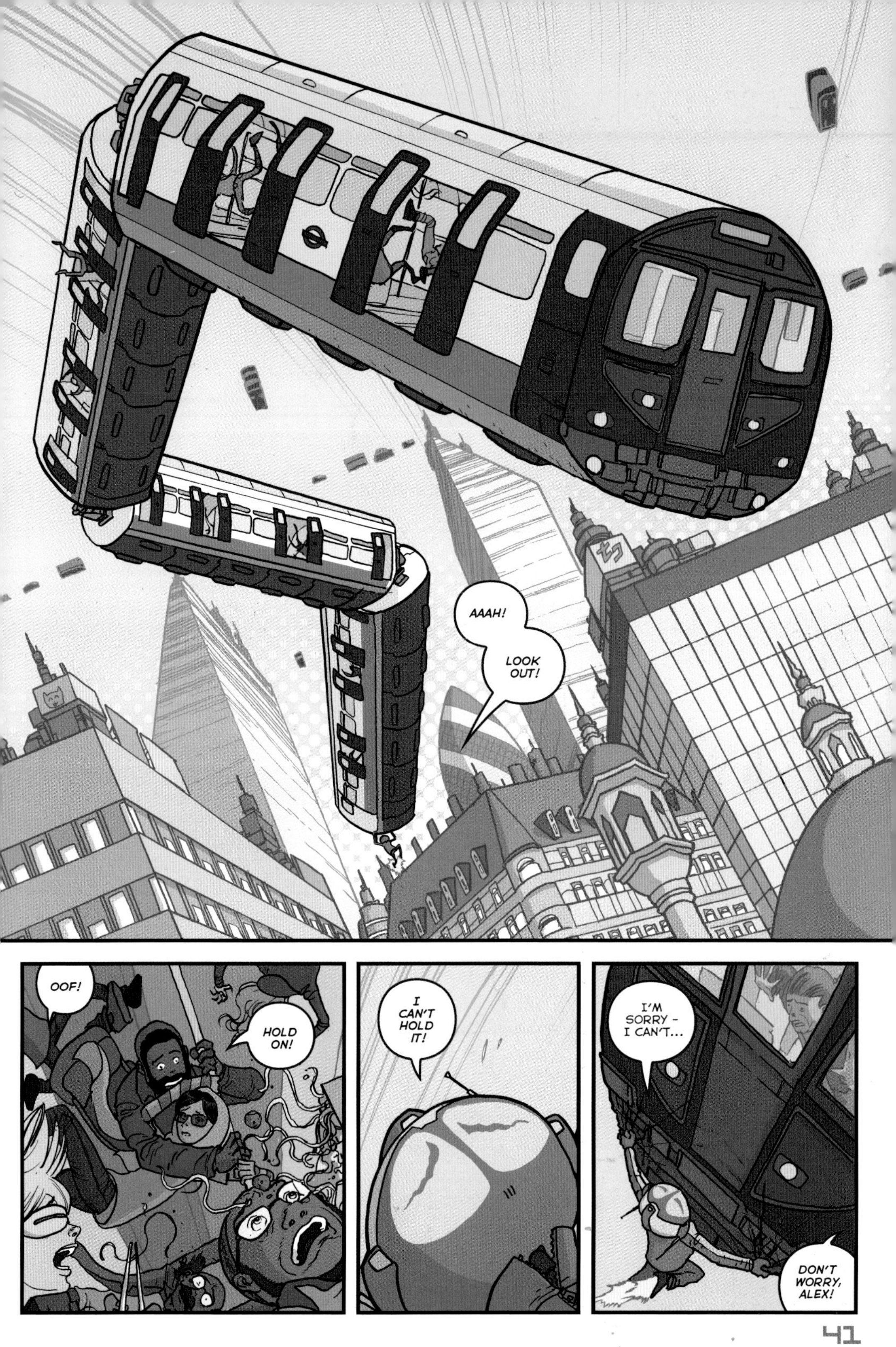
AAAH!
LOOK OUT!
OOF!
HOLD ON!
I CAN'T HOLD IT!
I'M SORRY - I CAN'T...
DON'T WORRY, ALEX!

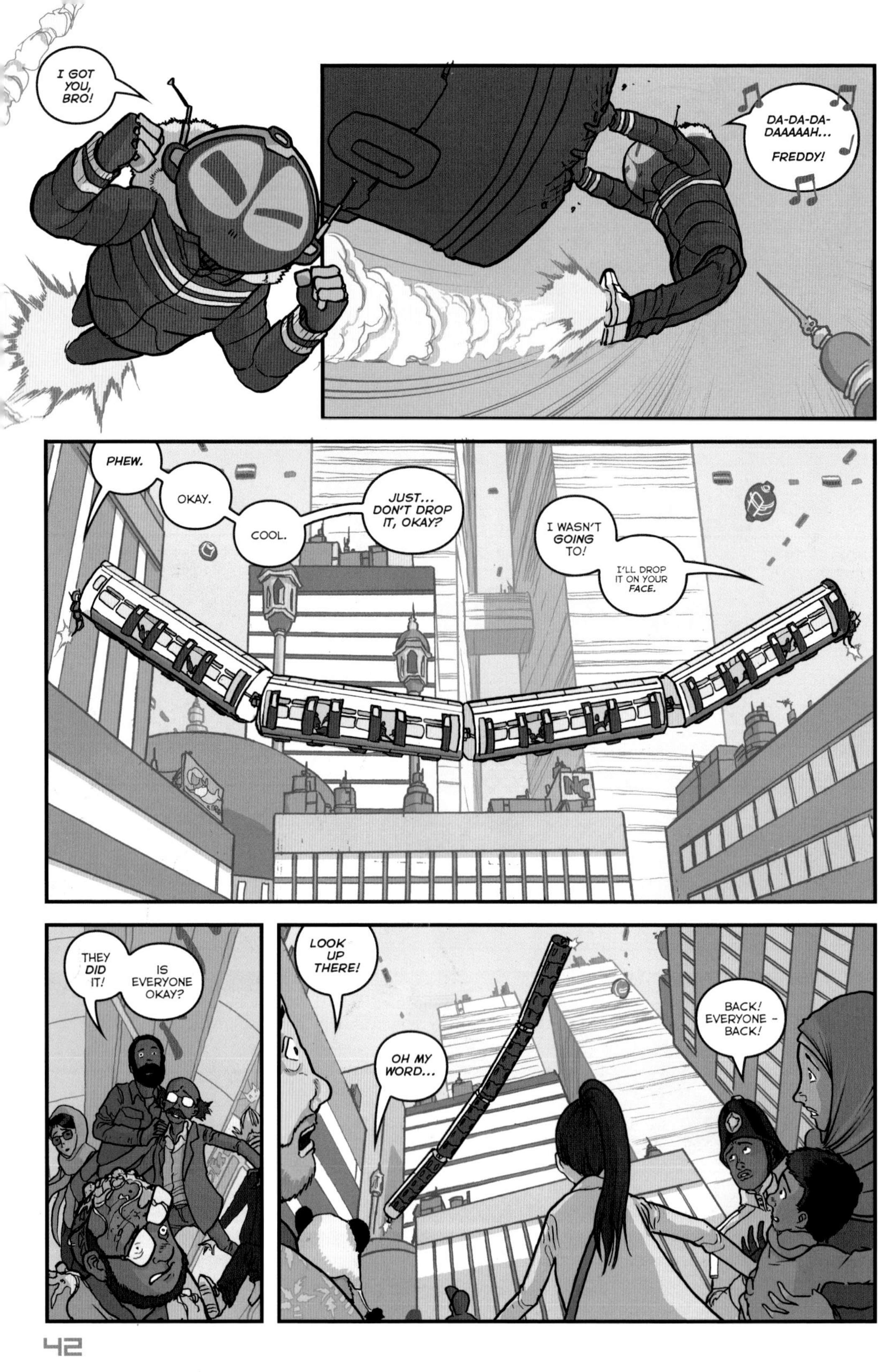
I GOT YOU, BRO!
DA-DA-DA-DAAAAAH... FREDDY!
PHEW.
OKAY.
COOL.
JUST... DON'T DROP IT, OKAY?
I WASN'T GOING TO!
I'LL DROP IT ON YOUR FACE.
THEY DID IT!
IS EVERYONE OKAY?
LOOK UP THERE!
OH MY WORD...
BACK! EVERYONE - BACK!

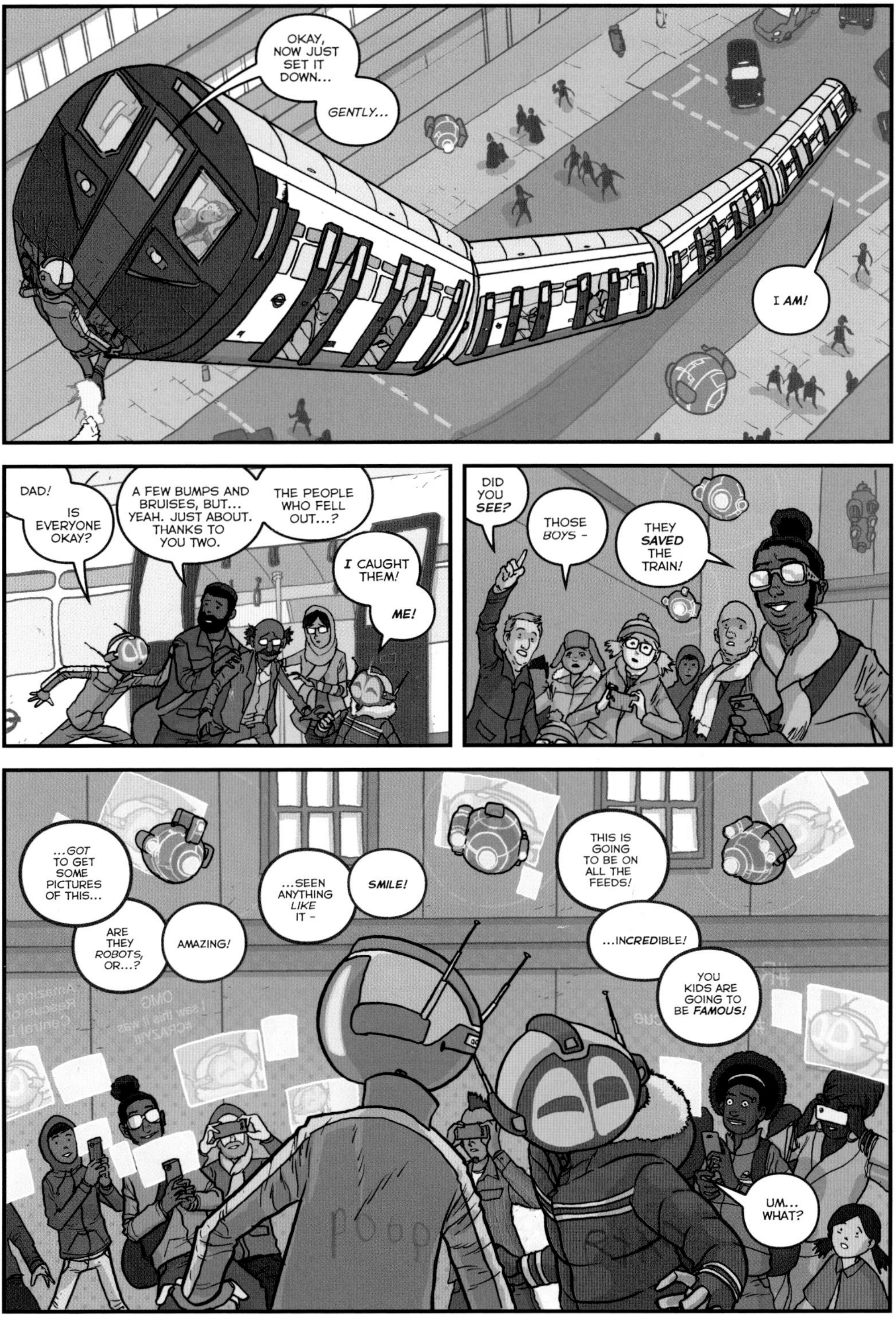
OKAY, NOW JUST SET IT DOWN...
GENTLY...
I AM!
DAD!
IS EVERYONE OKAY?
A FEW BUMPS AND BRUISES, BUT... YEAH. JUST ABOUT. THANKS TO YOU TWO.
THE PEOPLE WHO FELL OUT...?
I CAUGHT THEM!
ME!
DID YOU SEE?
THOSE BOYS -
THEY SAVED THE TRAIN!
...GOT TO GET SOME PICTURES OF THIS...
ARE THEY ROBOTS, OR...?
AMAZING!
...SEEN ANYTHING LIKE IT -
SMILE!
THIS IS GOING TO BE ON ALL THE FEEDS!
...INCREDIBLE!
YOU KIDS ARE GOING TO BE FAMOUS!
UM... WHAT?

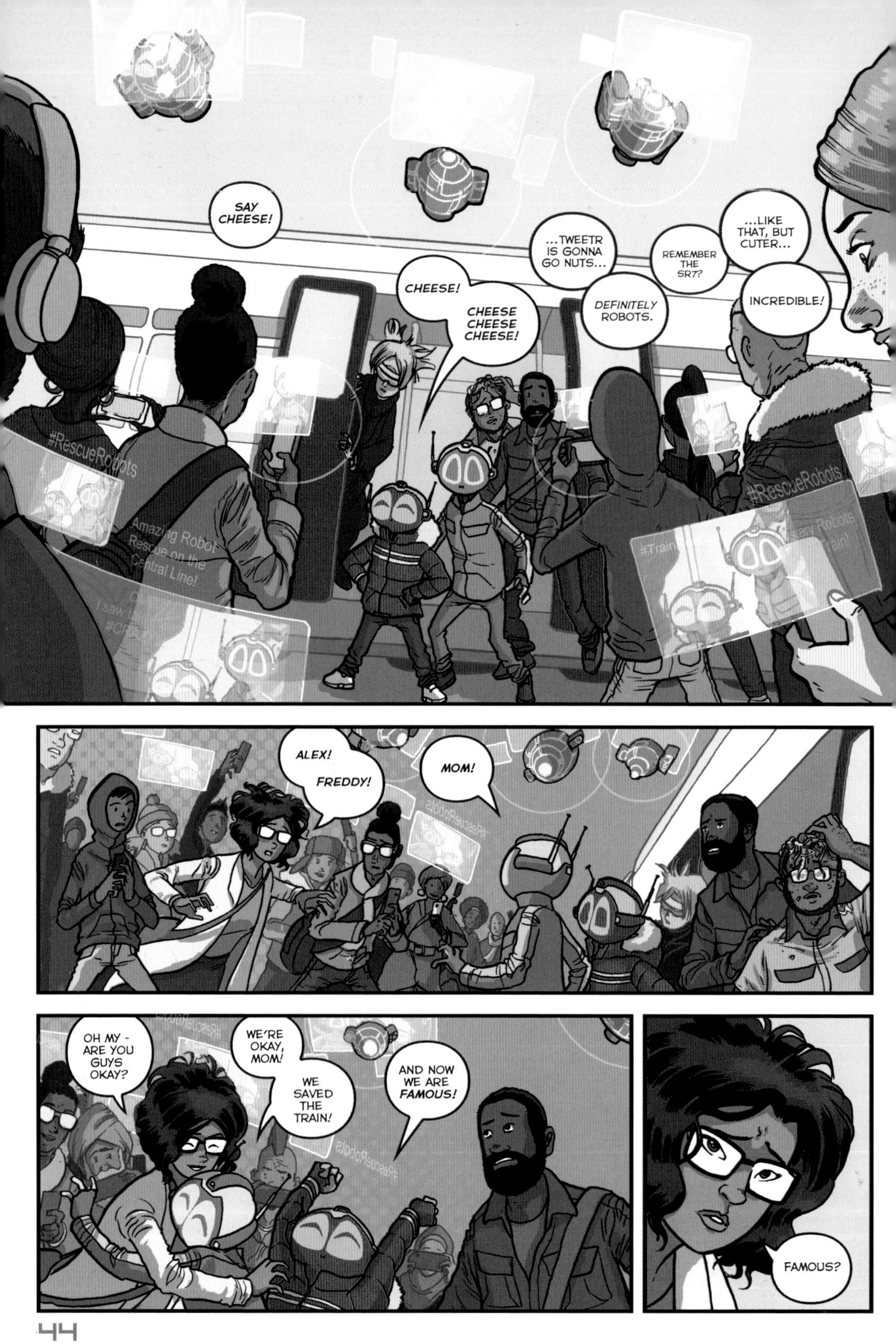
SAY CHEESE!
CHEESE!
CHEESE CHEESE CHEESE!
...TWEETR IS GONNA GO NUTS...
DEFINITELY ROBOTS.
REMEMBER THE SR7?
...LIKE THAT, BUT CUTER...
INCREDIBLE!
#RescueRobots
Amazing Robot Rescue on the Central Line!
#RescueRobots
ALEX!
FREDDY!
MOM!
OH MY - ARE YOU GUYS OKAY?
WE'RE OKAY, MOM!
WE SAVED THE TRAIN!
AND NOW WE ARE *FAMOUS!*
FAMOUS?

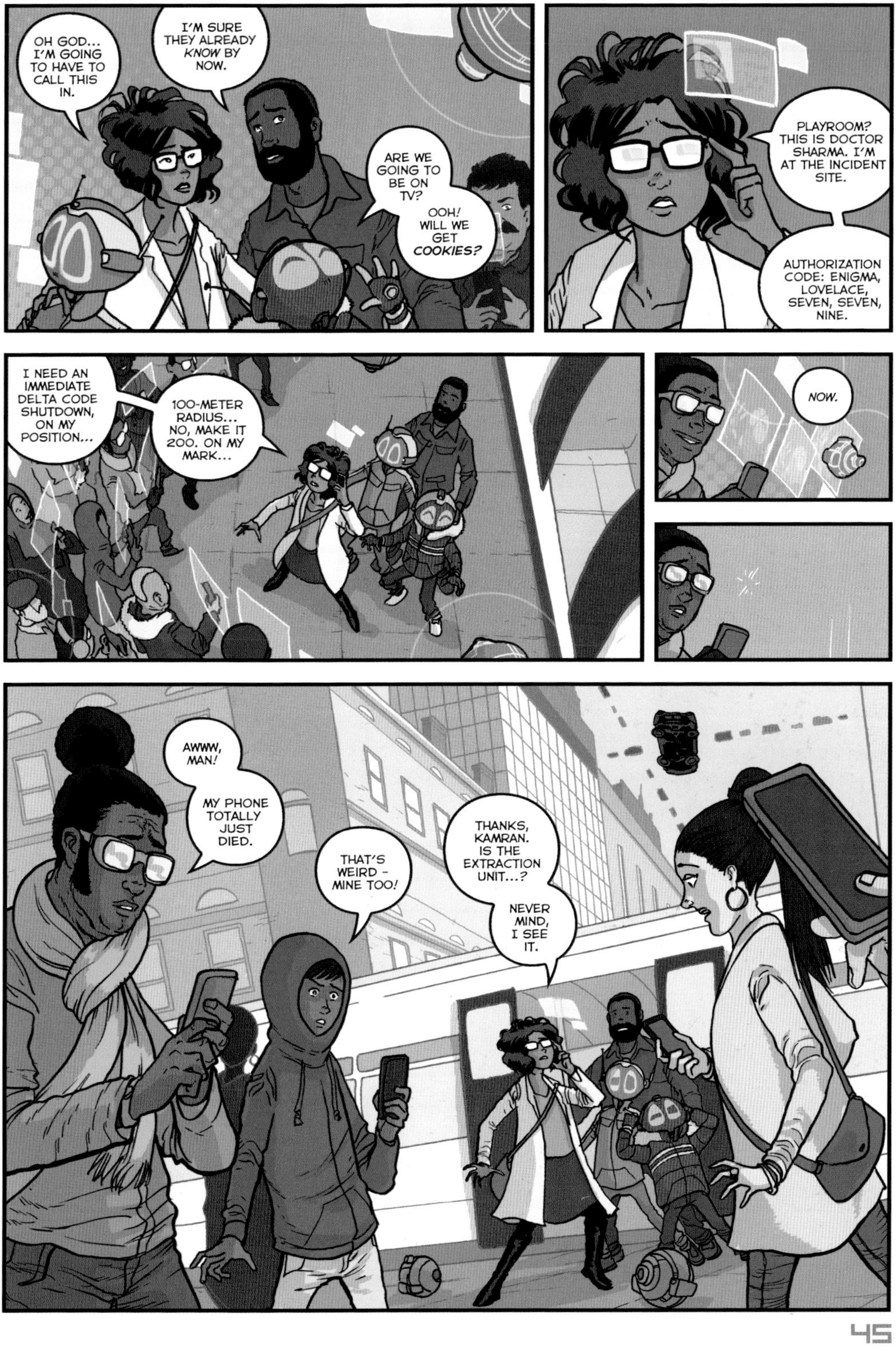
OH GOD... I'M GOING TO HAVE TO CALL THIS IN.
I'M SURE THEY ALREADY KNOW BY NOW.
ARE WE GOING TO BE ON TV?
OOH! WILL WE GET COOKIES?
PLAYROOM? THIS IS DOCTOR SHARMA. I'M AT THE INCIDENT SITE.
AUTHORIZATION CODE: ENIGMA, LOVELACE, SEVEN, SEVEN, NINE.
I NEED AN IMMEDIATE DELTA CODE SHUTDOWN, ON MY POSITION...
100-METER RADIUS... NO, MAKE IT 200. ON MY MARK...
NOW.
AWWW, MAN!
MY PHONE TOTALLY JUST DIED.
THAT'S WEIRD - MINE TOO!
THANKS, KAMRAN. IS THE EXTRACTION UNIT...?
NEVER MIND, I SEE IT.

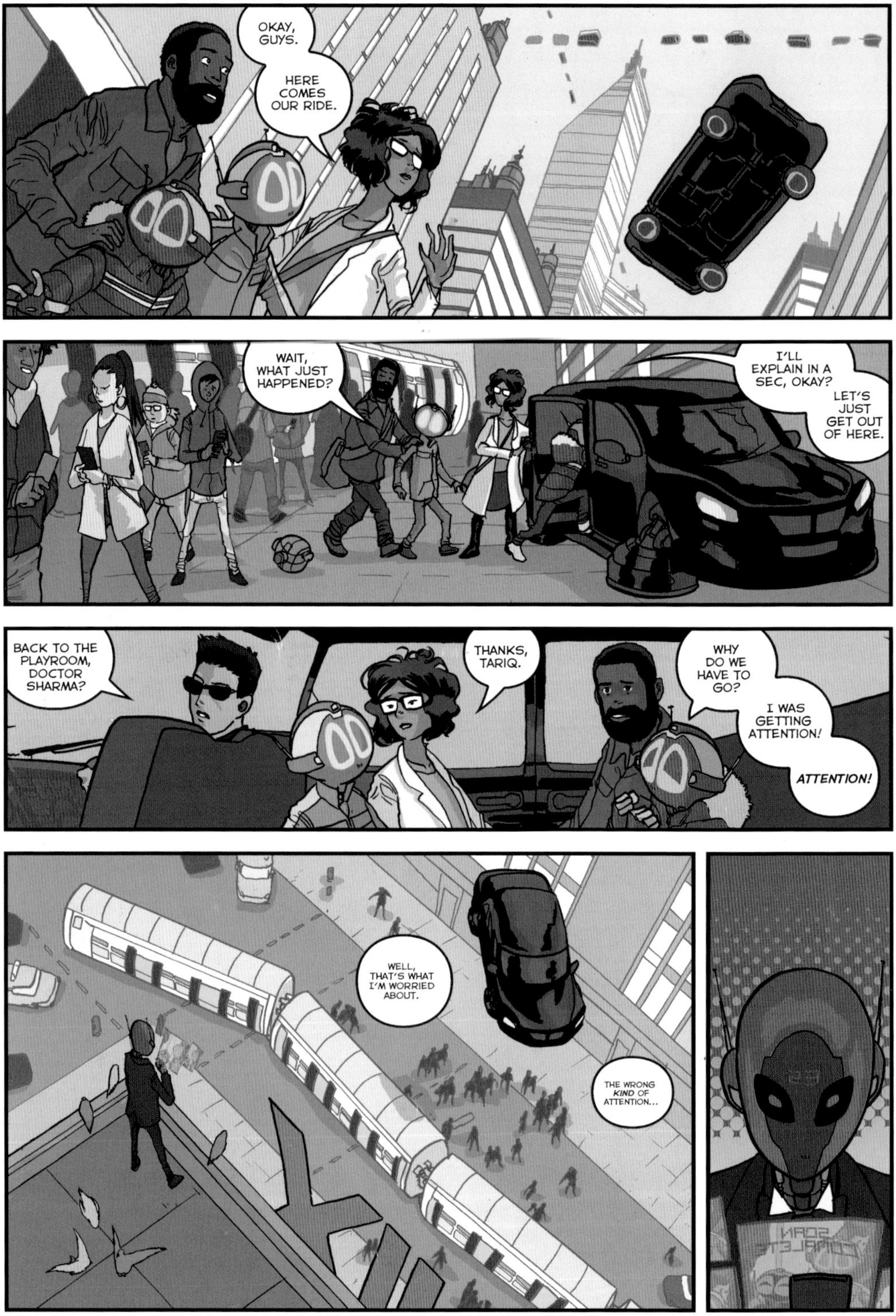
OKAY, GUYS.
HERE COMES OUR RIDE.
WAIT, WHAT JUST HAPPENED?
I'LL EXPLAIN IN A SEC, OKAY?
LET'S JUST GET OUT OF HERE.
BACK TO THE PLAYROOM, DOCTOR SHARMA?
THANKS, TARIQ.
WHY DO WE HAVE TO GO?
I WAS GETTING ATTENTION!
ATTENTION!
WELL, THAT'S WHAT I'M WORRIED ABOUT.
THE WRONG *KIND* OF ATTENTION...

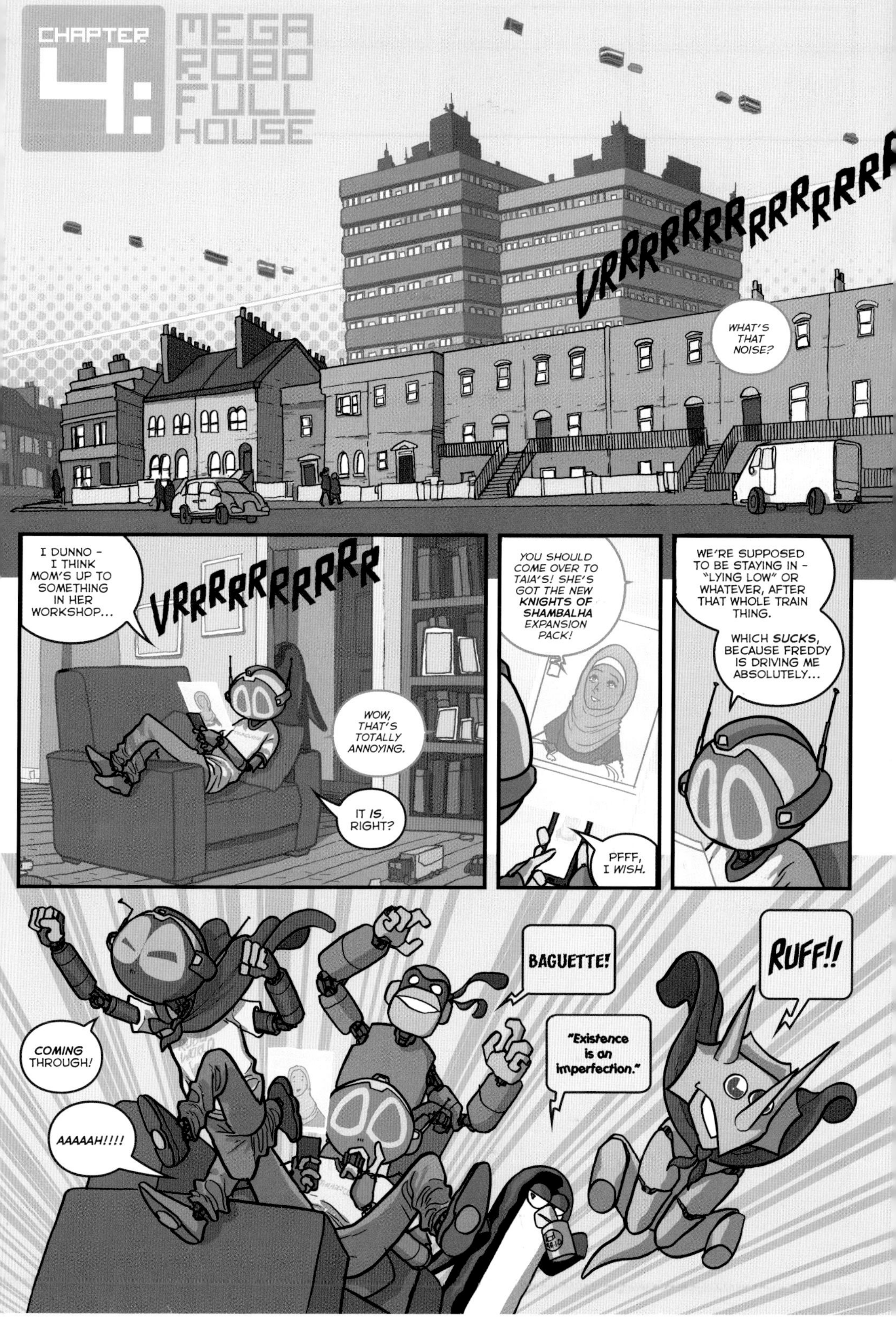
CHAPTER 4: MEGA ROBO FULL HOUSE
VRRRRRRRRRRRRRRR
WHAT'S THAT NOISE?
I DUNNO - I THINK MOM'S UP TO SOMETHING IN HER WORKSHOP...
VRRRRRRRRRR
WOW, THAT'S TOTALLY ANNOYING.
IT IS, RIGHT?
YOU SHOULD COME OVER TO TAIA'S! SHE'S GOT THE NEW KNIGHTS OF SHAMBALHA EXPANSION PACK!
PFFF, I WISH.
WE'RE SUPPOSED TO BE STAYING IN - "LYING LOW" OR WHATEVER, AFTER THAT WHOLE TRAIN THING.
WHICH SUCKS, BECAUSE FREDDY IS DRIVING ME ABSOLUTELY...
COMING THROUGH!
AAAAAH!!!!
BAGUETTE!
"Existence is an imperfection."
RUFF!!

...SEE WHAT I MEAN?

LIKE FREDDY ON HIS OWN WASN'T ANNOYING ENOUGH, NOW HE'S GOT HIS TRICERATOPS DOG, HIS INSANE GORILLA AND HIS...*STUPID PHILOSOPHY PENGUIN.*

VR RARR

AND IT'S LIKE THIS *ALL DAY.*

ALL RIGHT, MR. GRUMPYPANTS.

...SORRY. I'M JUST *TIRED.* I DIDN'T GET MUCH SLEEP.

ARE YOU OKAY, ALEX?

YEAH. JUST...

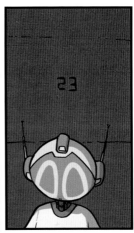

23

...BAD DREAMS.

IS IT... THE SAME ONE AGAIN?

YOU SHOULD TALK TO YOUR MOM AND DAD ABOUT IT...

I DUNNO. I DON'T WANT THEM TO WORRY. IT'S...

WAH*!!*

COMING THROUGH!

RUFF!

ALORS!

KRAK!

THAT'S IT!

MOOOOM!

VRRRRRRRRRR

VRRRR--

...MOM?

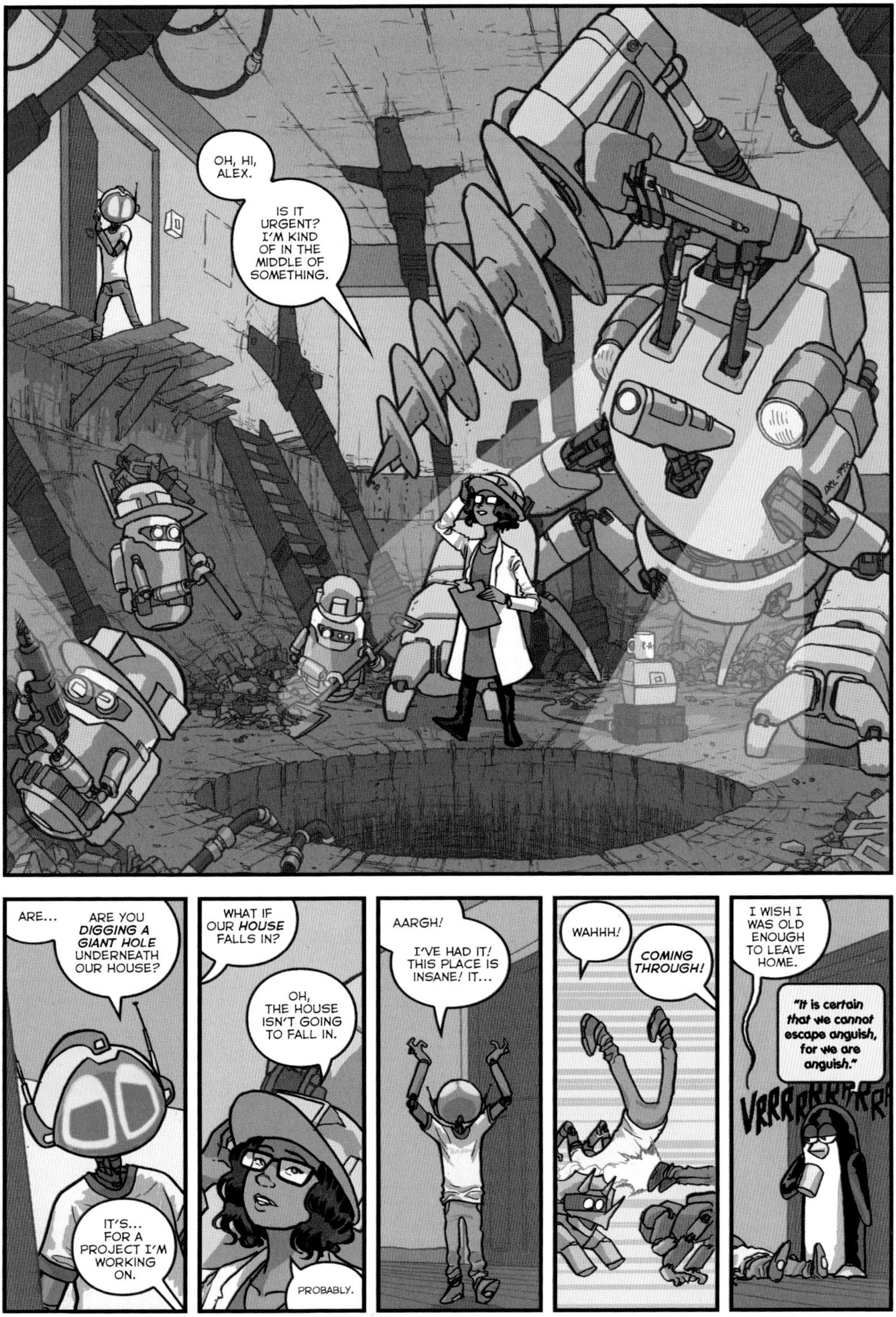
OH, HI, ALEX.
IS IT URGENT? I'M KIND OF IN THE MIDDLE OF SOMETHING.
ARE...
ARE YOU **DIGGING A GIANT HOLE** UNDERNEATH OUR HOUSE?
IT'S... FOR A PROJECT I'M WORKING ON.
WHAT IF OUR **HOUSE** FALLS IN?
OH, THE HOUSE ISN'T GOING TO FALL IN.
PROBABLY.
AARGH!
I'VE HAD IT! THIS PLACE IS INSANE! IT...
WAHHH!
COMING THROUGH!
I WISH I WAS OLD ENOUGH TO LEAVE HOME.
"It is certain that we cannot escape anguish, for we are anguish."
VRRRRRRRRRRA

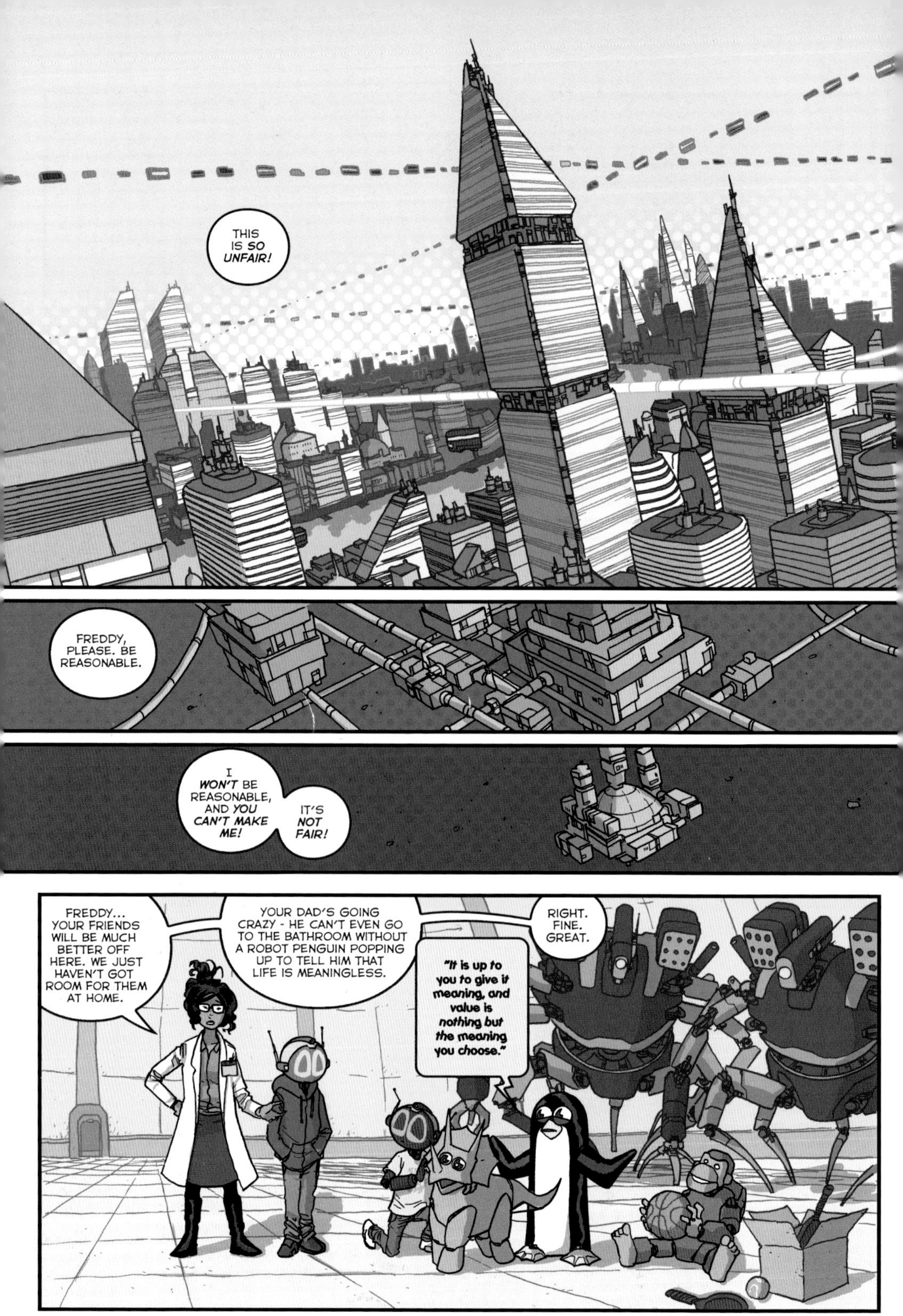
THIS IS SO UNFAIR!
FREDDY, PLEASE. BE REASONABLE.
I WON'T BE REASONABLE, AND YOU CAN'T MAKE ME!
IT'S NOT FAIR!
FREDDY... YOUR FRIENDS WILL BE MUCH BETTER OFF HERE. WE JUST HAVEN'T GOT ROOM FOR THEM AT HOME.
YOUR DAD'S GOING CRAZY - HE CAN'T EVEN GO TO THE BATHROOM WITHOUT A ROBOT PENGUIN POPPING UP TO TELL HIM THAT LIFE IS MEANINGLESS.
"It is up to you to give it meaning, and value is nothing but the meaning you choose."
RIGHT. FINE. GREAT.

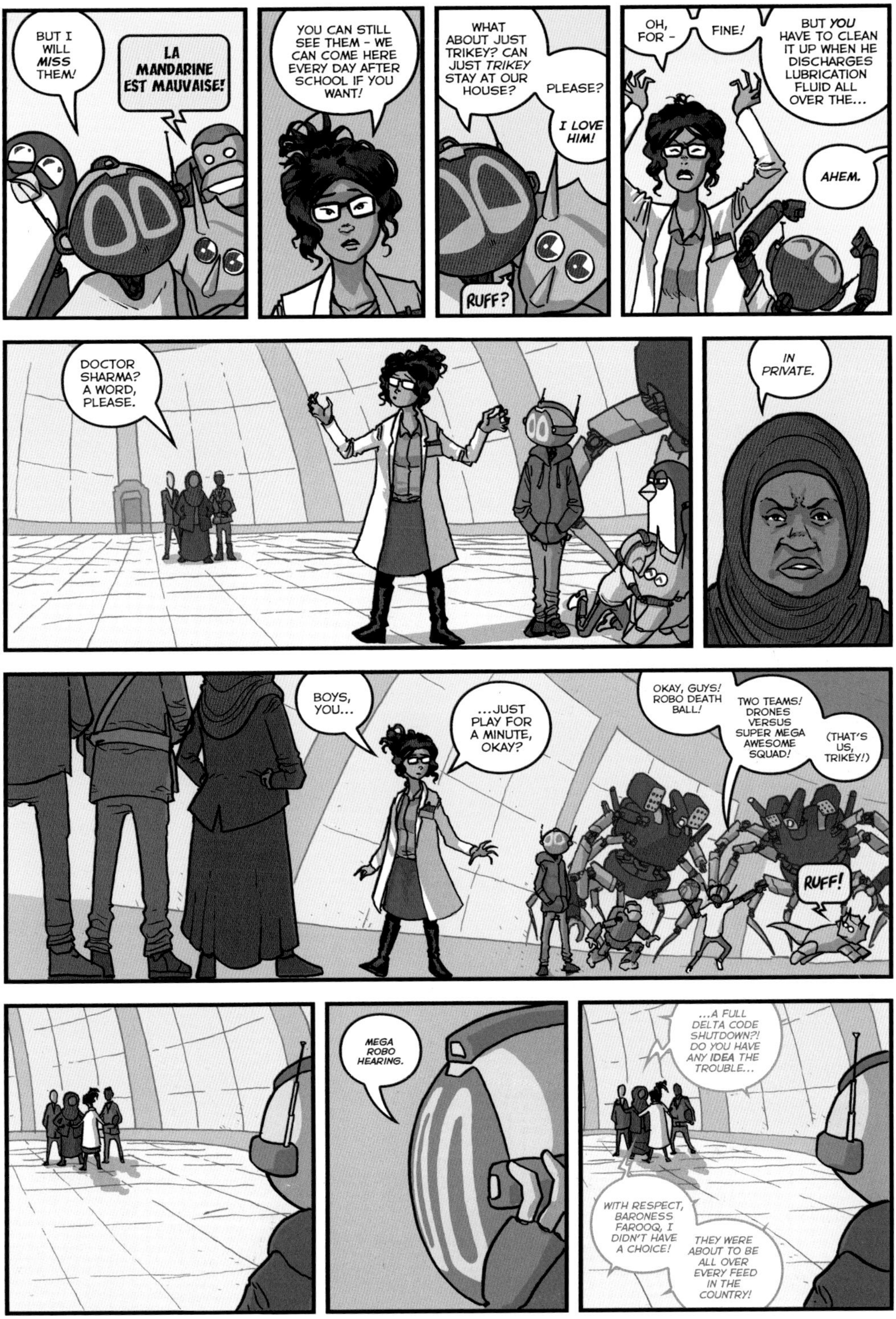
BUT I WILL *MISS* THEM!
LA MANDARINE EST MAUVAISE!
YOU CAN STILL SEE THEM - WE CAN COME HERE EVERY DAY AFTER SCHOOL IF YOU WANT!
WHAT ABOUT JUST TRIKEY? CAN JUST *TRIKEY* STAY AT OUR HOUSE?
PLEASE?
I LOVE HIM!
RUFF?
OH, FOR -
FINE!
BUT *YOU* HAVE TO CLEAN IT UP WHEN HE DISCHARGES LUBRICATION FLUID ALL OVER THE...
AHEM.
DOCTOR SHARMA? A WORD, PLEASE.
IN PRIVATE.
BOYS, YOU...
...JUST PLAY FOR A MINUTE, OKAY?
OKAY, GUYS! ROBO DEATH BALL!
TWO TEAMS! DRONES VERSUS SUPER MEGA AWESOME SQUAD!
(THAT'S US, TRIKEY!)
RUFF!
MEGA ROBO HEARING.
...A FULL DELTA CODE SHUTDOWN?! DO YOU HAVE ANY *IDEA* THE TROUBLE...
WITH RESPECT, BARONESS FAROOQ, I DIDN'T HAVE A CHOICE!
THEY WERE ABOUT TO BE ALL OVER EVERY FEED IN THE COUNTRY!

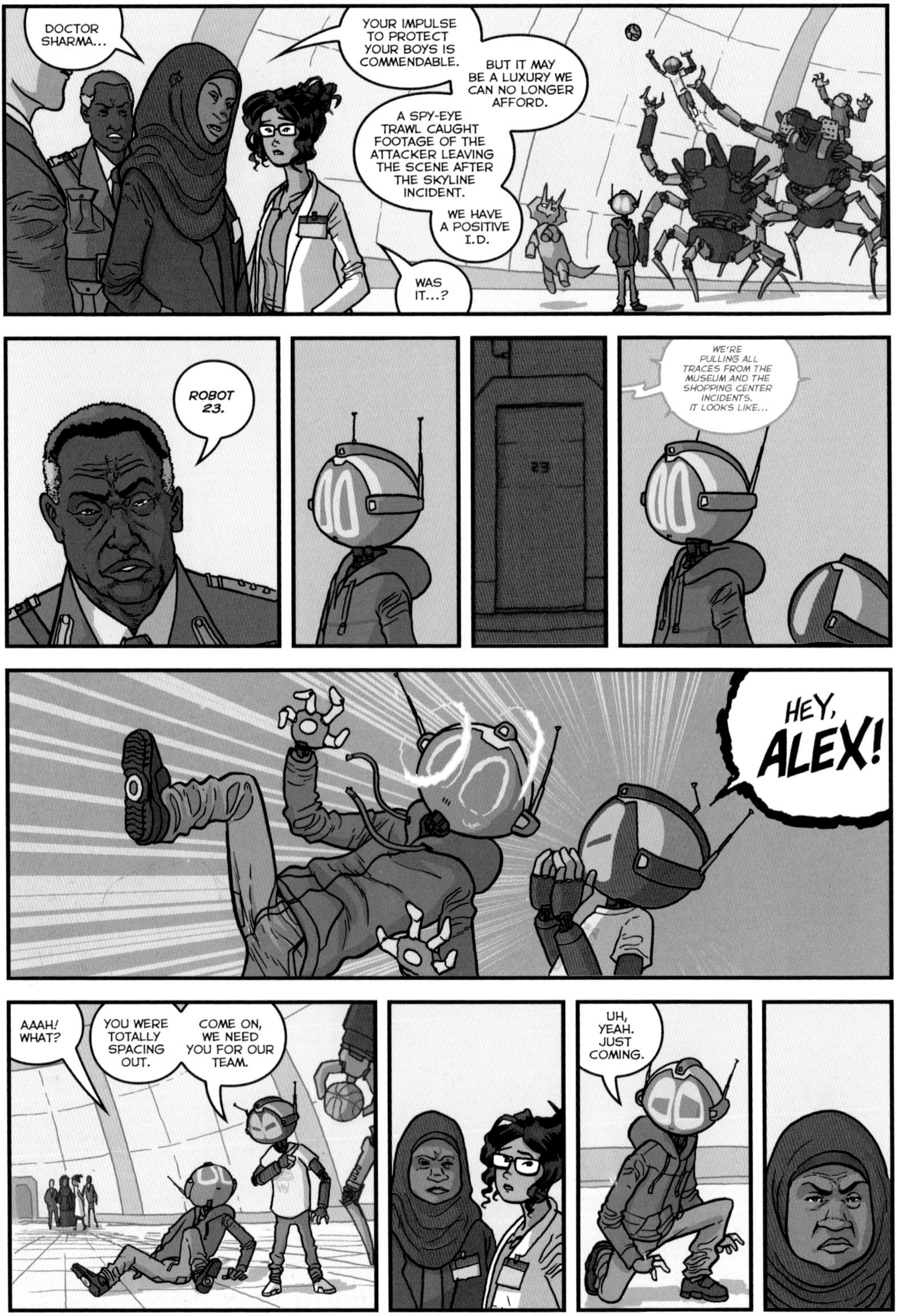
DOCTOR SHARMA...
YOUR IMPULSE TO PROTECT YOUR BOYS IS COMMENDABLE.
BUT IT MAY BE A LUXURY WE CAN NO LONGER AFFORD.
A SPY-EYE TRAWL CAUGHT FOOTAGE OF THE ATTACKER LEAVING THE SCENE AFTER THE SKYLINE INCIDENT.
WE HAVE A POSITIVE I.D.
WAS IT...?
ROBOT 23.
23
WE'RE PULLING ALL TRACES FROM THE MUSEUM AND THE SHOPPING CENTER INCIDENTS. IT LOOKS LIKE...
HEY, ALEX!
AAAH! WHAT?
YOU WERE TOTALLY SPACING OUT.
COME ON, WE NEED YOU FOR OUR TEAM.
UH, YEAH. JUST COMING.

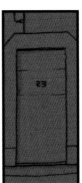

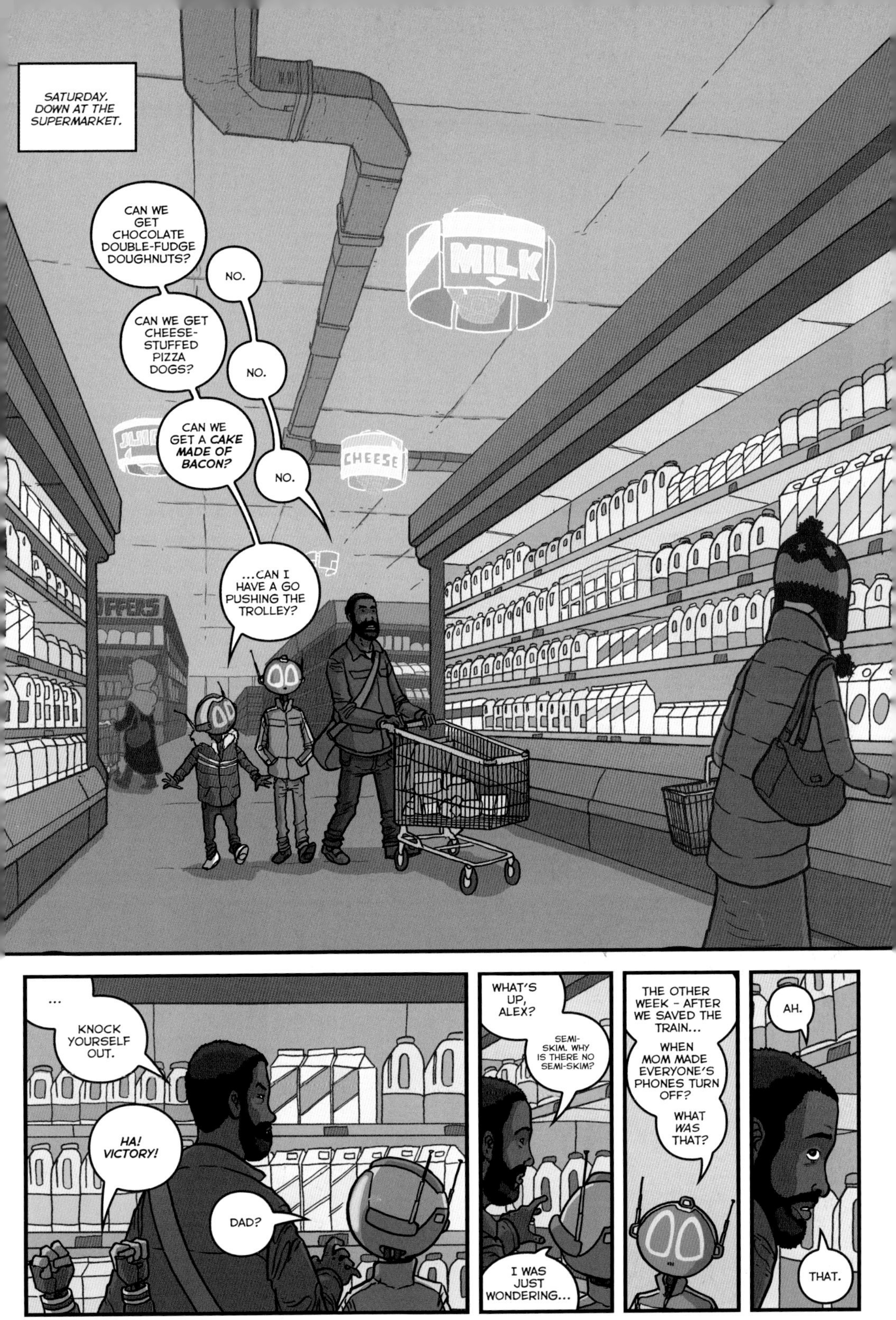
SATURDAY. DOWN AT THE SUPERMARKET.
CAN WE GET CHOCOLATE DOUBLE-FUDGE DOUGHNUTS?
NO.
CAN WE GET CHEESE-STUFFED PIZZA DOGS?
NO.
CAN WE GET A *CAKE MADE OF BACON?*
NO.
...CAN I HAVE A GO PUSHING THE TROLLEY?
MILK
CHEESE
...
KNOCK YOURSELF OUT.
HA! VICTORY!
DAD?
WHAT'S UP, ALEX?
SEMI-SKIM. WHY IS THERE NO SEMI-SKIM?
I WAS JUST WONDERING...
THE OTHER WEEK - AFTER WE SAVED THE TRAIN...
WHEN MOM MADE EVERYONE'S PHONES TURN OFF?
WHAT *WAS* THAT?
AH.
THAT.

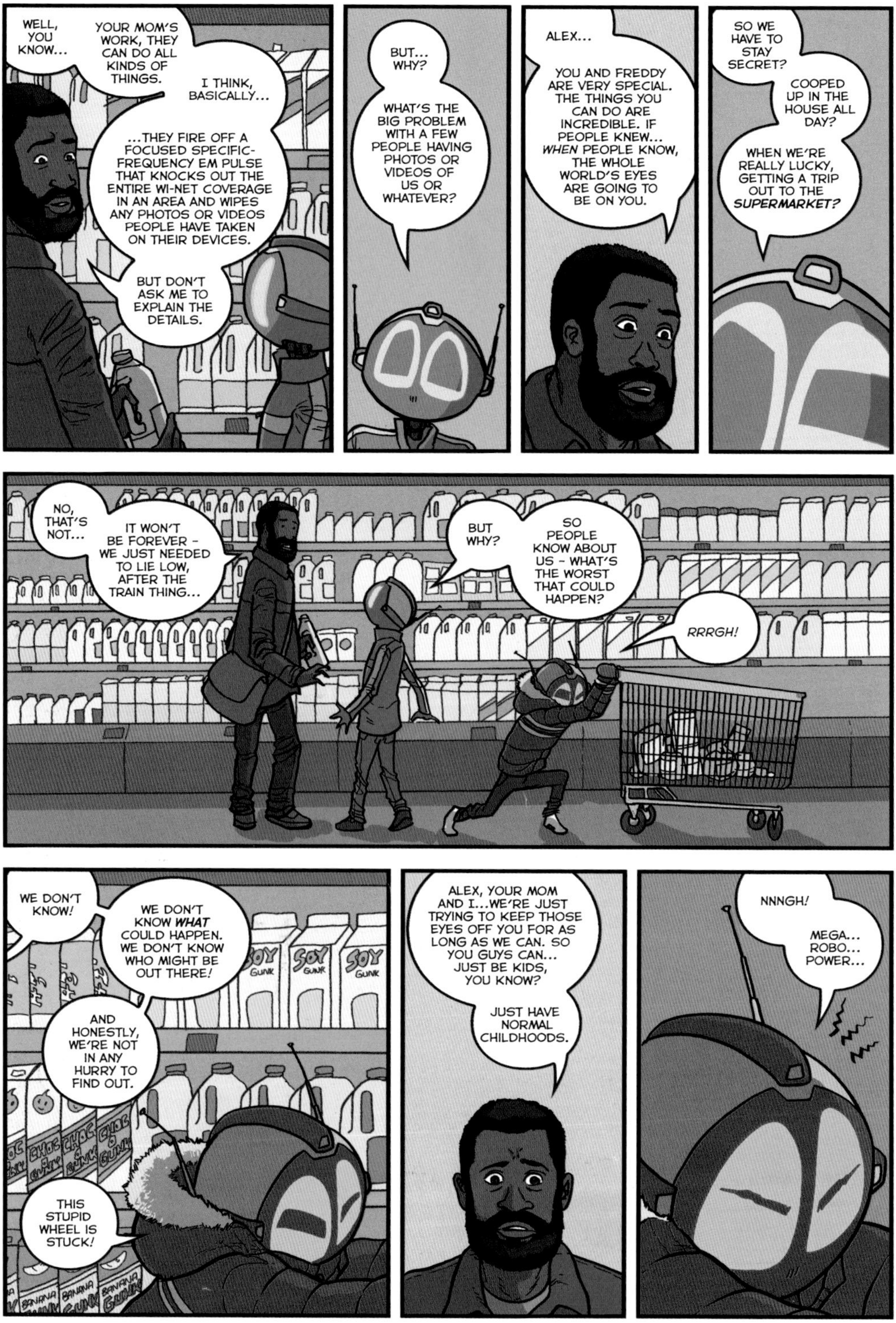
WELL, YOU KNOW...
YOUR MOM'S WORK, THEY CAN DO ALL KINDS OF THINGS.
I THINK, BASICALLY...
...THEY FIRE OFF A FOCUSED SPECIFIC-FREQUENCY EM PULSE THAT KNOCKS OUT THE ENTIRE WI-NET COVERAGE IN AN AREA AND WIPES ANY PHOTOS OR VIDEOS PEOPLE HAVE TAKEN ON THEIR DEVICES.
BUT DON'T ASK ME TO EXPLAIN THE DETAILS.
BUT... WHY?
WHAT'S THE BIG PROBLEM WITH A FEW PEOPLE HAVING PHOTOS OR VIDEOS OF US OR WHATEVER?
ALEX...
YOU AND FREDDY ARE VERY SPECIAL. THE THINGS YOU CAN DO ARE INCREDIBLE. IF PEOPLE KNEW... *WHEN* PEOPLE KNOW, THE WHOLE WORLD'S EYES ARE GOING TO BE ON YOU.
SO WE HAVE TO STAY SECRET?
COOPED UP IN THE HOUSE ALL DAY?
WHEN WE'RE REALLY LUCKY, GETTING A TRIP OUT TO THE ***SUPERMARKET?***
NO, THAT'S NOT...
IT WON'T BE FOREVER - WE JUST NEEDED TO LIE LOW, AFTER THE TRAIN THING...
BUT WHY?
SO PEOPLE KNOW ABOUT US - WHAT'S THE WORST THAT COULD HAPPEN?
RRRGH!
WE DON'T KNOW!
WE DON'T KNOW ***WHAT*** COULD HAPPEN. WE DON'T KNOW WHO MIGHT BE OUT THERE!
AND HONESTLY, WE'RE NOT IN ANY HURRY TO FIND OUT.
THIS STUPID WHEEL IS STUCK!
SOY GUNK
CHOC & GUNK
BANANA GUNK
ALEX, YOUR MOM AND I...WE'RE JUST TRYING TO KEEP THOSE EYES OFF YOU FOR AS LONG AS WE CAN. SO YOU GUYS CAN... JUST BE KIDS, YOU KNOW?
JUST HAVE NORMAL CHILDHOODS.
NNNGH!
MEGA... ROBO... POWER...

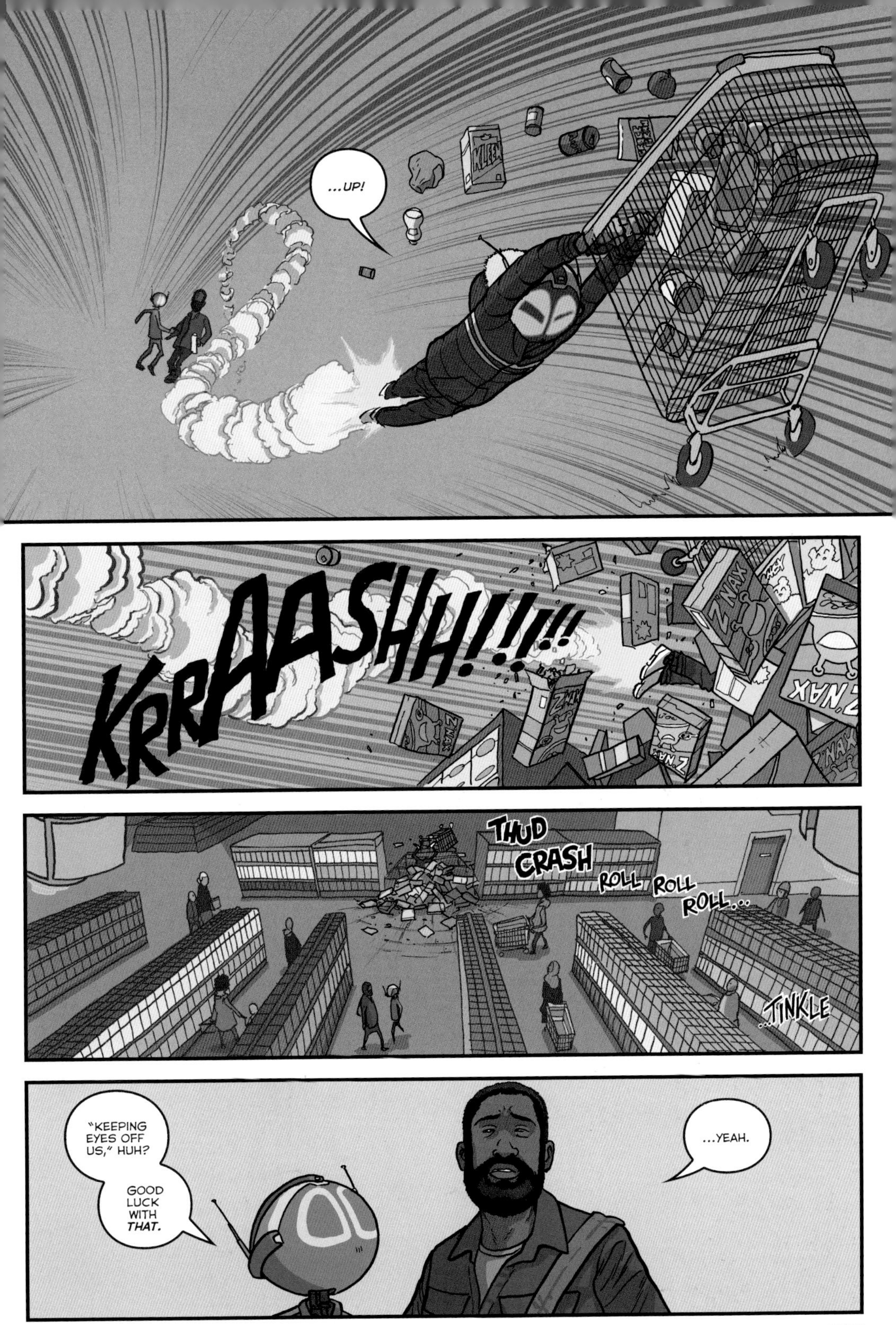
...UP!
KRRAASHH!!!!!!
THUD
CRASH
ROLL ROLL
ROLL...
...TINKLE
"KEEPING EYES OFF US," HUH?
GOOD LUCK WITH *THAT.*
...YEAH.

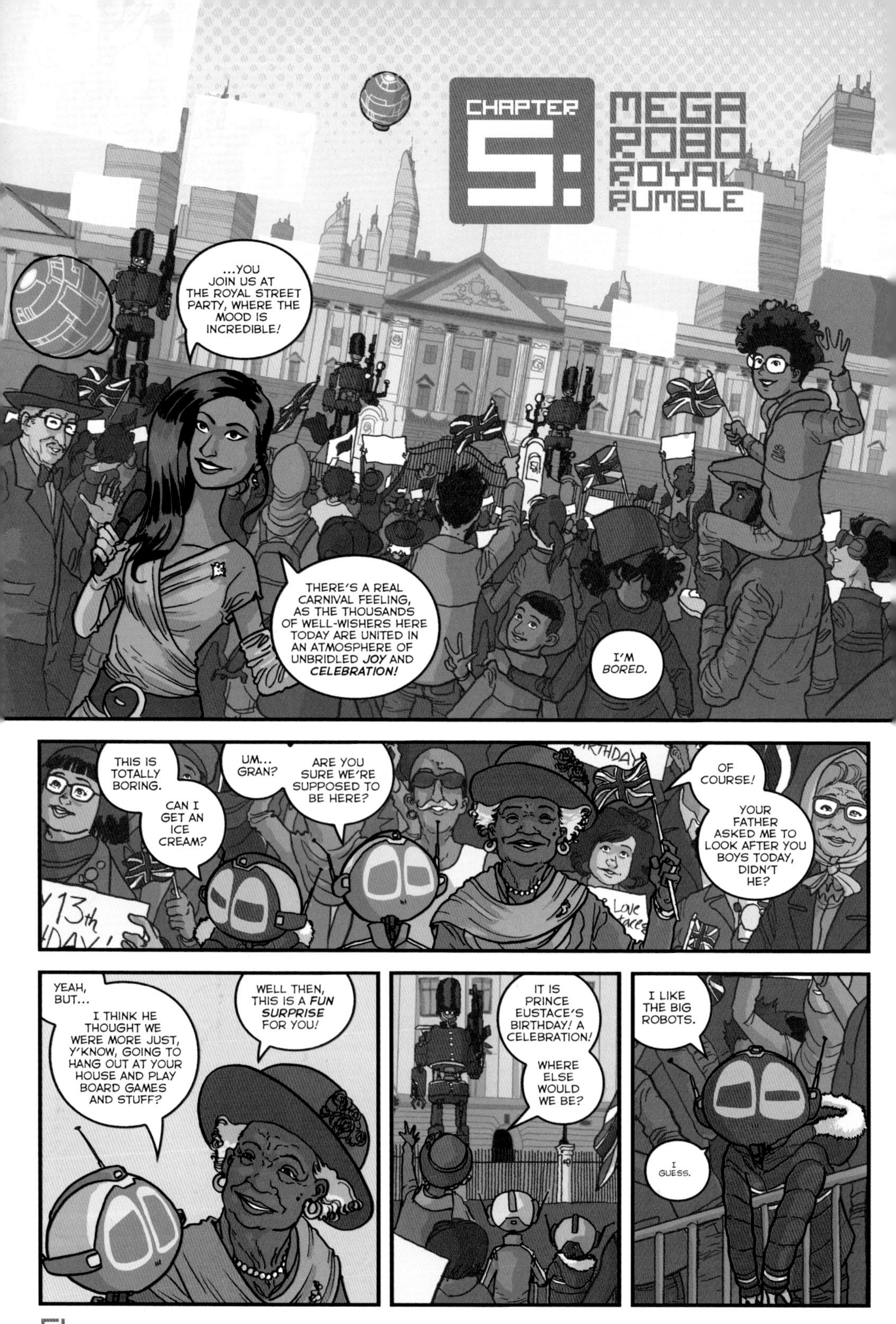
CHAPTER 5: MEGA ROBO ROYAL RUMBLE
...YOU JOIN US AT THE ROYAL STREET PARTY, WHERE THE MOOD IS INCREDIBLE!
THERE'S A REAL CARNIVAL FEELING, AS THE THOUSANDS OF WELL-WISHERS HERE TODAY ARE UNITED IN AN ATMOSPHERE OF UNBRIDLED JOY AND CELEBRATION!
I'M BORED.
THIS IS TOTALLY BORING.
CAN I GET AN ICE CREAM?
UM... GRAN?
ARE YOU SURE WE'RE SUPPOSED TO BE HERE?
OF COURSE!
YOUR FATHER ASKED ME TO LOOK AFTER YOU BOYS TODAY, DIDN'T HE?
YEAH, BUT...
I THINK HE THOUGHT WE WERE MORE JUST, Y'KNOW, GOING TO HANG OUT AT YOUR HOUSE AND PLAY BOARD GAMES AND STUFF?
WELL THEN, THIS IS A FUN SURPRISE FOR YOU!
IT IS PRINCE EUSTACE'S BIRTHDAY! A CELEBRATION!
WHERE ELSE WOULD WE BE?
I LIKE THE BIG ROBOTS.
I GUESS.

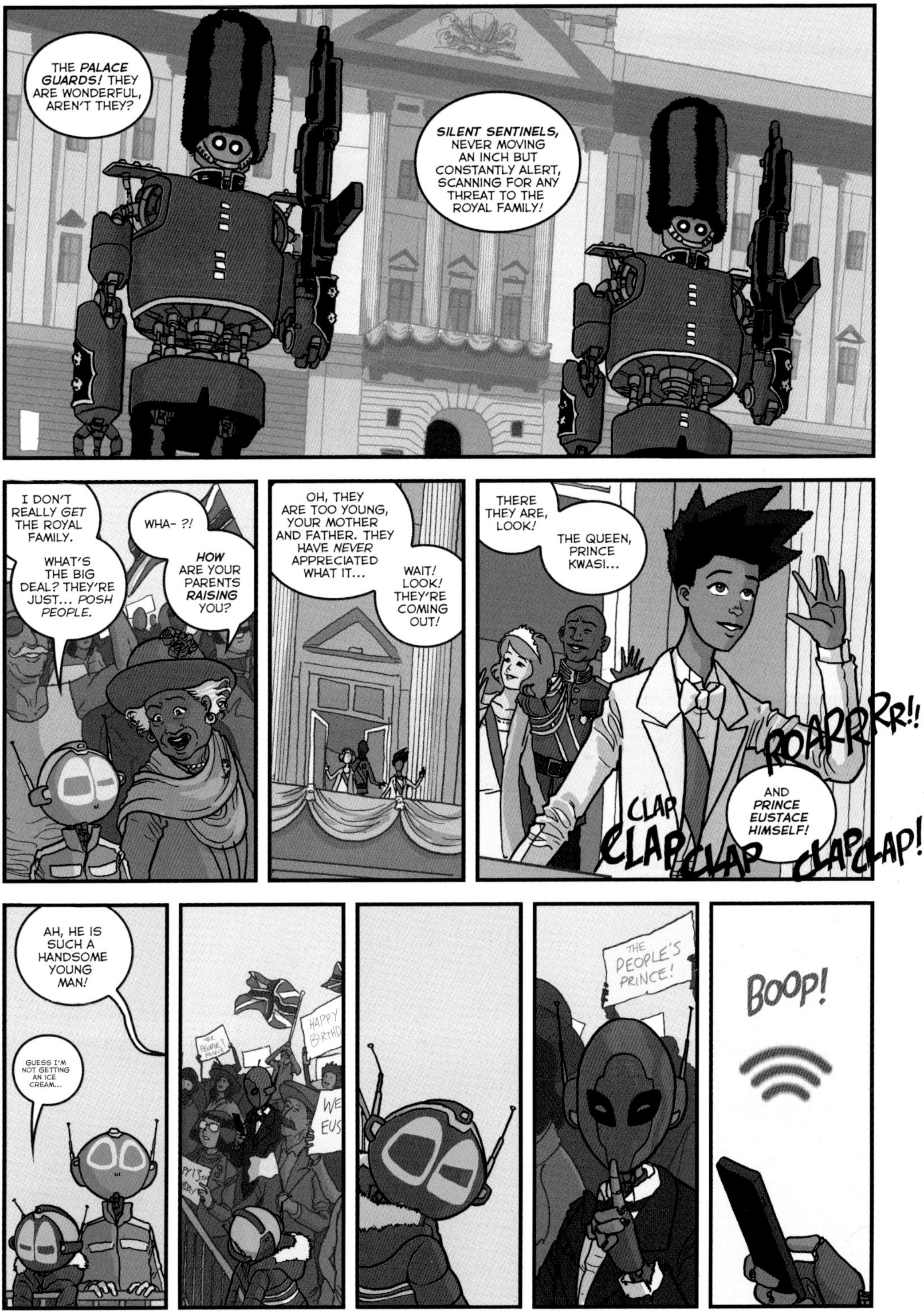
THE *PALACE GUARDS!* THEY ARE WONDERFUL, AREN'T THEY?
SILENT SENTINELS, NEVER MOVING AN INCH BUT CONSTANTLY ALERT, SCANNING FOR ANY THREAT TO THE ROYAL FAMILY!
I DON'T REALLY *GET* THE ROYAL FAMILY.
WHAT'S THE BIG DEAL? THEY'RE JUST... *POSH PEOPLE.*
WHA- ?!
HOW ARE YOUR PARENTS ***RAISING*** YOU?
OH, THEY ARE TOO YOUNG, YOUR MOTHER AND FATHER. THEY HAVE *NEVER* APPRECIATED WHAT IT...
WAIT! LOOK! THEY'RE COMING OUT!
THERE THEY ARE, LOOK!
THE QUEEN, PRINCE KWASI...
ROARRRR!!
AND ***PRINCE EUSTACE*** HIMSELF!
CLAP CLAP CLAP CLAP CLAP!
AH, HE IS SUCH A HANDSOME YOUNG MAN!
GUESS I'M NOT GETTING AN ICE CREAM...
THE PEOPLE'S PRINCE!
BOOP!

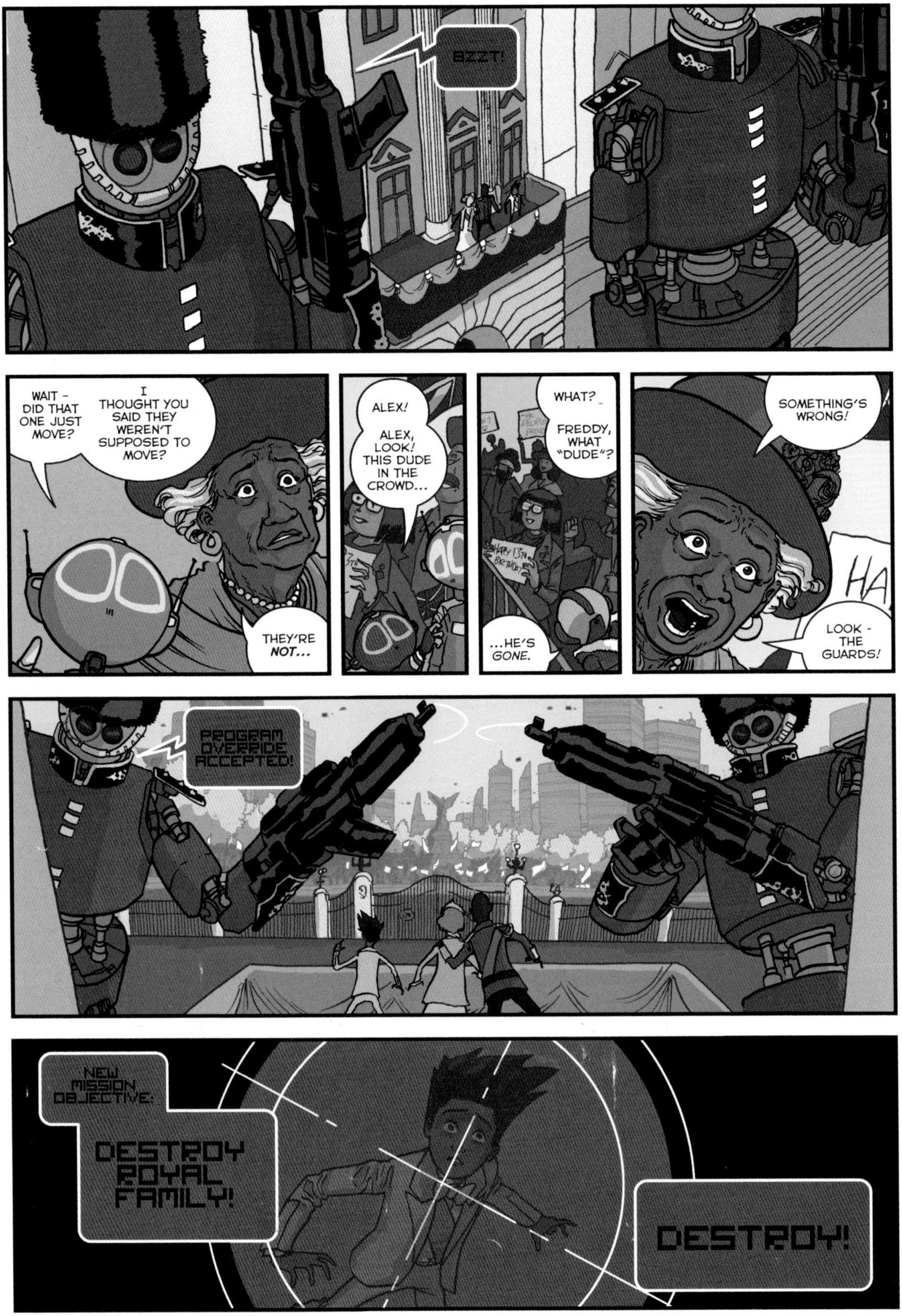
BZZT!
WAIT - DID THAT ONE JUST MOVE?
I THOUGHT YOU SAID THEY WEREN'T SUPPOSED TO MOVE?
THEY'RE NOT...
ALEX!
ALEX, LOOK! THIS DUDE IN THE CROWD...
WHAT?
FREDDY, WHAT "DUDE"?
...HE'S GONE.
HAPPY 13TH BIRTHDAY
SOMETHING'S WRONG!
LOOK - THE GUARDS!
PROGRAM OVERRIDE ACCEPTED!
NEW MISSION OBJECTIVE:
DESTROY ROYAL FAMILY!
DESTROY!

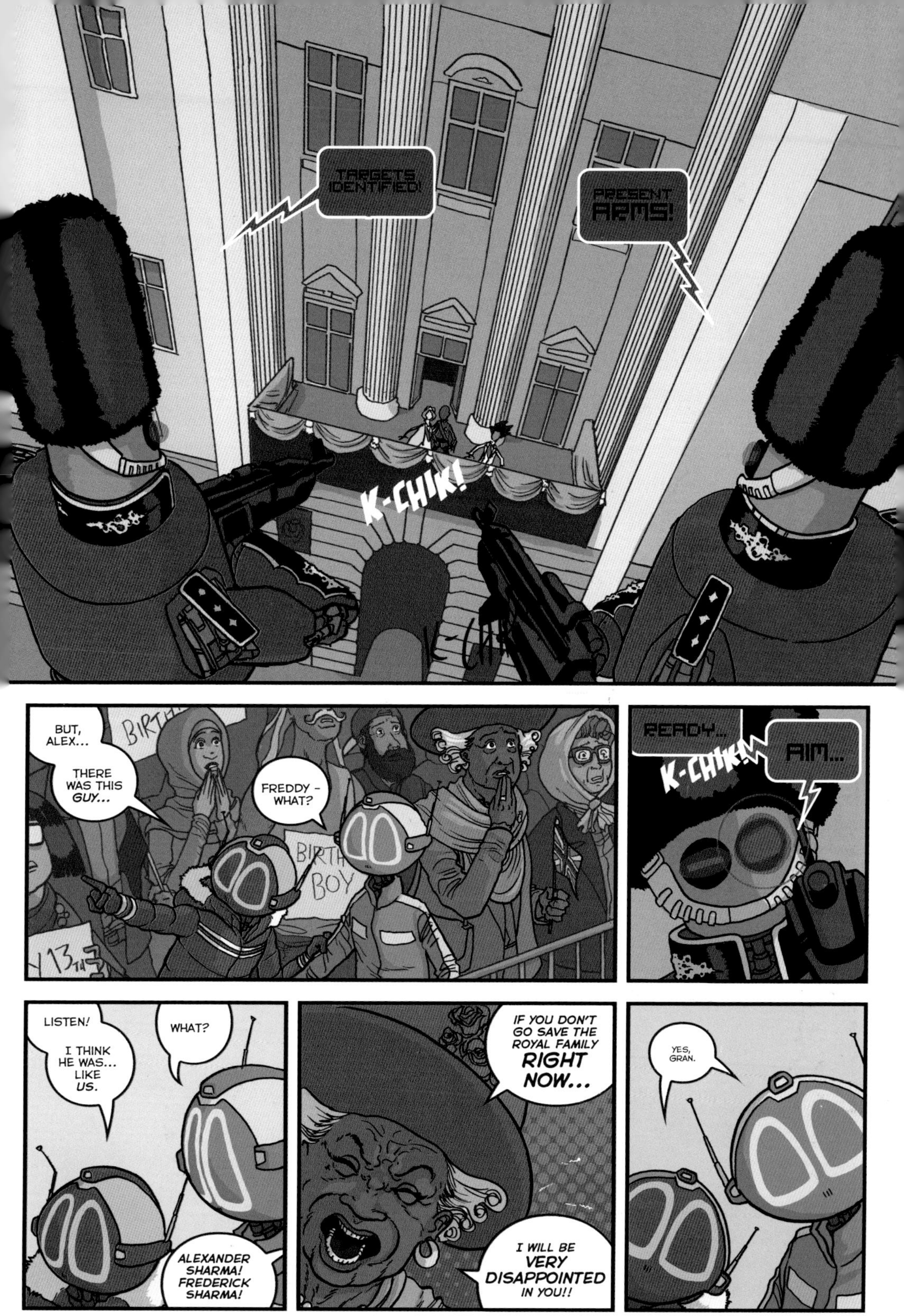
TARGETS IDENTIFIED!
PRESENT ARMS!
K-CHIK!
BUT, ALEX...
THERE WAS THIS *GUY*...
FREDDY - WHAT?
READY...
K-CHIK!
AIM...
LISTEN!
I THINK HE WAS... LIKE *US*.
WHAT?
ALEXANDER SHARMA! FREDERICK SHARMA!
IF YOU DON'T GO SAVE THE ROYAL FAMILY **RIGHT NOW...**
I WILL BE **VERY DISAPPOINTED** IN YOU!!
YES, GRAN.

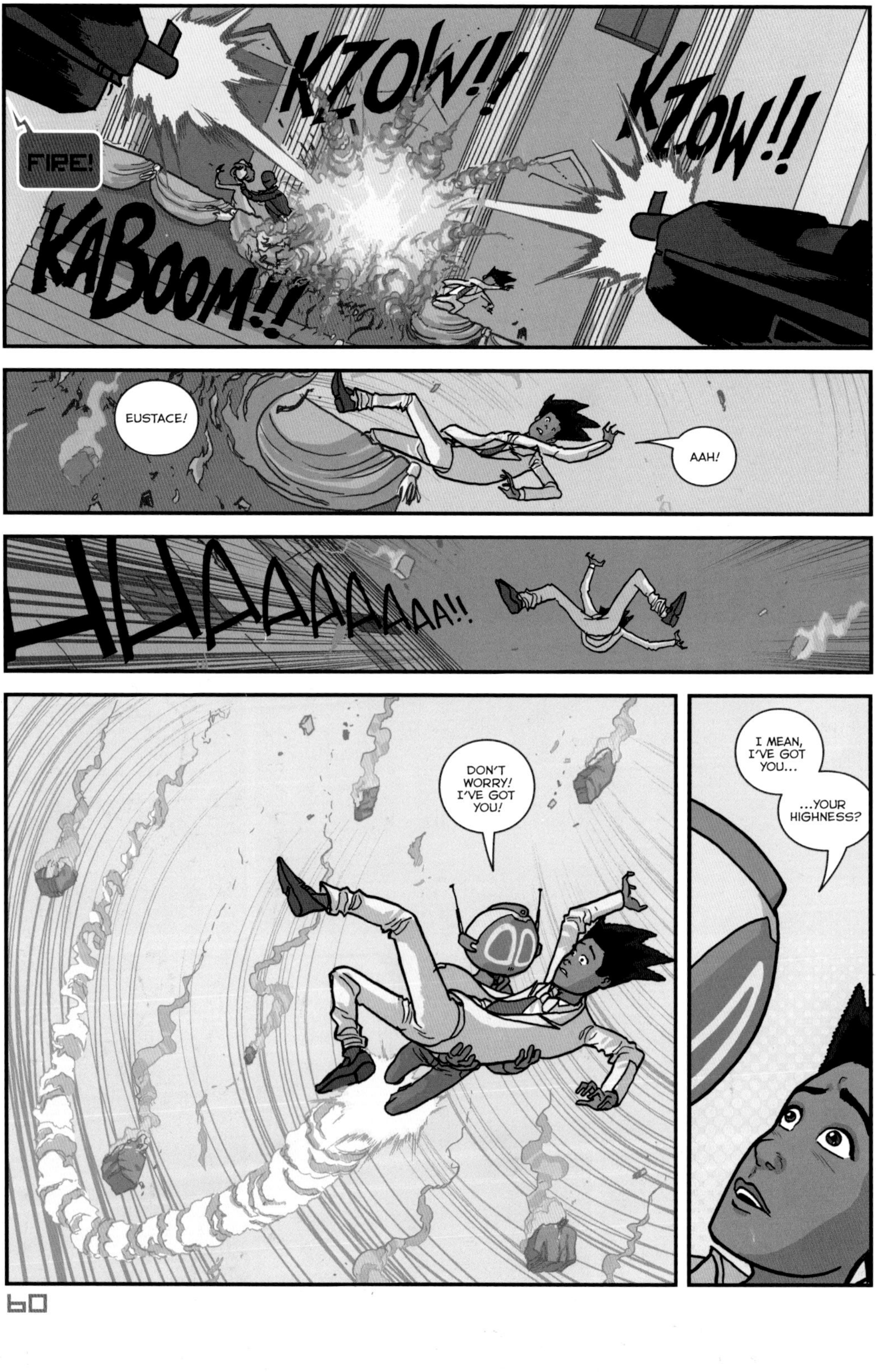
KZOW!!
FIRE!
KZOW!!
KABOOM!!
EUSTACE!
AAH!
HUAAAAAAAA!!
DON'T WORRY! I'VE GOT YOU!
I MEAN, I'VE GOT YOU...
...YOUR HIGHNESS?

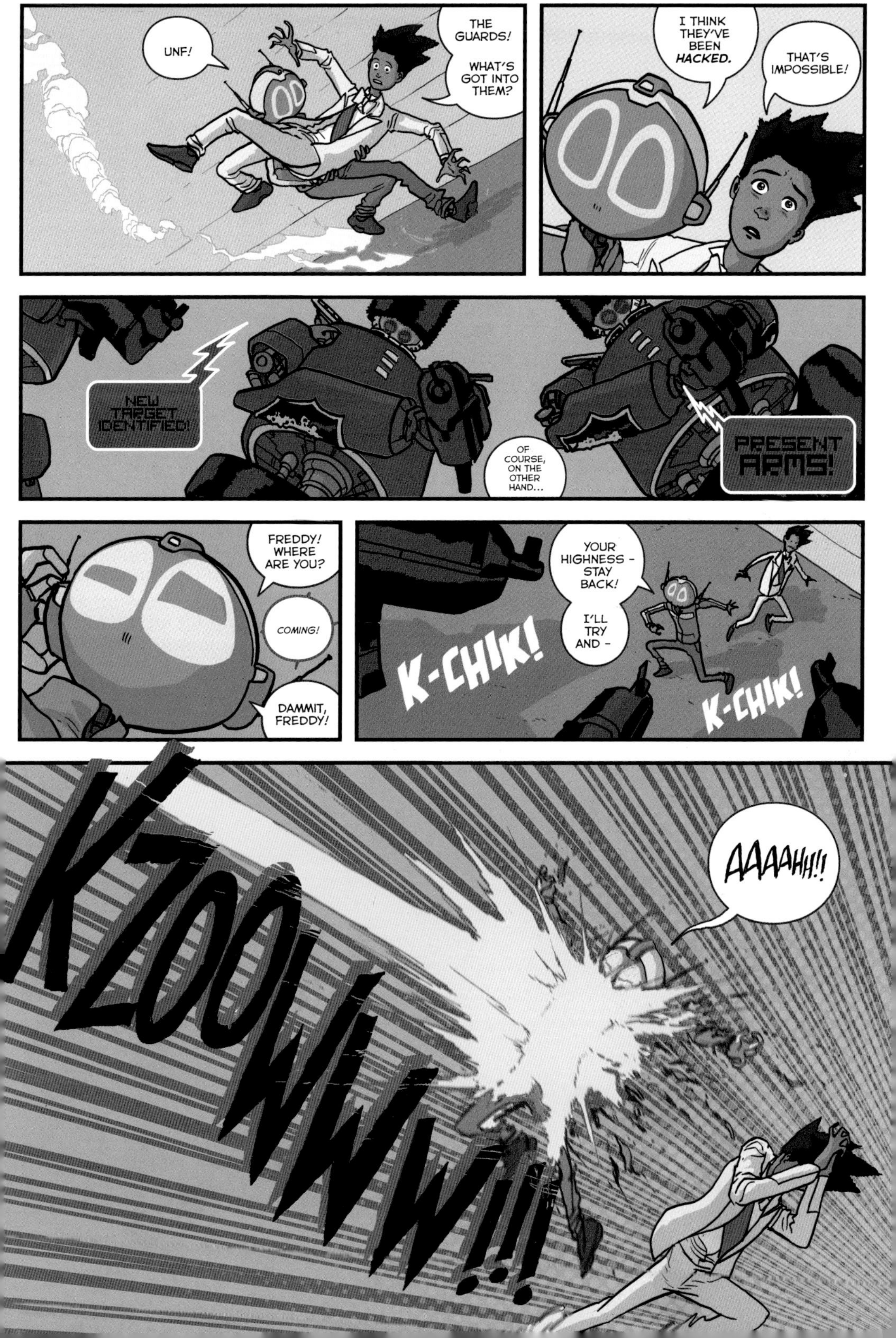
UNF!
THE GUARDS!
WHAT'S GOT INTO THEM?
I THINK THEY'VE BEEN HACKED.
THAT'S IMPOSSIBLE!
NEW TARGET IDENTIFIED!
OF COURSE, ON THE OTHER HAND...
PRESENT ARMS!
FREDDY! WHERE ARE YOU?
COMING!
DAMMIT, FREDDY!
YOUR HIGHNESS - STAY BACK!
I'LL TRY AND -
K-CHIK!
K-CHIK!
KZOOWWWW!!!
AAAAHH!!

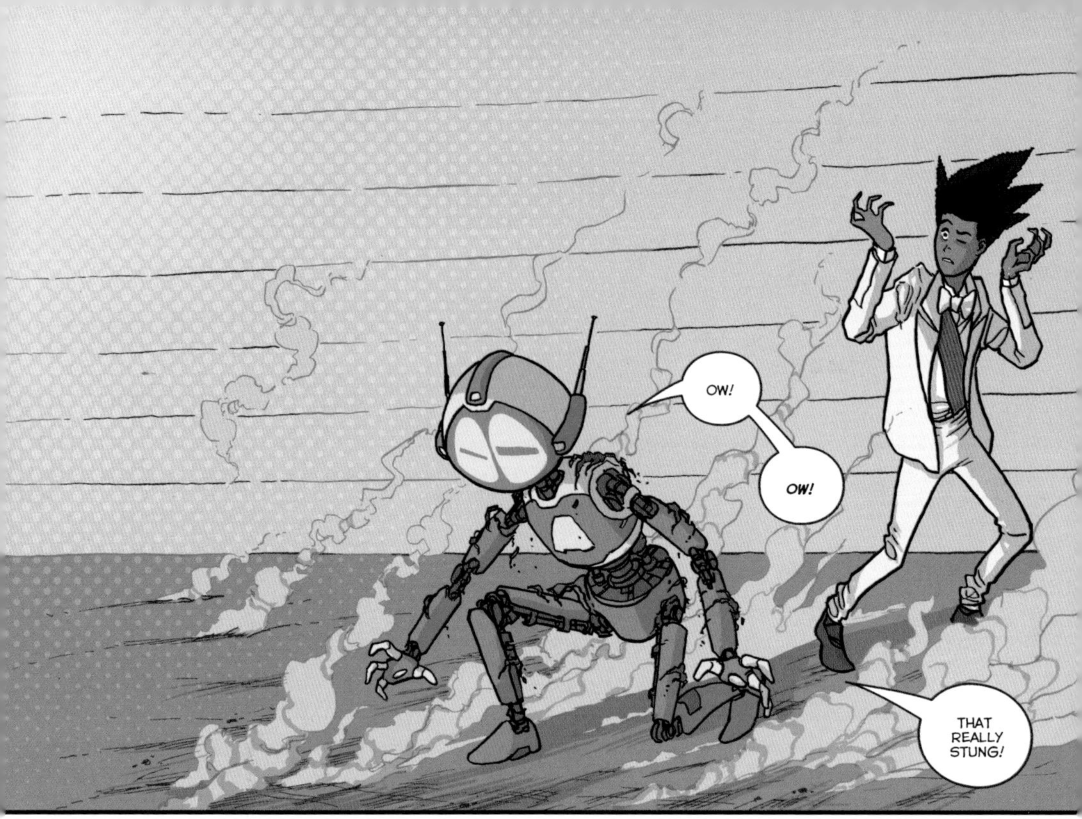
OW!
OW!
THAT REALLY STUNG!

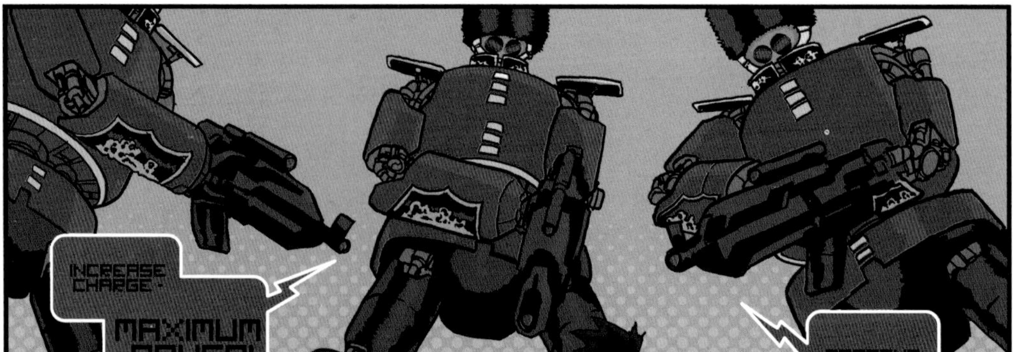
INCREASE CHARGE -
MAXIMUM POWER!
PRESENT ARMS!

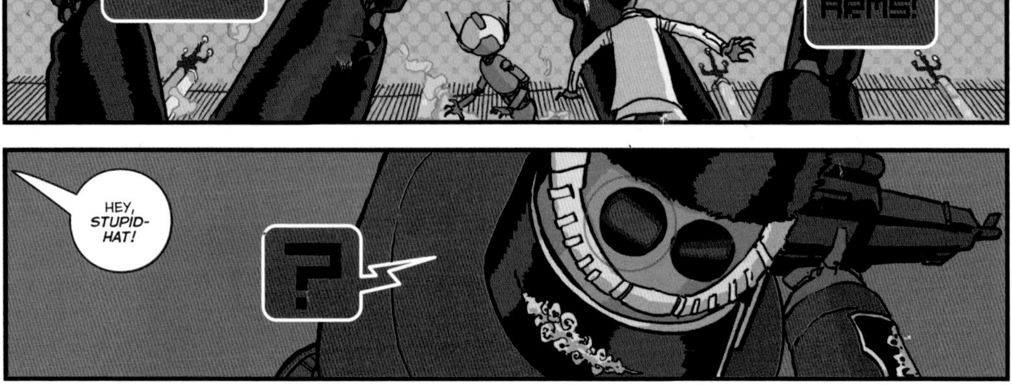
HEY, STUPID-HAT!
?

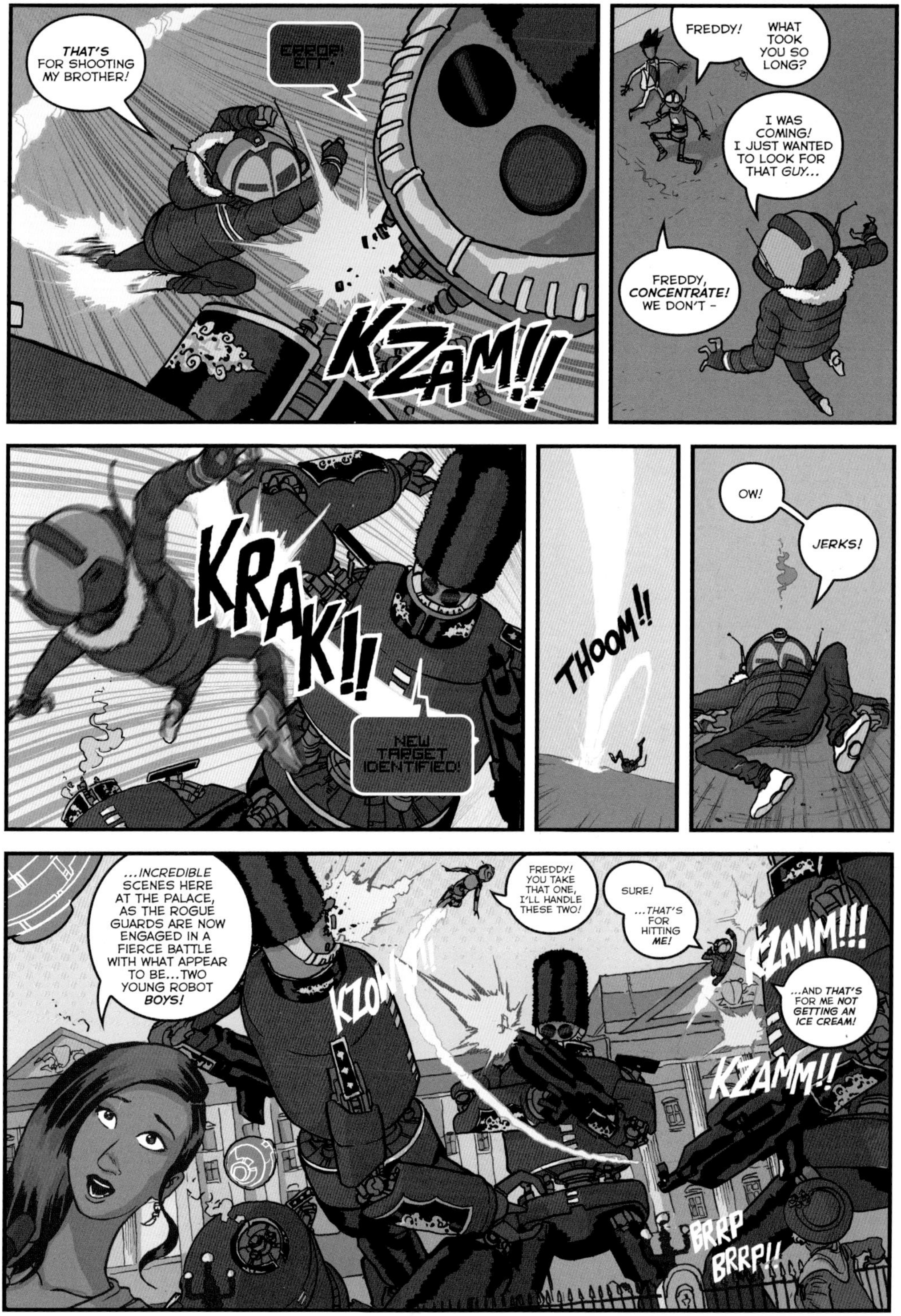
THAT'S FOR SHOOTING MY BROTHER!
ERROR! ERR-
KZAM!!
FREDDY! WHAT TOOK YOU SO LONG?
I WAS COMING! I JUST WANTED TO LOOK FOR THAT GUY...
FREDDY, CONCENTRATE! WE DON'T -
KRAK!!
NEW TARGET IDENTIFIED!
THOOM!!
OW!
JERKS!
...INCREDIBLE SCENES HERE AT THE PALACE, AS THE ROGUE GUARDS ARE NOW ENGAGED IN A FIERCE BATTLE WITH WHAT APPEAR TO BE...TWO YOUNG ROBOT BOYS!
FREDDY! YOU TAKE THAT ONE, I'LL HANDLE THESE TWO!
SURE!
...THAT'S FOR HITTING ME!
KZOW!!
KZAMM!!!
...AND THAT'S FOR ME NOT GETTING AN ICE CREAM!
KZAMM!!
BRRP BRRP!!

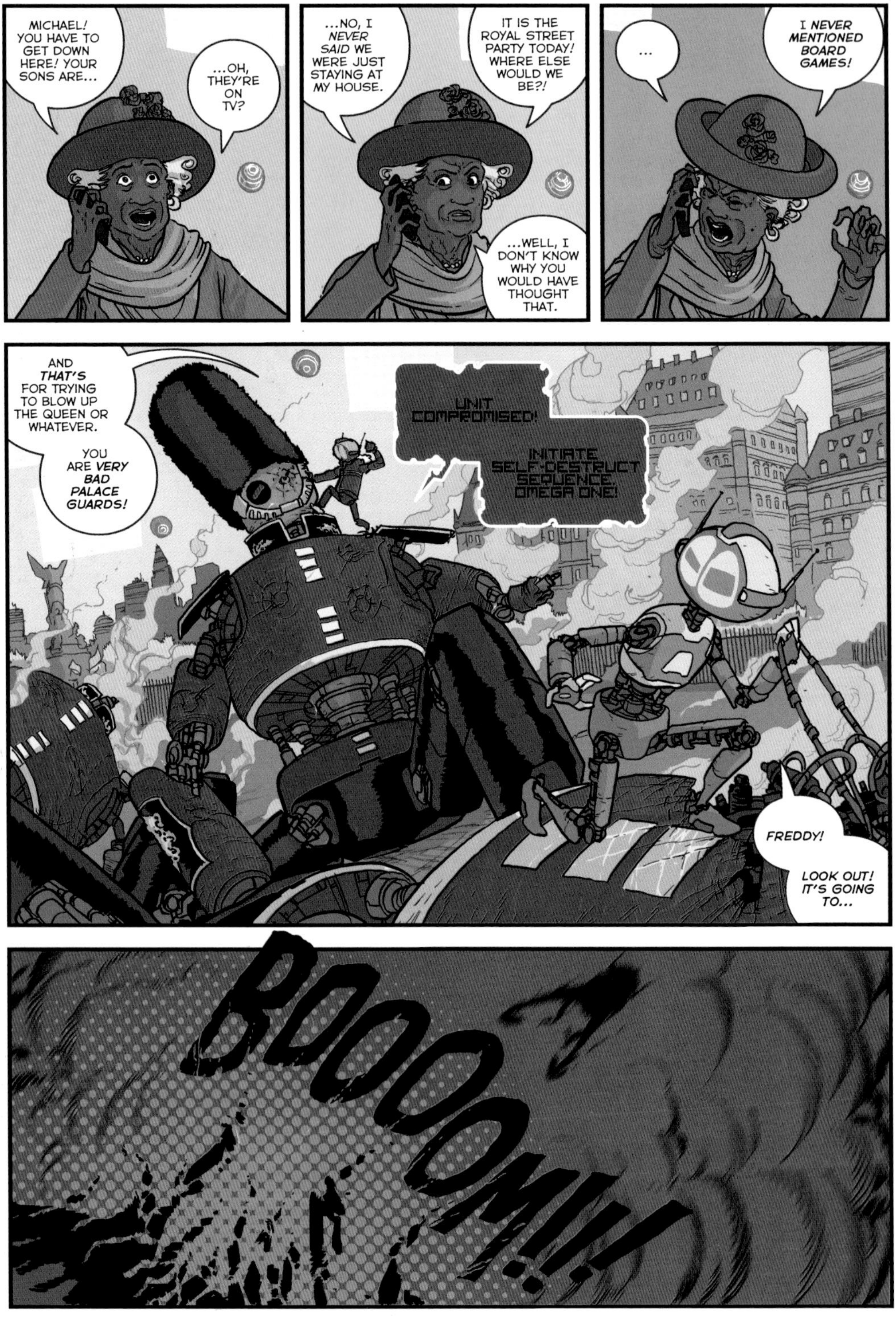
MICHAEL! YOU HAVE TO GET DOWN HERE! YOUR SONS ARE...
...OH, THEY'RE ON TV?
...NO, I NEVER SAID WE WERE JUST STAYING AT MY HOUSE.
IT IS THE ROYAL STREET PARTY TODAY! WHERE ELSE WOULD WE BE?!
...WELL, I DON'T KNOW WHY YOU WOULD HAVE THOUGHT THAT.
...
I NEVER MENTIONED BOARD GAMES!
AND THAT'S FOR TRYING TO BLOW UP THE QUEEN OR WHATEVER.
YOU ARE VERY BAD PALACE GUARDS!
UNIT COMPROMISED!
INITIATE SELF-DESTRUCT SEQUENCE, OMEGA ONE!
FREDDY!
LOOK OUT! IT'S GOING TO...
BOOOOM!!!

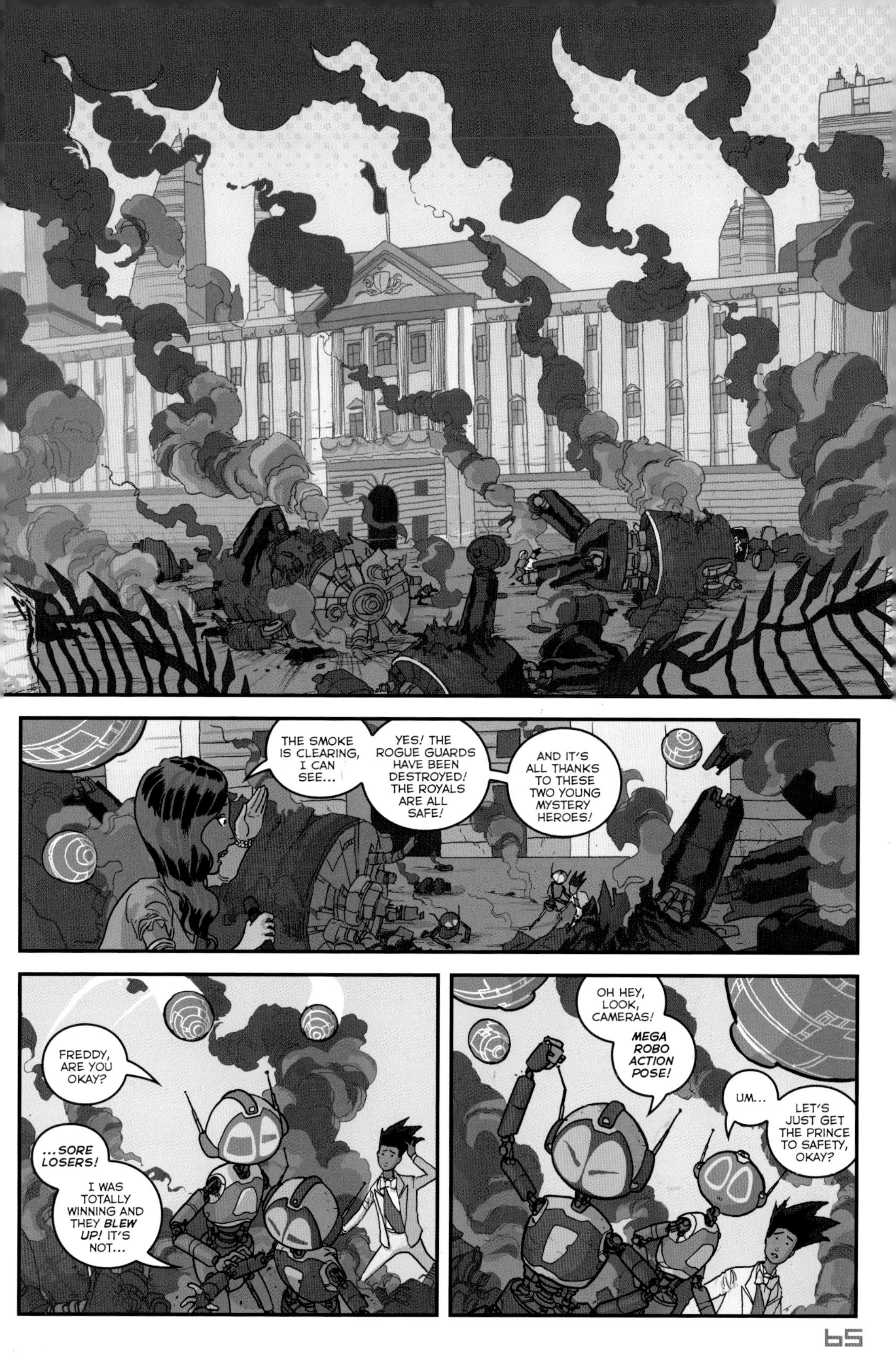
THE SMOKE IS CLEARING, I CAN SEE...
YES! THE ROGUE GUARDS HAVE BEEN DESTROYED! THE ROYALS ARE ALL SAFE!
AND IT'S ALL THANKS TO THESE TWO YOUNG MYSTERY HEROES!
FREDDY, ARE YOU OKAY?
...SORE LOSERS!
I WAS TOTALLY WINNING AND THEY BLEW UP! IT'S NOT...
OH HEY, LOOK, CAMERAS!
MEGA ROBO ACTION POSE!
UM...
LET'S JUST GET THE PRINCE TO SAFETY, OKAY?

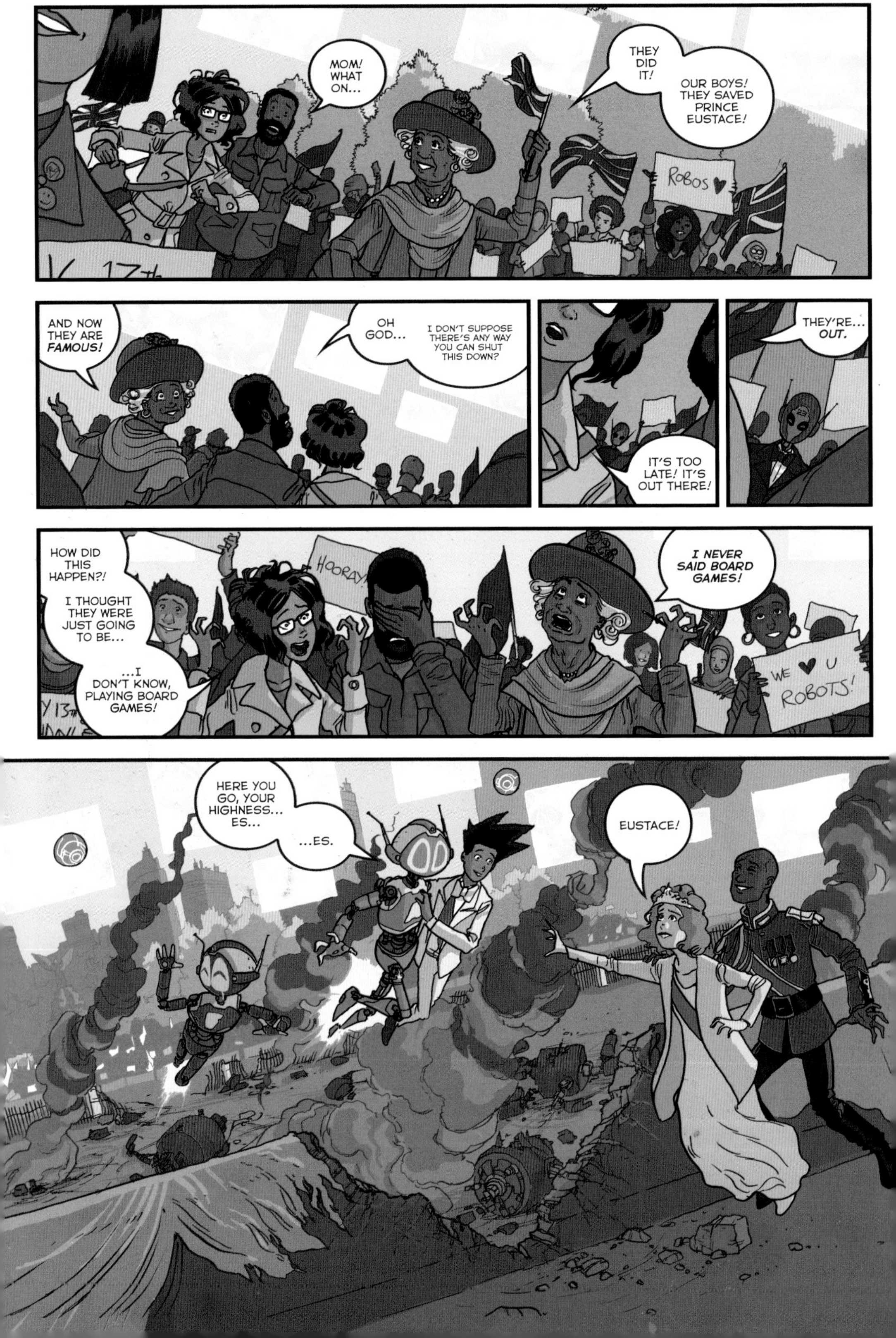
MOM! WHAT ON...
THEY DID IT!
OUR BOYS! THEY SAVED PRINCE EUSTACE!
ROBOS ♥
AND NOW THEY ARE *FAMOUS!*
OH GOD...
I DON'T SUPPOSE THERE'S ANY WAY YOU CAN SHUT THIS DOWN?
IT'S TOO LATE! IT'S OUT THERE!
THEY'RE... *OUT.*
HOW DID THIS HAPPEN?!
I THOUGHT THEY WERE JUST GOING TO BE...
...I DON'T KNOW, PLAYING BOARD GAMES!
HOORAY
I NEVER SAID BOARD GAMES!
WE ♥ U ROBOTS!
HERE YOU GO, YOUR HIGHNESS... ES...
...ES.
EUSTACE!

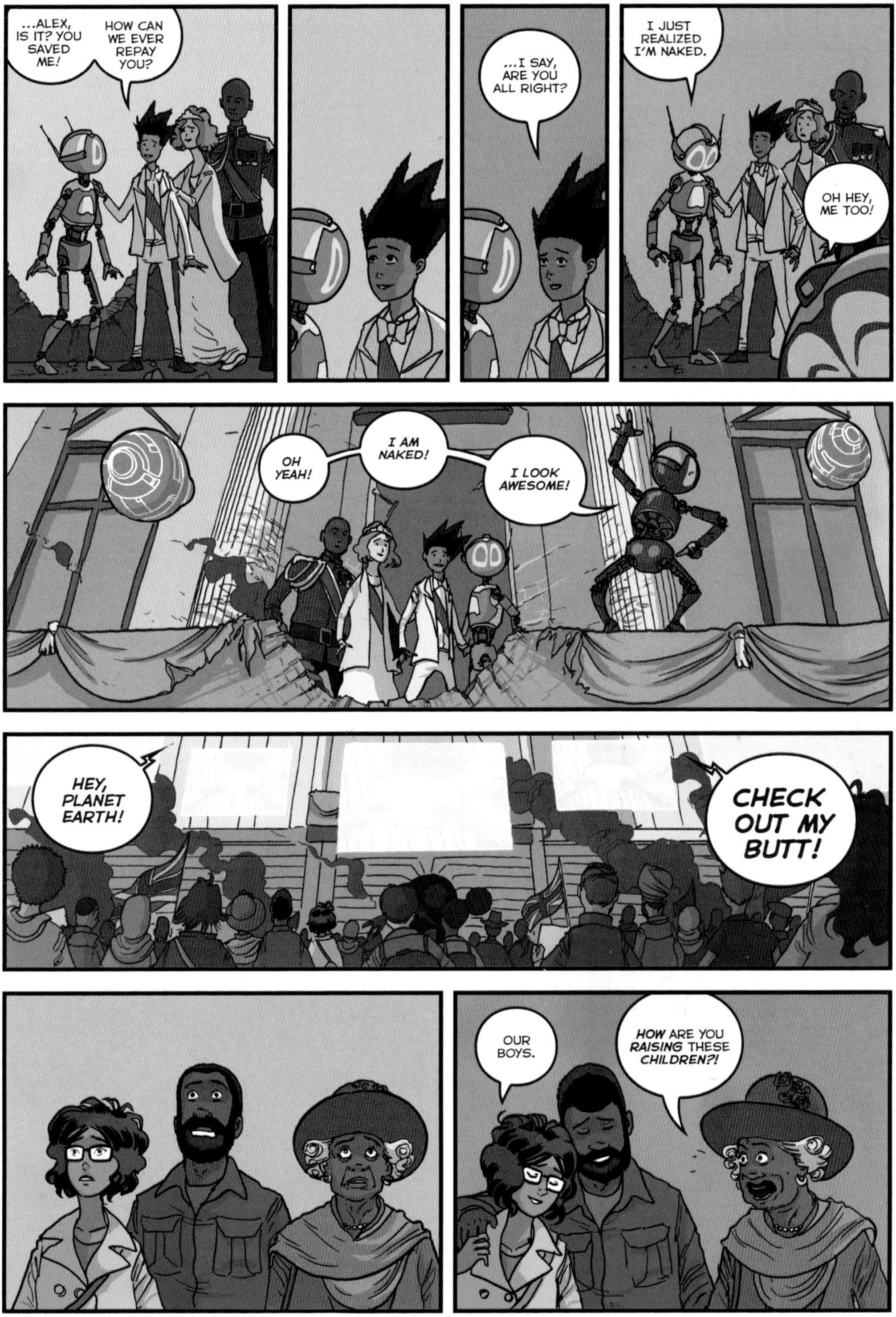
...ALEX, IS IT? YOU SAVED ME!
HOW CAN WE EVER REPAY YOU?
...I SAY, ARE YOU ALL RIGHT?
I JUST REALIZED I'M NAKED.
OH HEY, ME TOO!
OH YEAH!
I AM NAKED!
I LOOK AWESOME!
HEY, PLANET EARTH!
CHECK OUT MY BUTT!
OUR BOYS.
HOW ARE YOU RAISING THESE CHILDREN?!

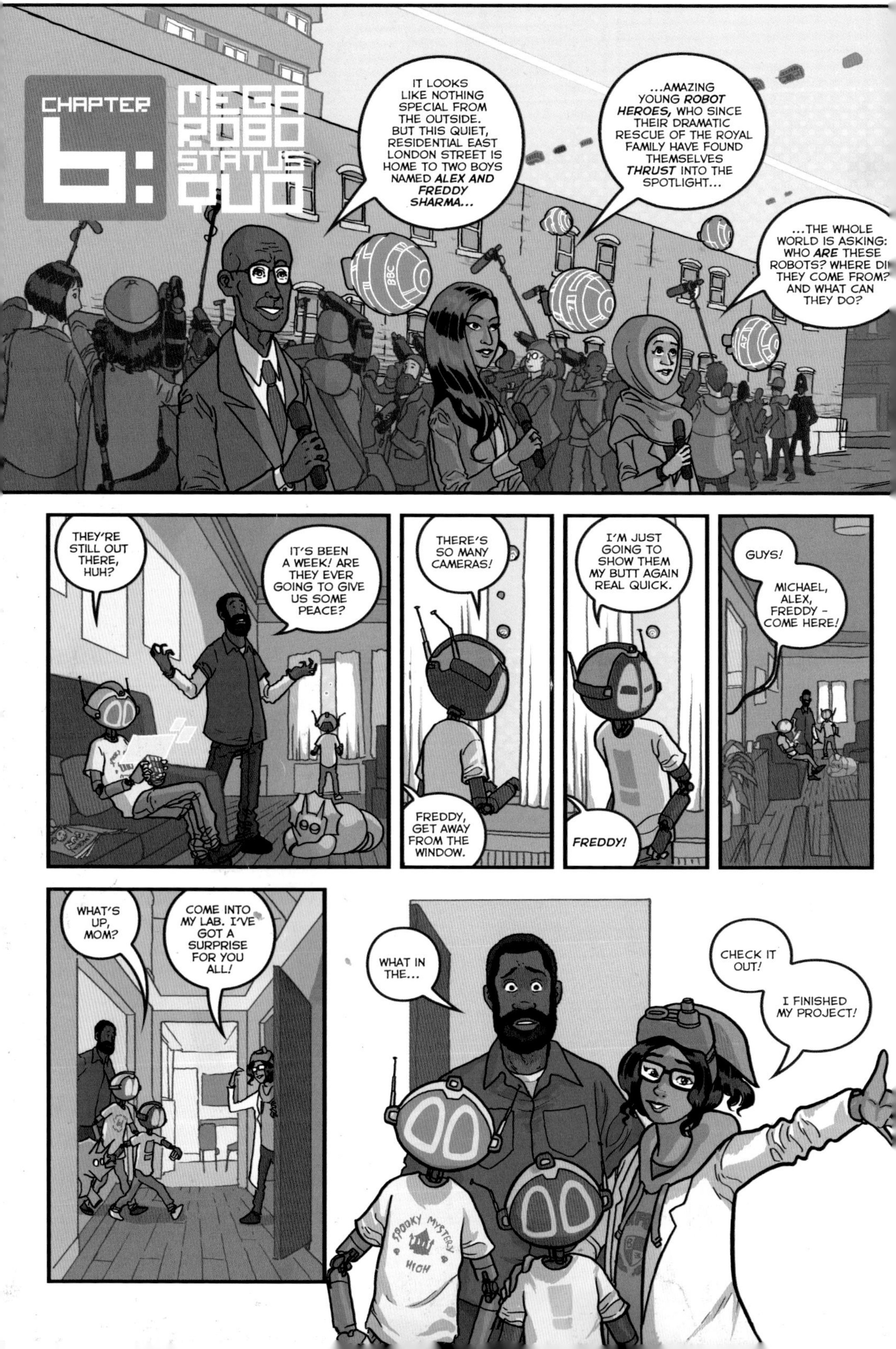
CHAPTER 6: MEGA ROBO STATUS QUO
IT LOOKS LIKE NOTHING SPECIAL FROM THE OUTSIDE. BUT THIS QUIET, RESIDENTIAL EAST LONDON STREET IS HOME TO TWO BOYS NAMED ALEX AND FREDDY SHARMA...
...AMAZING YOUNG ROBOT HEROES, WHO SINCE THEIR DRAMATIC RESCUE OF THE ROYAL FAMILY HAVE FOUND THEMSELVES THRUST INTO THE SPOTLIGHT...
...THE WHOLE WORLD IS ASKING: WHO ARE THESE ROBOTS? WHERE DI THEY COME FROM? AND WHAT CAN THEY DO?
BBC
THEY'RE STILL OUT THERE, HUH?
IT'S BEEN A WEEK! ARE THEY EVER GOING TO GIVE US SOME PEACE?
THERE'S SO MANY CAMERAS!
FREDDY, GET AWAY FROM THE WINDOW.
I'M JUST GOING TO SHOW THEM MY BUTT AGAIN REAL QUICK.
FREDDY!
GUYS!
MICHAEL, ALEX, FREDDY - COME HERE!
WHAT'S UP, MOM?
COME INTO MY LAB. I'VE GOT A SURPRISE FOR YOU ALL!
WHAT IN THE...
CHECK IT OUT!
I FINISHED MY PROJECT!
SPOOKY MYSTERY HIGH

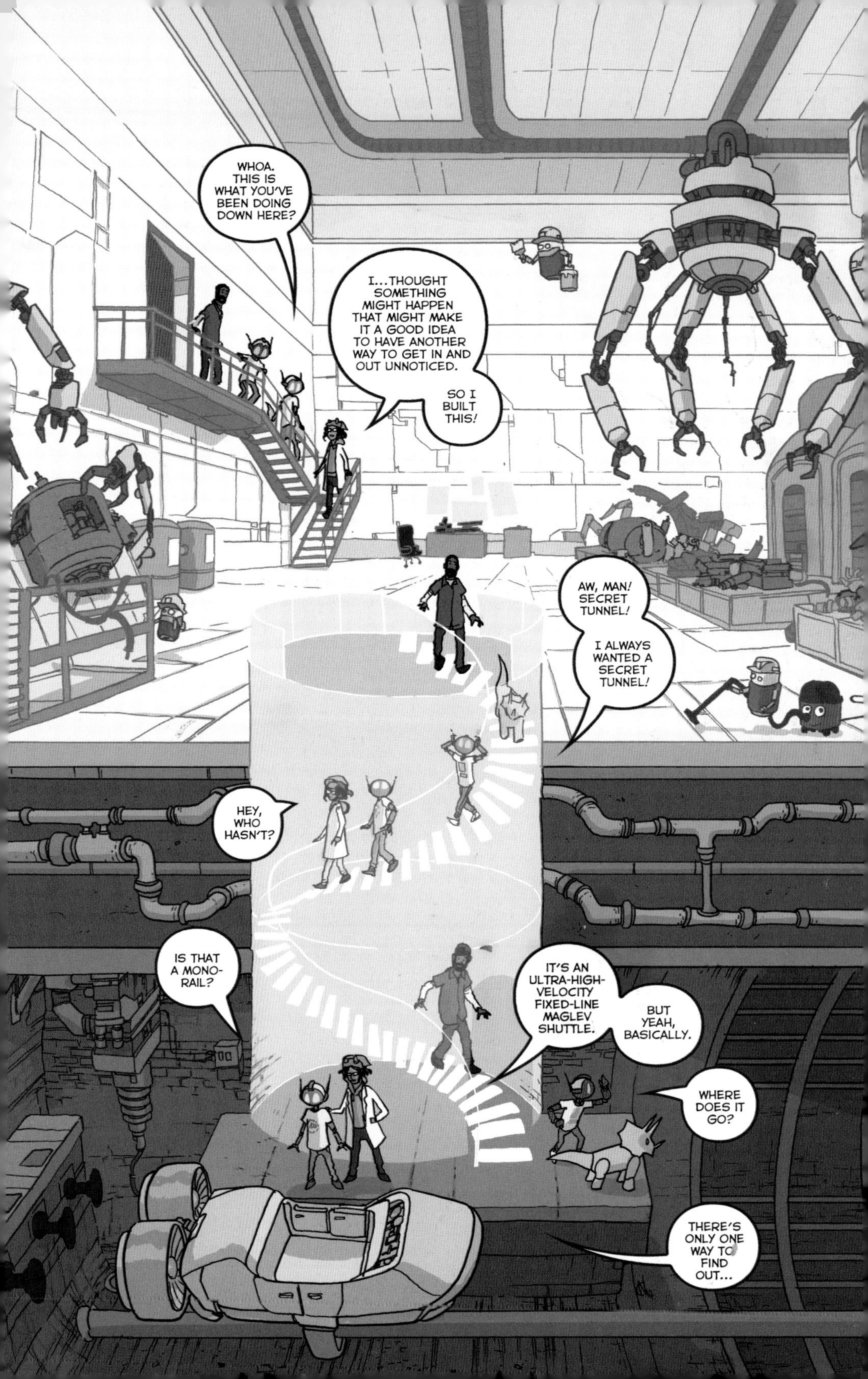
WHOA. THIS IS WHAT YOU'VE BEEN DOING DOWN HERE?
I...THOUGHT SOMETHING MIGHT HAPPEN THAT MIGHT MAKE IT A GOOD IDEA TO HAVE ANOTHER WAY TO GET IN AND OUT UNNOTICED.
SO I BUILT THIS!
AW, MAN! SECRET TUNNEL!
I ALWAYS WANTED A SECRET TUNNEL!
HEY, WHO HASN'T?
IS THAT A MONO-RAIL?
IT'S AN ULTRA-HIGH-VELOCITY FIXED-LINE MAGLEV SHUTTLE.
BUT YEAH, BASICALLY.
WHERE DOES IT GO?
THERE'S ONLY ONE WAY TO FIND OUT...

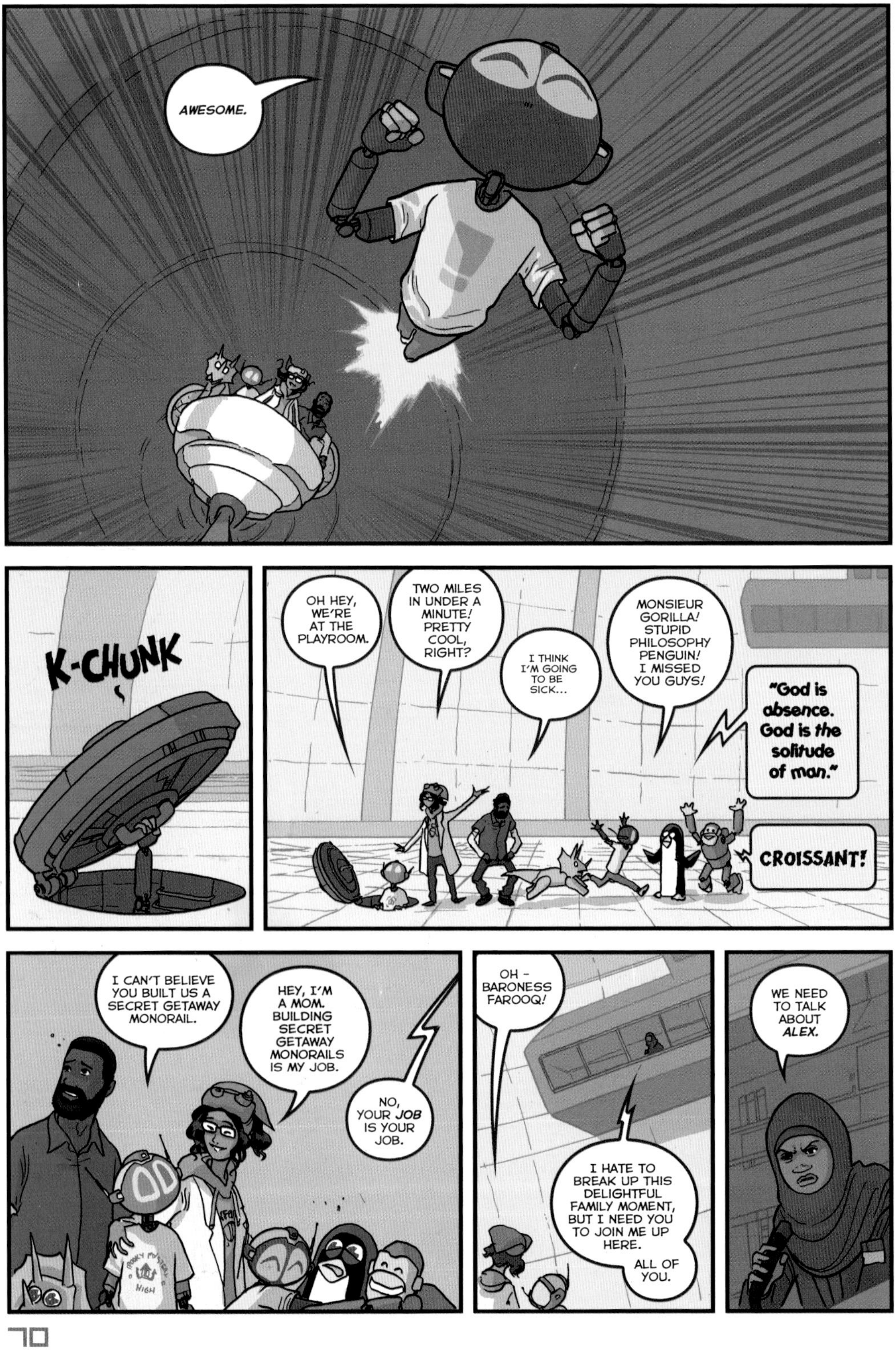
AWESOME.
K-CHUNK
OH HEY, WE'RE AT THE PLAYROOM.
TWO MILES IN UNDER A MINUTE! PRETTY COOL, RIGHT?
I THINK I'M GOING TO BE SICK...
MONSIEUR GORILLA! STUPID PHILOSOPHY PENGUIN! I MISSED YOU GUYS!
"God is absence. God is the solitude of man."
CROISSANT!
I CAN'T BELIEVE YOU BUILT US A SECRET GETAWAY MONORAIL.
HEY, I'M A MOM. BUILDING SECRET GETAWAY MONORAILS IS MY JOB.
NO, YOUR JOB IS YOUR JOB.
OH - BARONESS FAROOQ!
I HATE TO BREAK UP THIS DELIGHTFUL FAMILY MOMENT, BUT I NEED YOU TO JOIN ME UP HERE.
ALL OF YOU.
WE NEED TO TALK ABOUT ALEX.

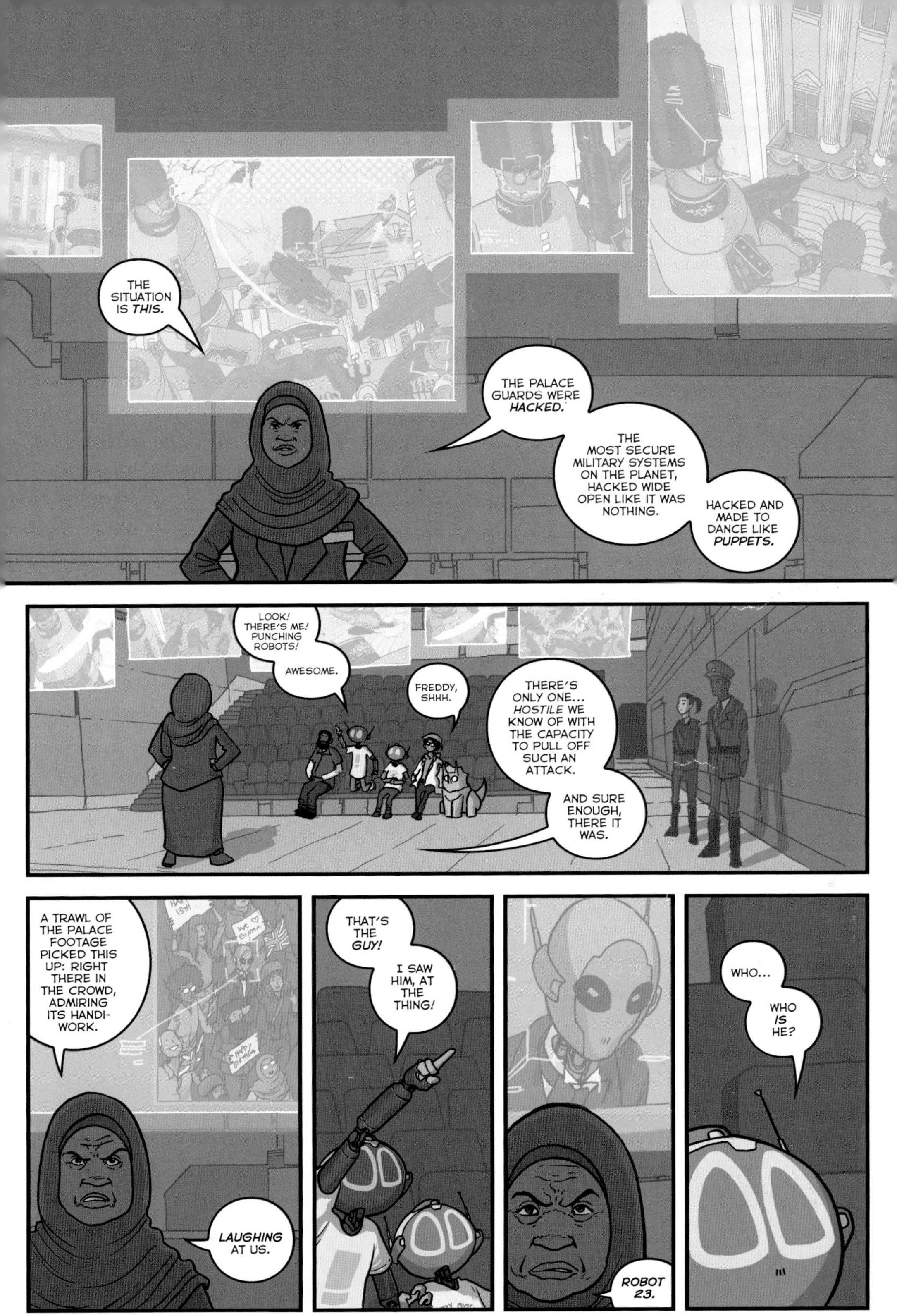
THE SITUATION IS *THIS.*
THE PALACE GUARDS WERE *HACKED.*
THE MOST SECURE MILITARY SYSTEMS ON THE PLANET, HACKED WIDE OPEN LIKE IT WAS NOTHING.
HACKED AND MADE TO DANCE LIKE *PUPPETS.*
LOOK! THERE'S ME! PUNCHING ROBOTS!
AWESOME.
FREDDY, SHHH.
THERE'S ONLY ONE... *HOSTILE* WE KNOW OF WITH THE CAPACITY TO PULL OFF SUCH AN ATTACK.
AND SURE ENOUGH, THERE IT WAS.
A TRAWL OF THE PALACE FOOTAGE PICKED THIS UP: RIGHT THERE IN THE CROWD, ADMIRING ITS HANDI-WORK.
LAUGHING AT US.
THAT'S THE *GUY!*
I SAW HIM, AT THE THING!
ROBOT 23.
WHO...
WHO *IS* HE?

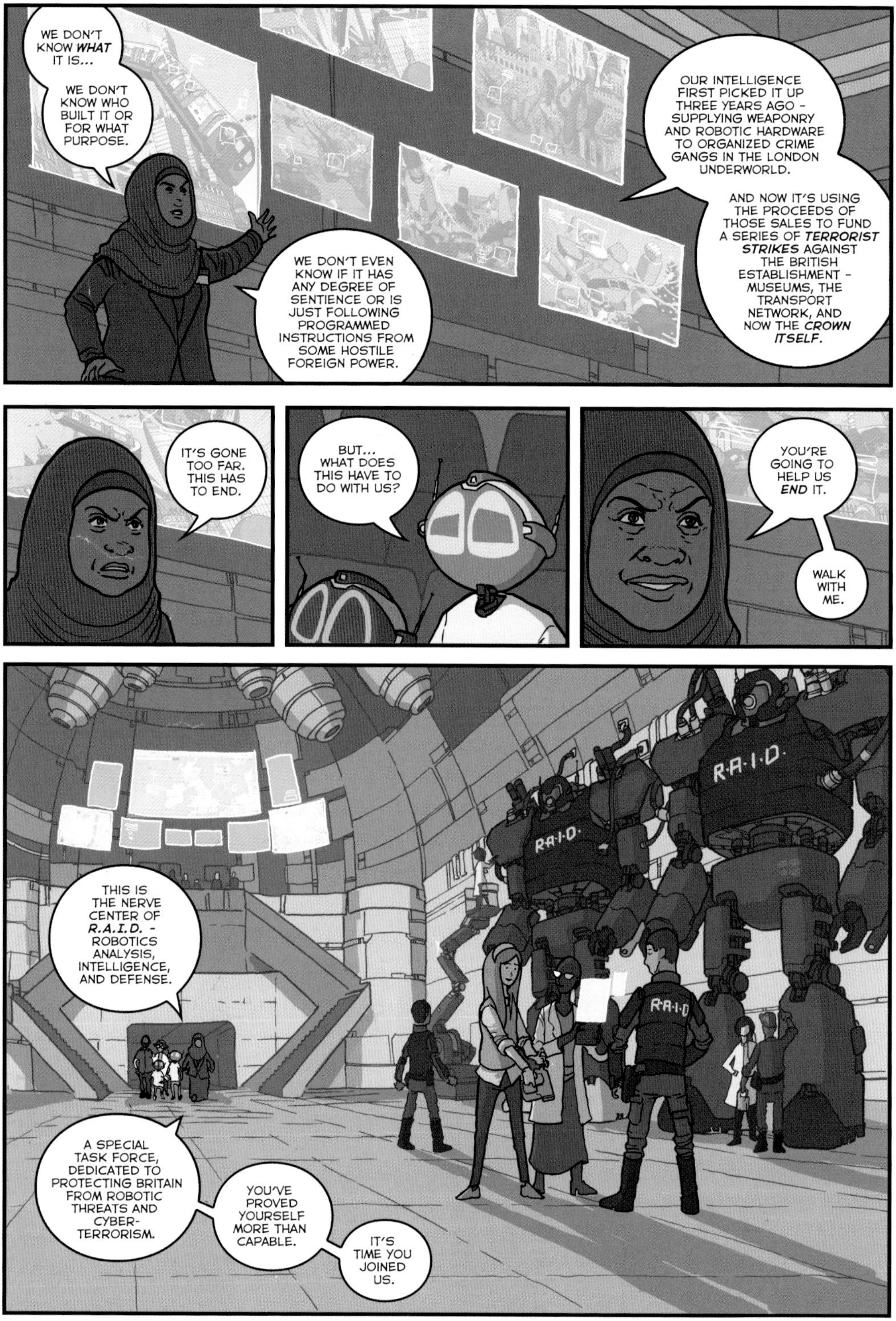
WE DON'T KNOW *WHAT* IT IS...
WE DON'T KNOW WHO BUILT IT OR FOR WHAT PURPOSE.
WE DON'T EVEN KNOW IF IT HAS ANY DEGREE OF SENTIENCE OR IS JUST FOLLOWING PROGRAMMED INSTRUCTIONS FROM SOME HOSTILE FOREIGN POWER.
OUR INTELLIGENCE FIRST PICKED IT UP THREE YEARS AGO - SUPPLYING WEAPONRY AND ROBOTIC HARDWARE TO ORGANIZED CRIME GANGS IN THE LONDON UNDERWORLD.
AND NOW IT'S USING THE PROCEEDS OF THOSE SALES TO FUND A SERIES OF *TERRORIST STRIKES* AGAINST THE BRITISH ESTABLISHMENT - MUSEUMS, THE TRANSPORT NETWORK, AND NOW THE *CROWN ITSELF*.
IT'S GONE TOO FAR. THIS HAS TO END.
BUT... WHAT DOES THIS HAVE TO DO WITH US?
YOU'RE GOING TO HELP US *END* IT.
WALK WITH ME.
R·A·I·D·
R·A·I·D·
R·A·I·D
THIS IS THE NERVE CENTER OF *R.A.I.D.* - ROBOTICS ANALYSIS, INTELLIGENCE, AND DEFENSE.
A SPECIAL TASK FORCE, DEDICATED TO PROTECTING BRITAIN FROM ROBOTIC THREATS AND CYBER-TERRORISM.
YOU'VE PROVED YOURSELF MORE THAN CAPABLE.
IT'S TIME YOU JOINED US.

YOU'D BE BACKED UP ON MISSIONS BY A FULL TEAM OF AGENTS AND COMMANDO MECHS...
R-A-I-D
IS THAT SUSIE?
SHE'S OUR BABY-SITTER!
HI, ALEX! HI, FREDDY!
AGENT NICHOLS IS A SCIENTIFIC ATTACHÉ TO THE FIELD TEAM.
SHE'LL STILL BE BABYSITTING YOU, IN A SENSE. THERE'LL JUST BE... MORE GUNFIRE AND EXPLOSIONS.
SO WHAT DO YOU SAY, ALEX? ARE YOU READY TO STEP UP? TO BECOME AN *AGENT OF R.A.I.D.?*
ALEX...
I KNOW THIS IS A LOT TO TAKE IN. DON'T LET THEM PRESSURE YOU.
YOU DON'T HAVE TO DO *ANYTHING* YOU DON'T WANT TO.
ACTUALLY, I THINK YOU'LL FIND...
SPOOKY MYSTERY HIGH
NO, IT'S FINE. I...
I WANT TO. TO HELP.
TO... FIND THAT GUY.
AWWW YEAH!
THIS IS SO AWESOME!
WE GET TO BE *MEGA ROBO SECRET AGENTS!*
SPOOKY MYSTERY HIGH
YOU...?
OH NO, NOT YOU. JUST ALEX.
YOURE STILL MUCH TOO YOUNG.
WHAT?!

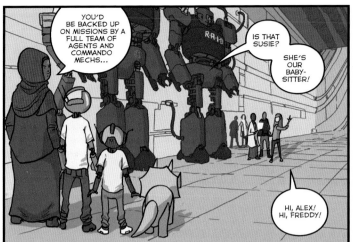

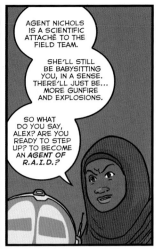

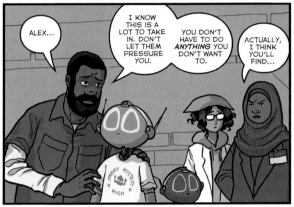

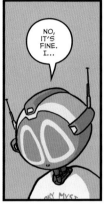

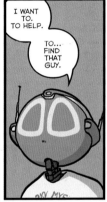

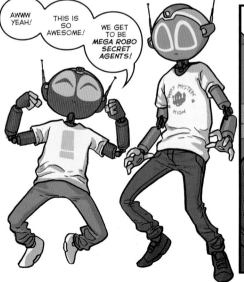

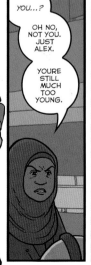

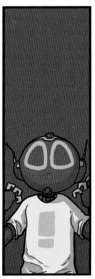

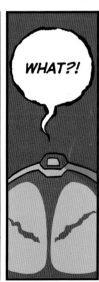

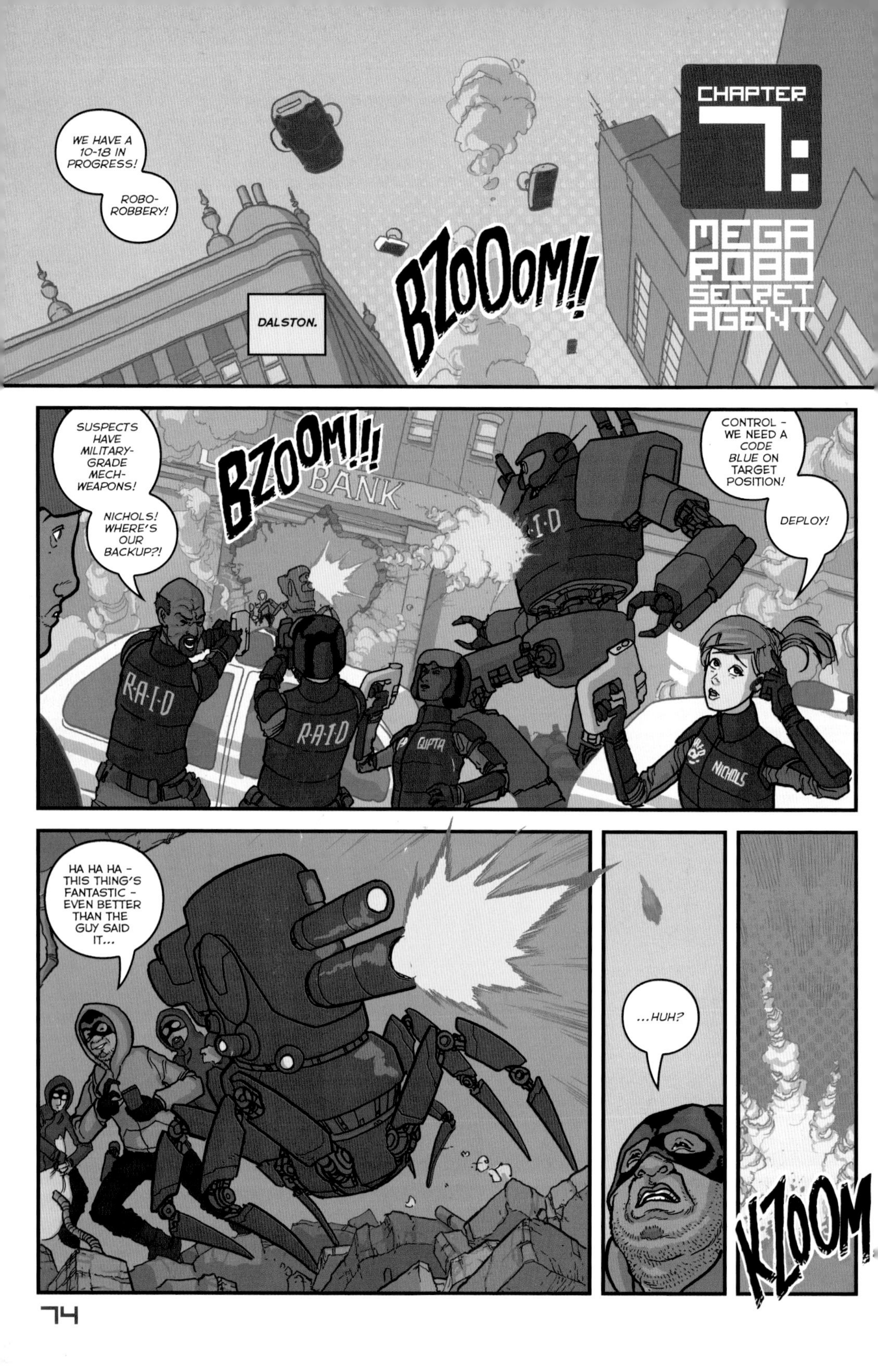
CHAPTER 7:
MEGA ROBO SECRET AGENT
WE HAVE A 10-18 IN PROGRESS!
ROBO-ROBBERY!
DALSTON.
BZOOOM!!
SUSPECTS HAVE MILITARY-GRADE MECH-WEAPONS!
NICHOLS! WHERE'S OUR BACKUP?!
BZOOM!!!
BANK
CONTROL - WE NEED A CODE BLUE ON TARGET POSITION!
DEPLOY!
R-A-I-D
R-A-I-D
GUPTA
NICHOLS
HA HA HA - THIS THING'S FANTASTIC - EVEN BETTER THAN THE GUY SAID IT...
...HUH?
KZOOM

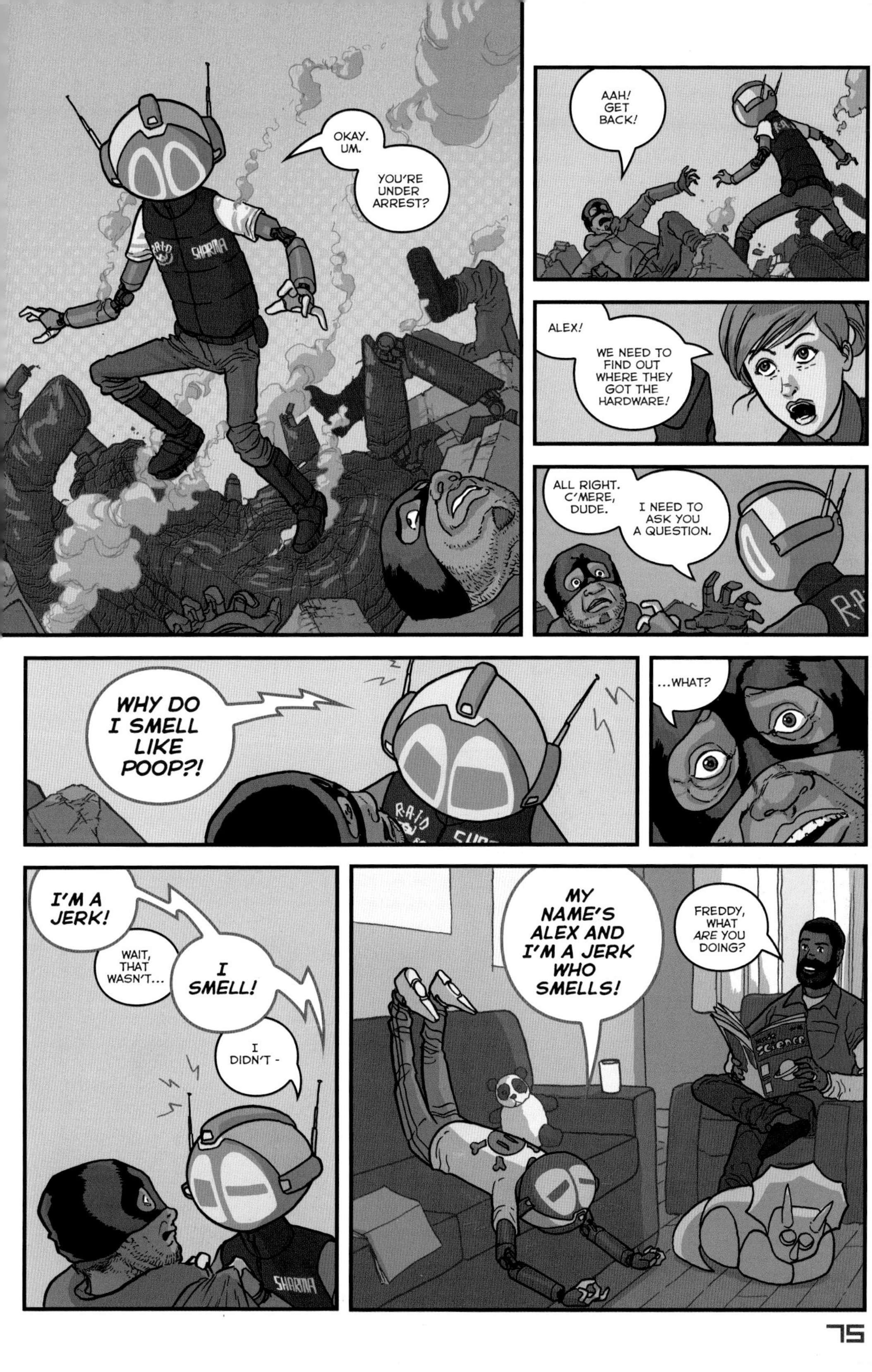
OKAY. UM.
YOU'RE UNDER ARREST?
AAH! GET BACK!
ALEX!
WE NEED TO FIND OUT WHERE THEY GOT THE HARDWARE!
ALL RIGHT. C'MERE, DUDE.
I NEED TO ASK YOU A QUESTION.
WHY DO I SMELL LIKE POOP?!
...WHAT?
I'M A JERK!
WAIT, THAT WASN'T...
I SMELL!
I DIDN'T -
MY NAME'S ALEX AND I'M A JERK WHO SMELLS!
FREDDY, WHAT ARE YOU DOING?

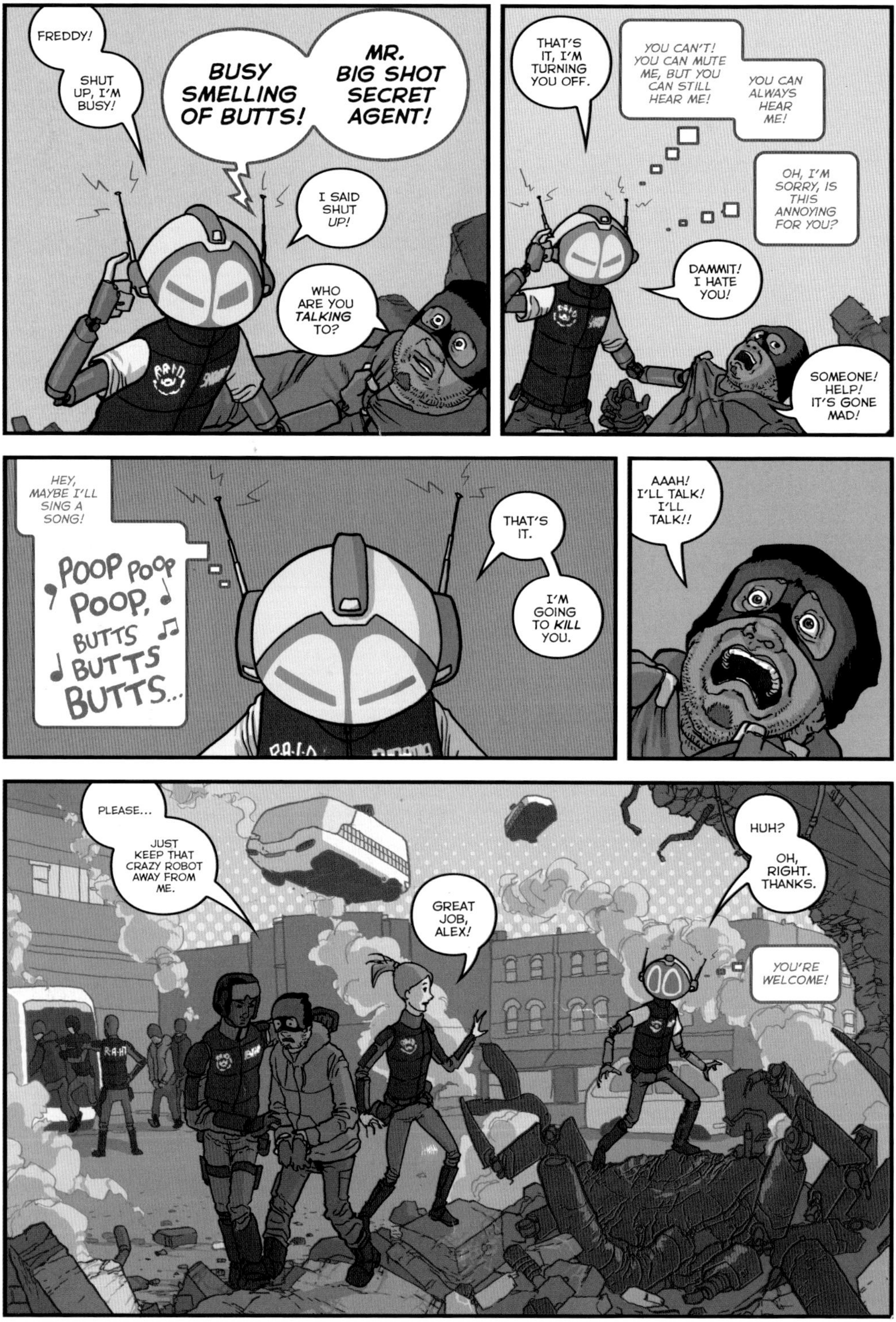

FREDDY!
SHUT UP, I'M BUSY!
BUSY SMELLING OF BUTTS!
MR. BIG SHOT SECRET AGENT!
I SAID SHUT UP!
WHO ARE YOU TALKING TO?
THAT'S IT, I'M TURNING YOU OFF.
YOU CAN'T! YOU CAN MUTE ME, BUT YOU CAN STILL HEAR ME!
YOU CAN ALWAYS HEAR ME!
OH, I'M SORRY, IS THIS ANNOYING FOR YOU?
DAMMIT! I HATE YOU!
SOMEONE! HELP! IT'S GONE MAD!
HEY, MAYBE I'LL SING A SONG!
POOP POOP POOP, BUTTS BUTTS BUTTS...
THAT'S IT.
I'M GOING TO KILL YOU.
AAAH! I'LL TALK! I'LL TALK!!
PLEASE...
JUST KEEP THAT CRAZY ROBOT AWAY FROM ME.
GREAT JOB, ALEX!
HUH?
OH, RIGHT. THANKS.
YOU'RE WELCOME!

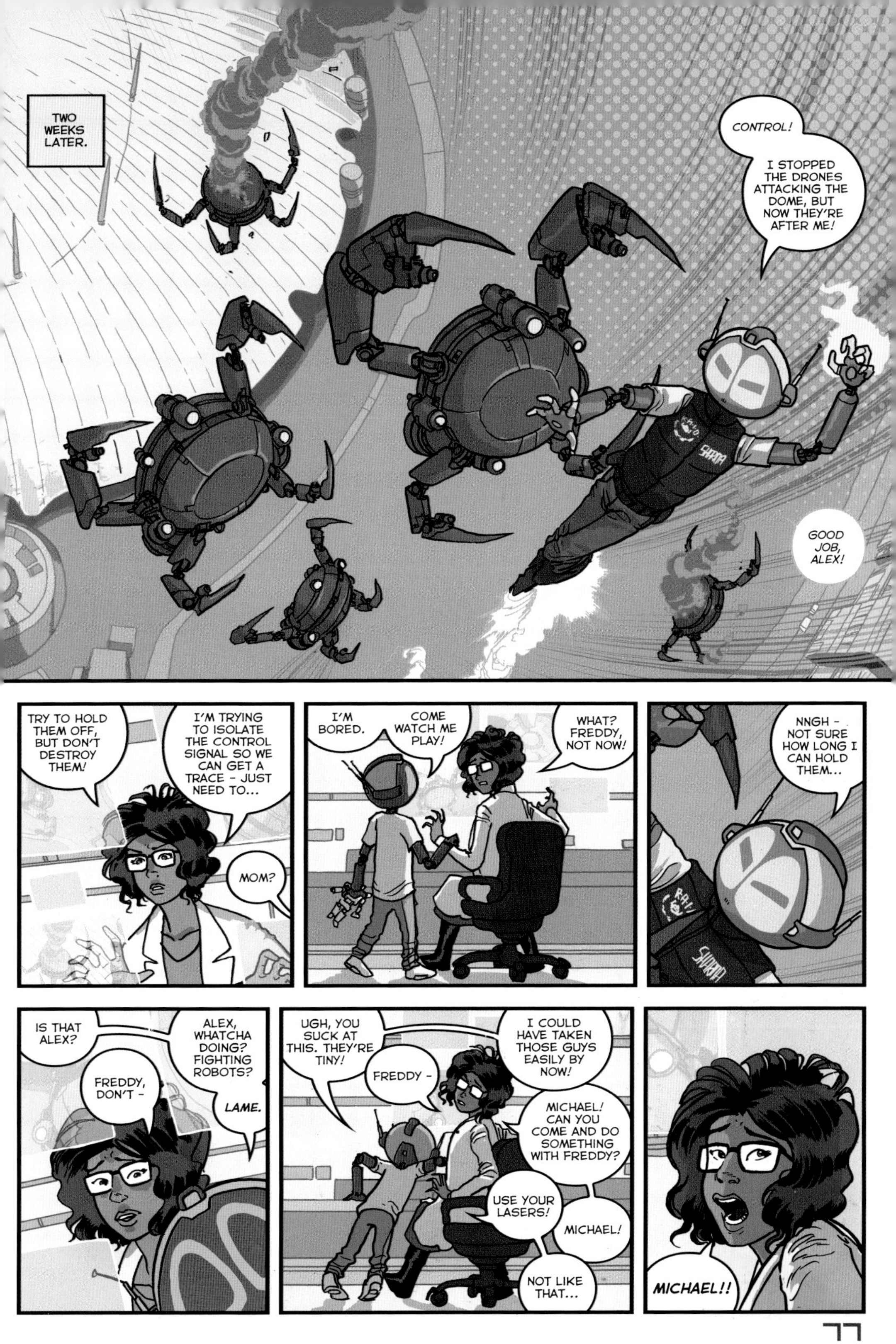

TWO WEEKS LATER.
CONTROL!
I STOPPED THE DRONES ATTACKING THE DOME, BUT NOW THEY'RE AFTER ME!
GOOD JOB, ALEX!
TRY TO HOLD THEM OFF, BUT DON'T DESTROY THEM!
I'M TRYING TO ISOLATE THE CONTROL SIGNAL SO WE CAN GET A TRACE - JUST NEED TO...
MOM?
I'M BORED.
COME WATCH ME PLAY!
WHAT? FREDDY, NOT NOW!
NNGH - NOT SURE HOW LONG I CAN HOLD THEM...
IS THAT ALEX?
ALEX, WHATCHA DOING? FIGHTING ROBOTS?
FREDDY, DON'T -
LAME.
UGH, YOU SUCK AT THIS. THEY'RE TINY!
FREDDY -
I COULD HAVE TAKEN THOSE GUYS EASILY BY NOW!
MICHAEL! CAN YOU COME AND DO SOMETHING WITH FREDDY?
USE YOUR LASERS!
MICHAEL!
NOT LIKE THAT...
MICHAEL!!

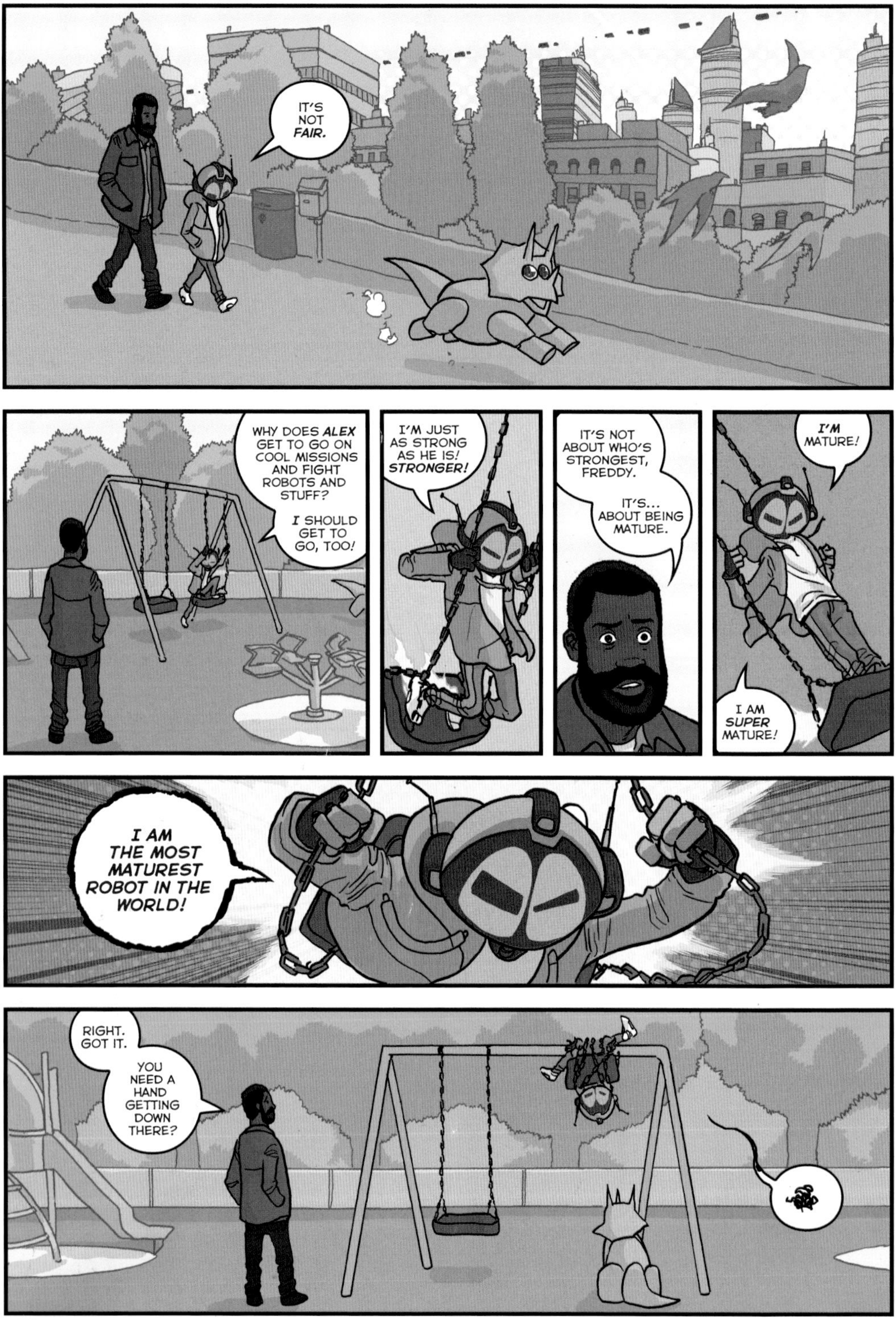
IT'S NOT FAIR.
WHY DOES ALEX GET TO GO ON COOL MISSIONS AND FIGHT ROBOTS AND STUFF?
I SHOULD GET TO GO, TOO!
I'M JUST AS STRONG AS HE IS! STRONGER!
IT'S NOT ABOUT WHO'S STRONGEST, FREDDY.
IT'S... ABOUT BEING MATURE.
I'M MATURE!
I AM SUPER MATURE!
I AM THE MOST MATUREST ROBOT IN THE WORLD!
RIGHT. GOT IT.
YOU NEED A HAND GETTING DOWN THERE?

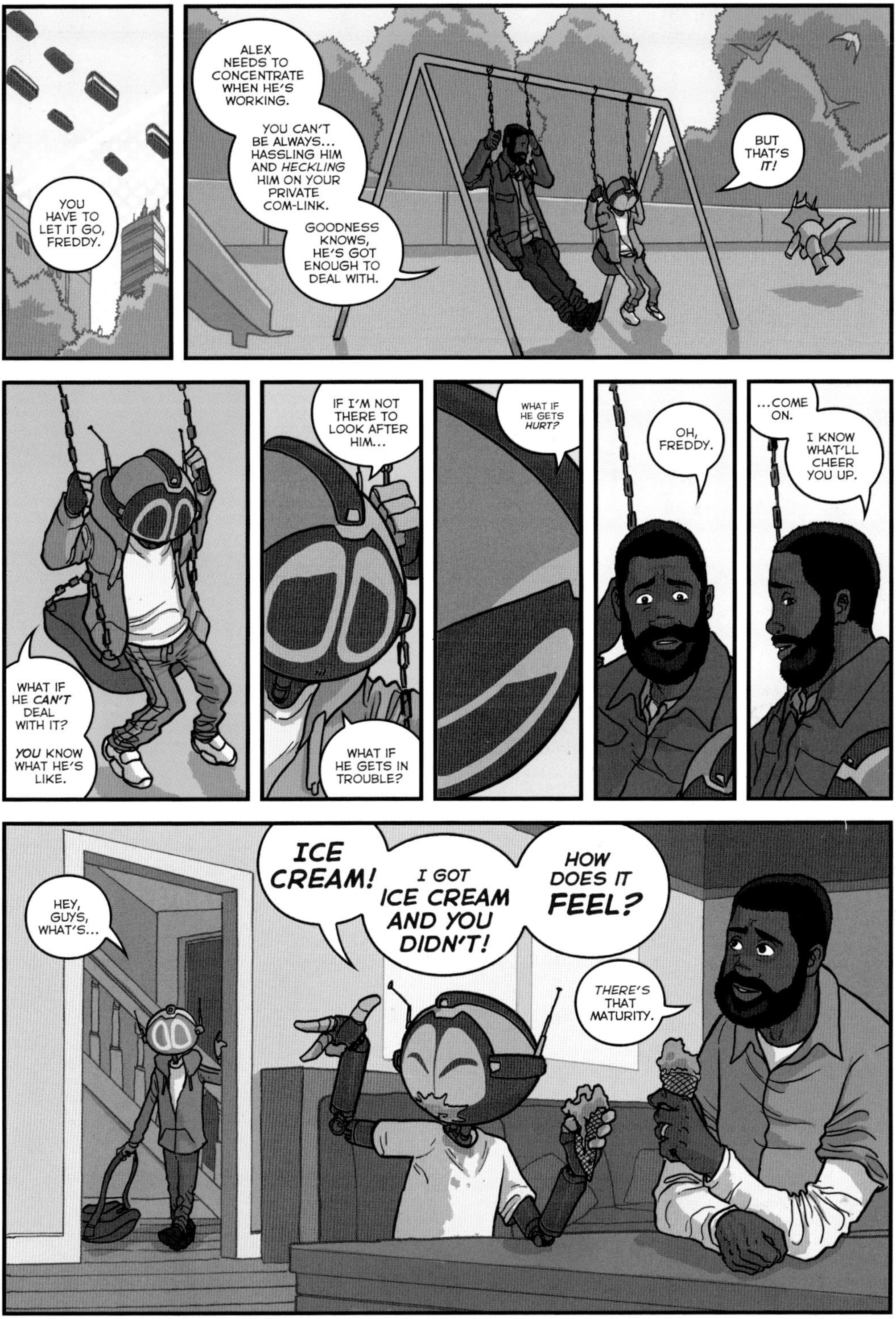
YOU HAVE TO LET IT GO, FREDDY.
ALEX NEEDS TO CONCENTRATE WHEN HE'S WORKING.
YOU CAN'T BE ALWAYS... HASSLING HIM AND HECKLING HIM ON YOUR PRIVATE COM-LINK.
GOODNESS KNOWS, HE'S GOT ENOUGH TO DEAL WITH.
BUT THAT'S IT!
WHAT IF HE CAN'T DEAL WITH IT?
YOU KNOW WHAT HE'S LIKE.
IF I'M NOT THERE TO LOOK AFTER HIM...
WHAT IF HE GETS IN TROUBLE?
WHAT IF HE GETS HURT?
OH, FREDDY.
...COME ON.
I KNOW WHAT'LL CHEER YOU UP.
HEY, GUYS, WHAT'S...
ICE CREAM!
I GOT ICE CREAM AND YOU DIDN'T!
HOW DOES IT FEEL?
THERE'S THAT MATURITY.

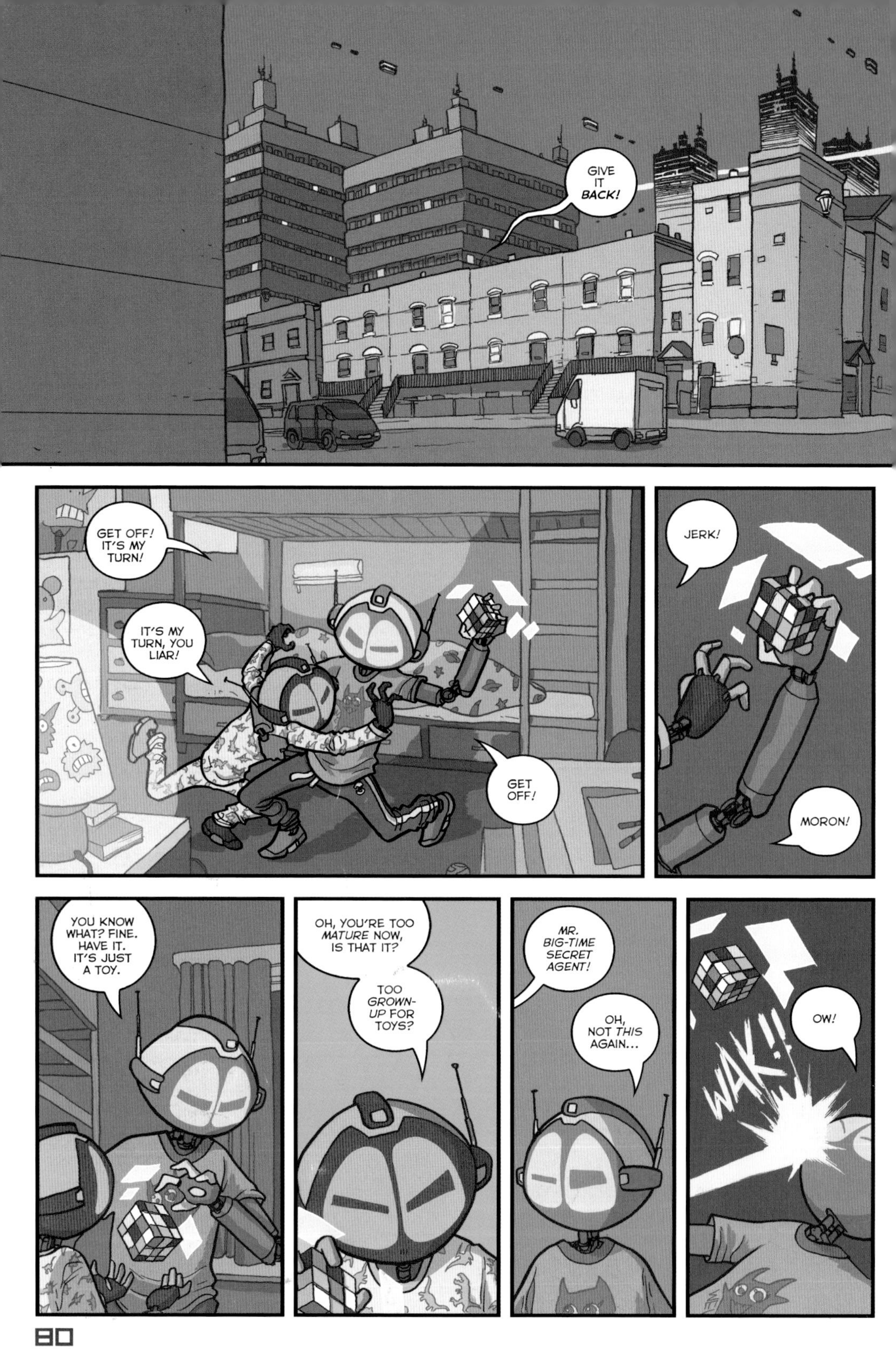
GIVE IT BACK!
GET OFF! IT'S MY TURN!
IT'S MY TURN, YOU LIAR!
GET OFF!
JERK!
MORON!
YOU KNOW WHAT? FINE. HAVE IT. IT'S JUST A TOY.
OH, YOU'RE TOO MATURE NOW, IS THAT IT?
TOO GROWN-UP FOR TOYS?
MR. BIG-TIME SECRET AGENT!
OH, NOT THIS AGAIN...
WAK!!
OW!

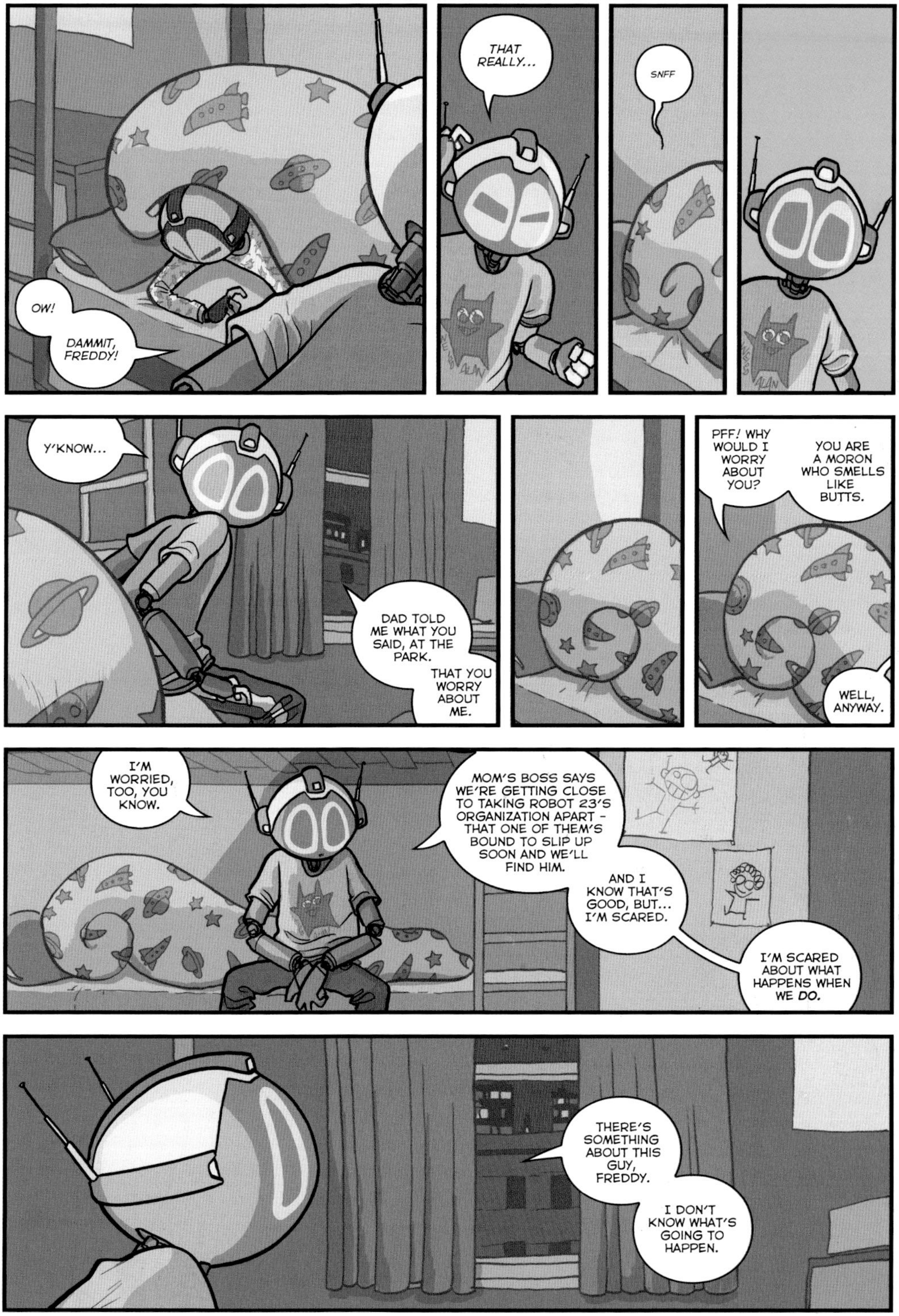
OW!
DAMMIT, FREDDY!
THAT REALLY...
SNFF
Y'KNOW...
DAD TOLD ME WHAT YOU SAID, AT THE PARK.
THAT YOU WORRY ABOUT ME.
PFF! WHY WOULD I WORRY ABOUT YOU?
YOU ARE A MORON WHO SMELLS LIKE BUTTS.
WELL, ANYWAY.
I'M WORRIED, TOO, YOU KNOW.
MOM'S BOSS SAYS WE'RE GETTING CLOSE TO TAKING ROBOT 23'S ORGANIZATION APART - THAT ONE OF THEM'S BOUND TO SLIP UP SOON AND WE'LL FIND HIM.
AND I KNOW THAT'S GOOD, BUT... I'M SCARED.
I'M SCARED ABOUT WHAT HAPPENS WHEN WE *DO.*
THERE'S SOMETHING ABOUT THIS GUY, FREDDY.
I DON'T KNOW WHAT'S GOING TO HAPPEN.

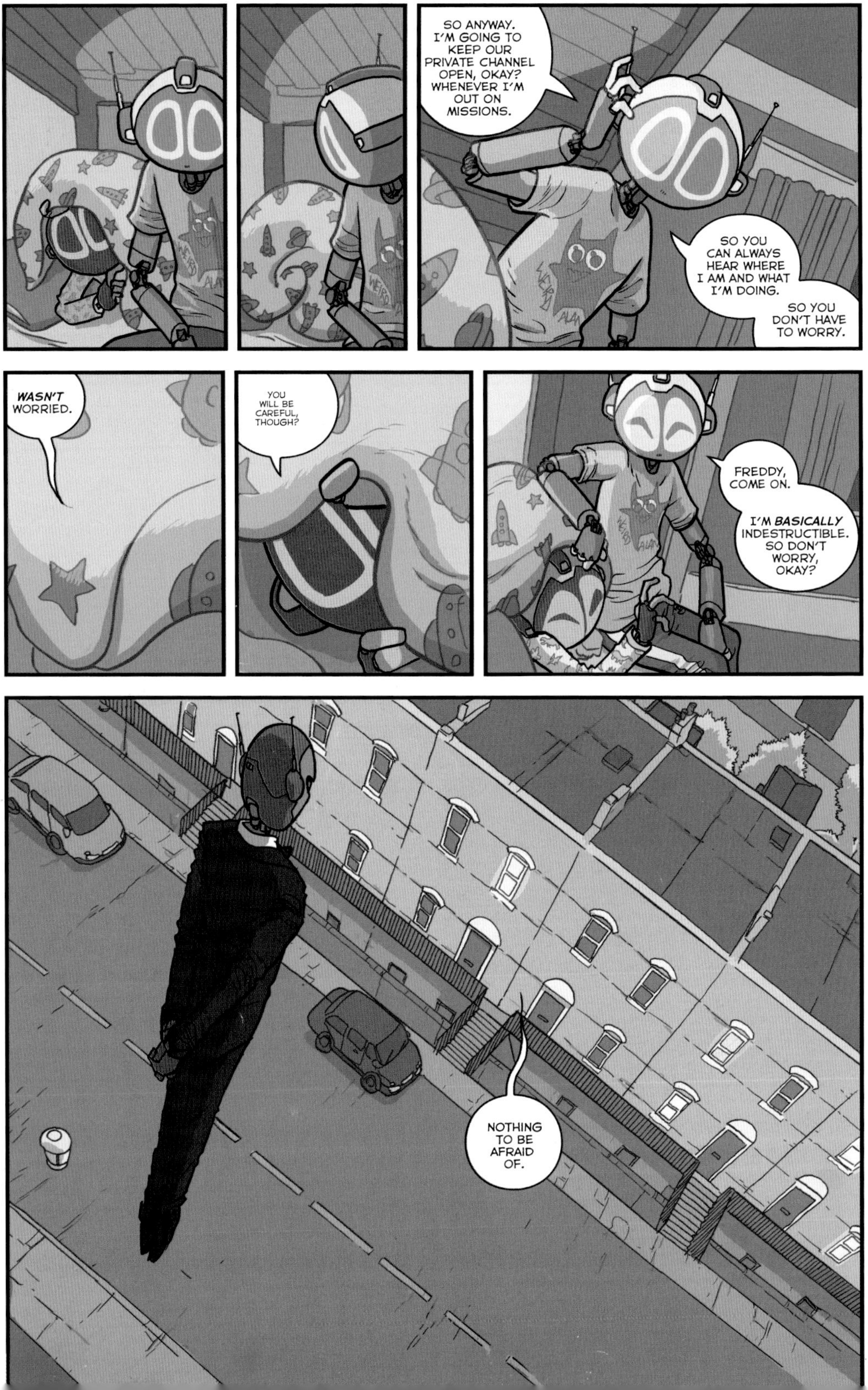
SO ANYWAY. I'M GOING TO KEEP OUR PRIVATE CHANNEL OPEN, OKAY? WHENEVER I'M OUT ON MISSIONS.
SO YOU CAN ALWAYS HEAR WHERE I AM AND WHAT I'M DOING.
SO YOU DON'T HAVE TO WORRY.
WASN'T WORRIED.
YOU WILL BE CAREFUL, THOUGH?
FREDDY, COME ON.
I'M *BASICALLY* INDESTRUCTIBLE. SO DON'T WORRY, OKAY?
NOTHING TO BE AFRAID OF.

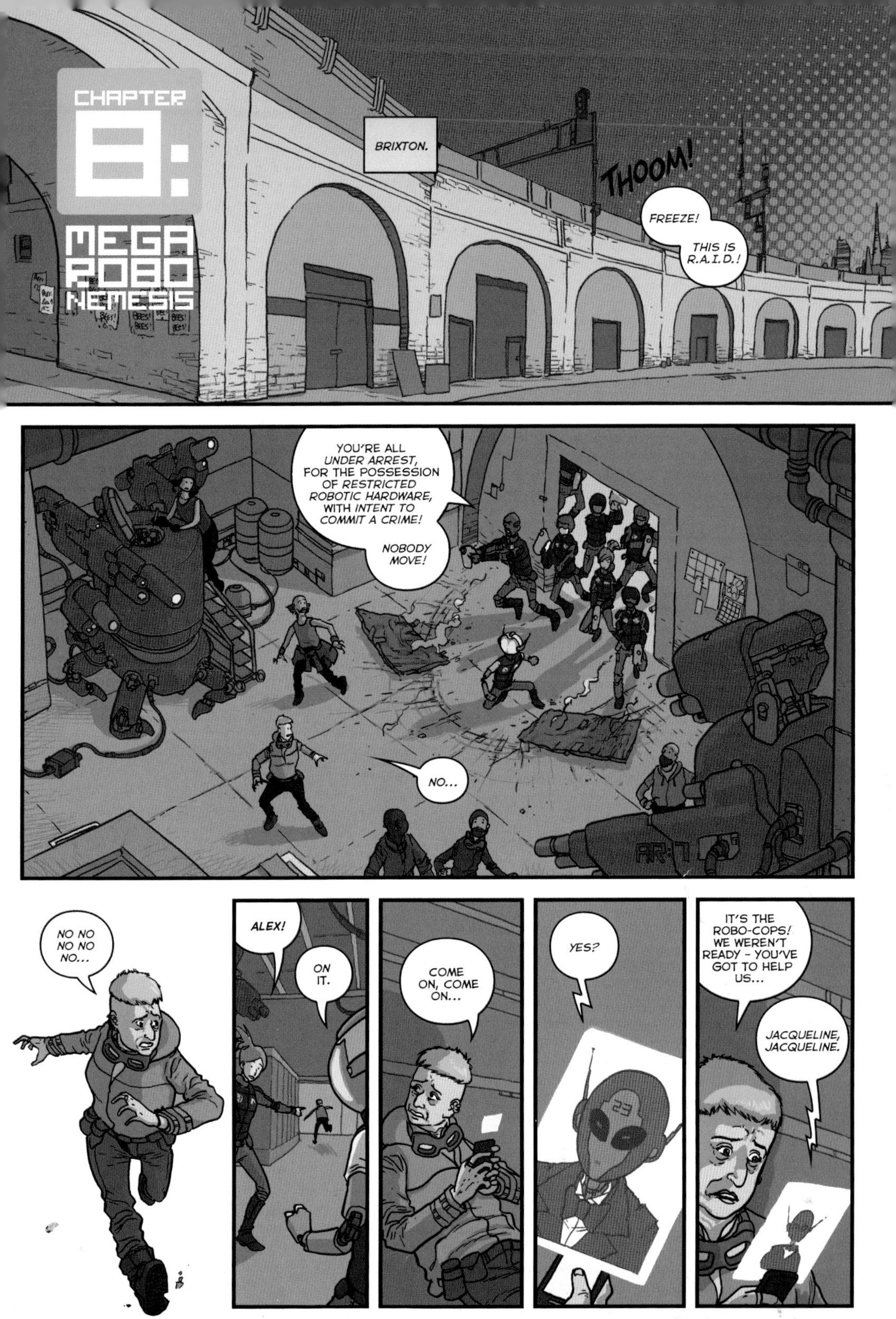
CHAPTER 8:
MEGA ROBO NEMESIS
BRIXTON.
THOOM!
FREEZE!
THIS IS R.A.I.D.!
YOU'RE ALL UNDER ARREST, FOR THE POSSESSION OF RESTRICTED ROBOTIC HARDWARE, WITH INTENT TO COMMIT A CRIME!
NOBODY MOVE!
NO...
NO NO NO NO NO...
ALEX!
ON IT.
COME ON, COME ON...
YES?
IT'S THE ROBO-COPS! WE WEREN'T READY - YOU'VE GOT TO HELP US...
JACQUELINE, JACQUELINE.

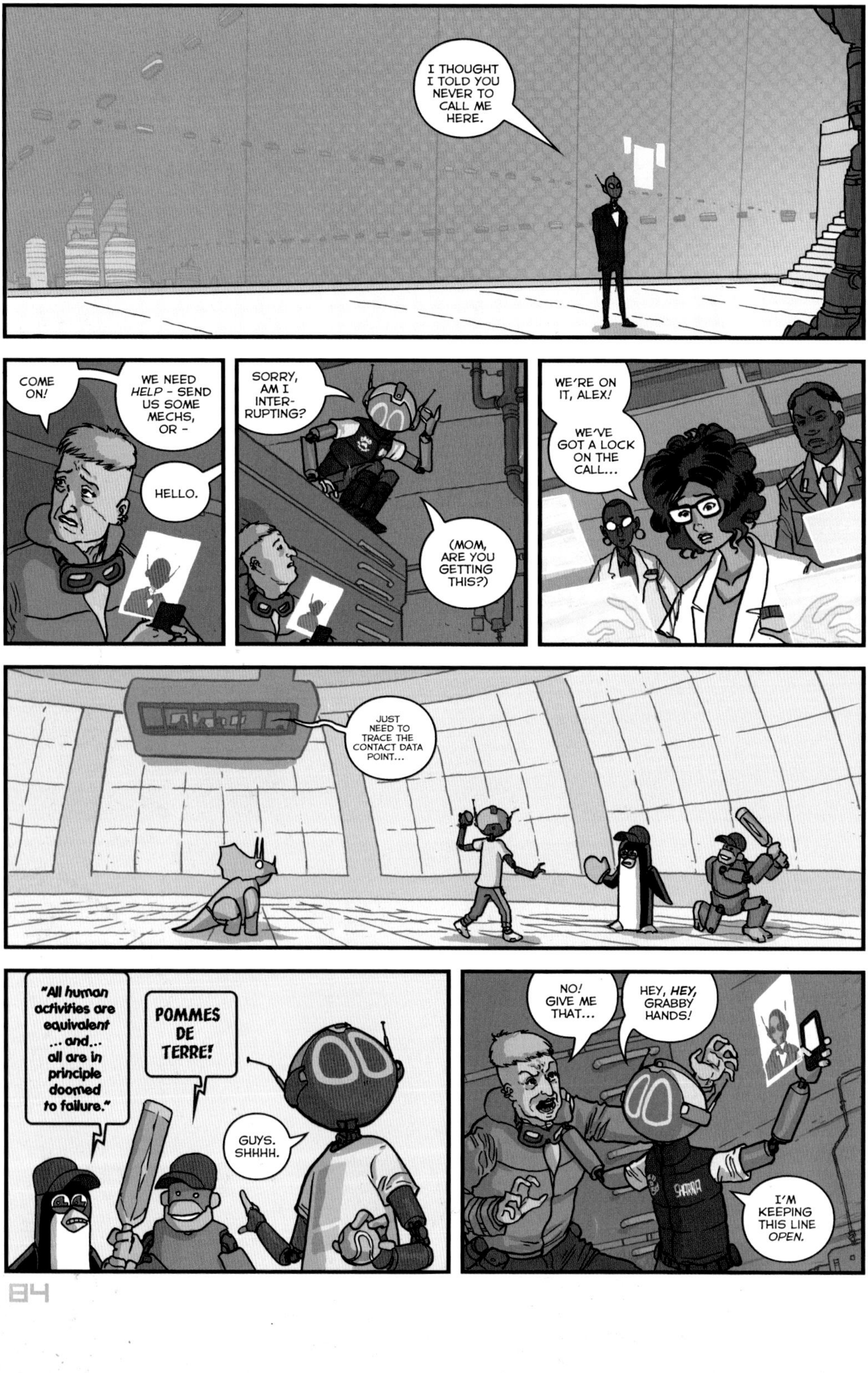
I THOUGHT I TOLD YOU NEVER TO CALL ME HERE.
COME ON!
WE NEED HELP - SEND US SOME MECHS, OR -
HELLO.
SORRY, AM I INTER-RUPTING?
(MOM, ARE YOU GETTING THIS?)
WE'RE ON IT, ALEX!
WE'VE GOT A LOCK ON THE CALL...
JUST NEED TO TRACE THE CONTACT DATA POINT...
"All human activities are equivalent ... and... all are in principle doomed to failure."
POMMES DE TERRE!
GUYS. SHHHH.
NO! GIVE ME THAT...
HEY, HEY, GRABBY HANDS!
I'M KEEPING THIS LINE OPEN.

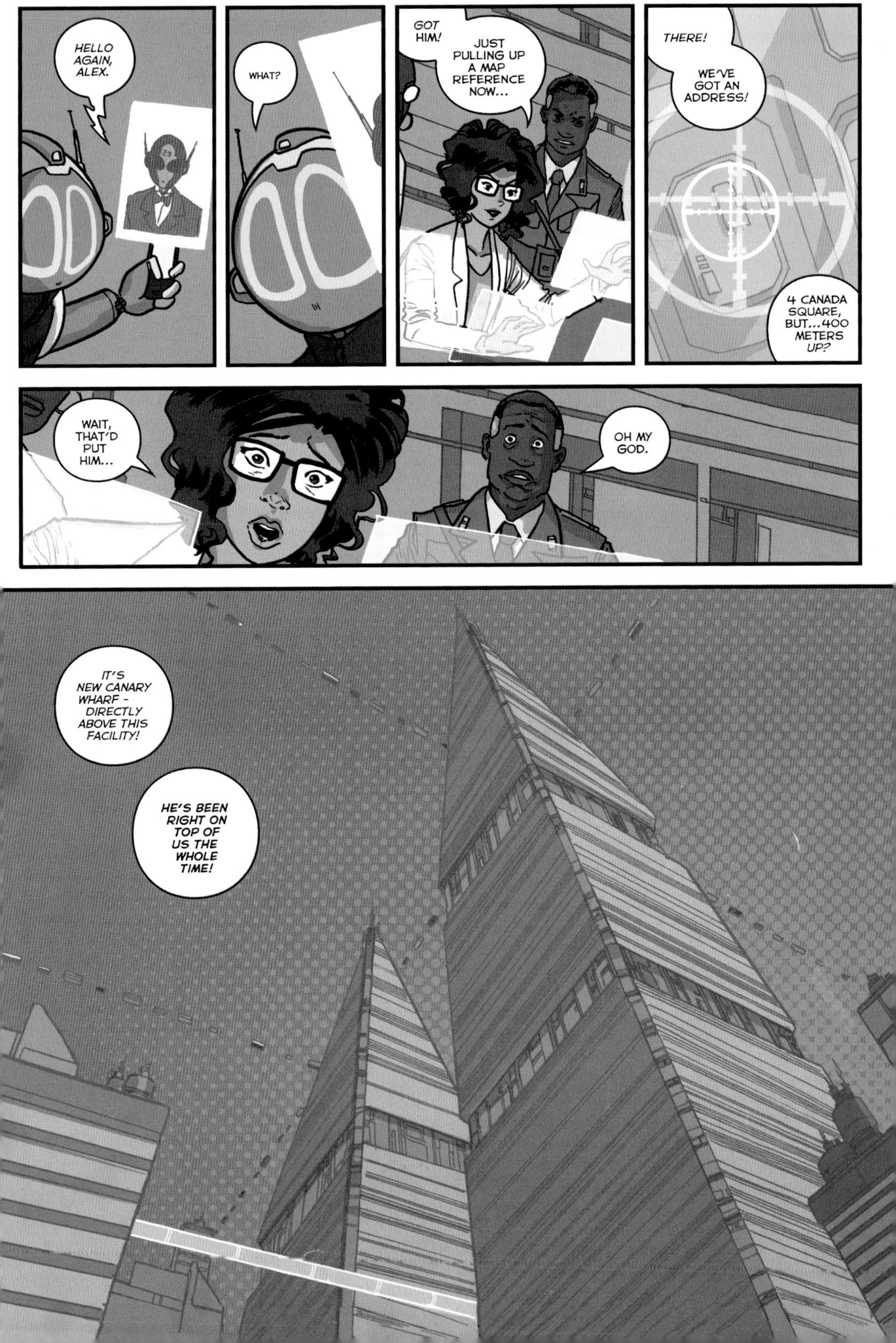
HELLO AGAIN, ALEX.
WHAT?
GOT HIM!
JUST PULLING UP A MAP REFERENCE NOW...
THERE!
WE'VE GOT AN ADDRESS!
4 CANADA SQUARE, BUT...400 METERS UP?
WAIT, THAT'D PUT HIM...
OH MY GOD.
IT'S NEW CANARY WHARF - DIRECTLY ABOVE THIS FACILITY!
HE'S BEEN RIGHT ON TOP OF US THE WHOLE TIME!

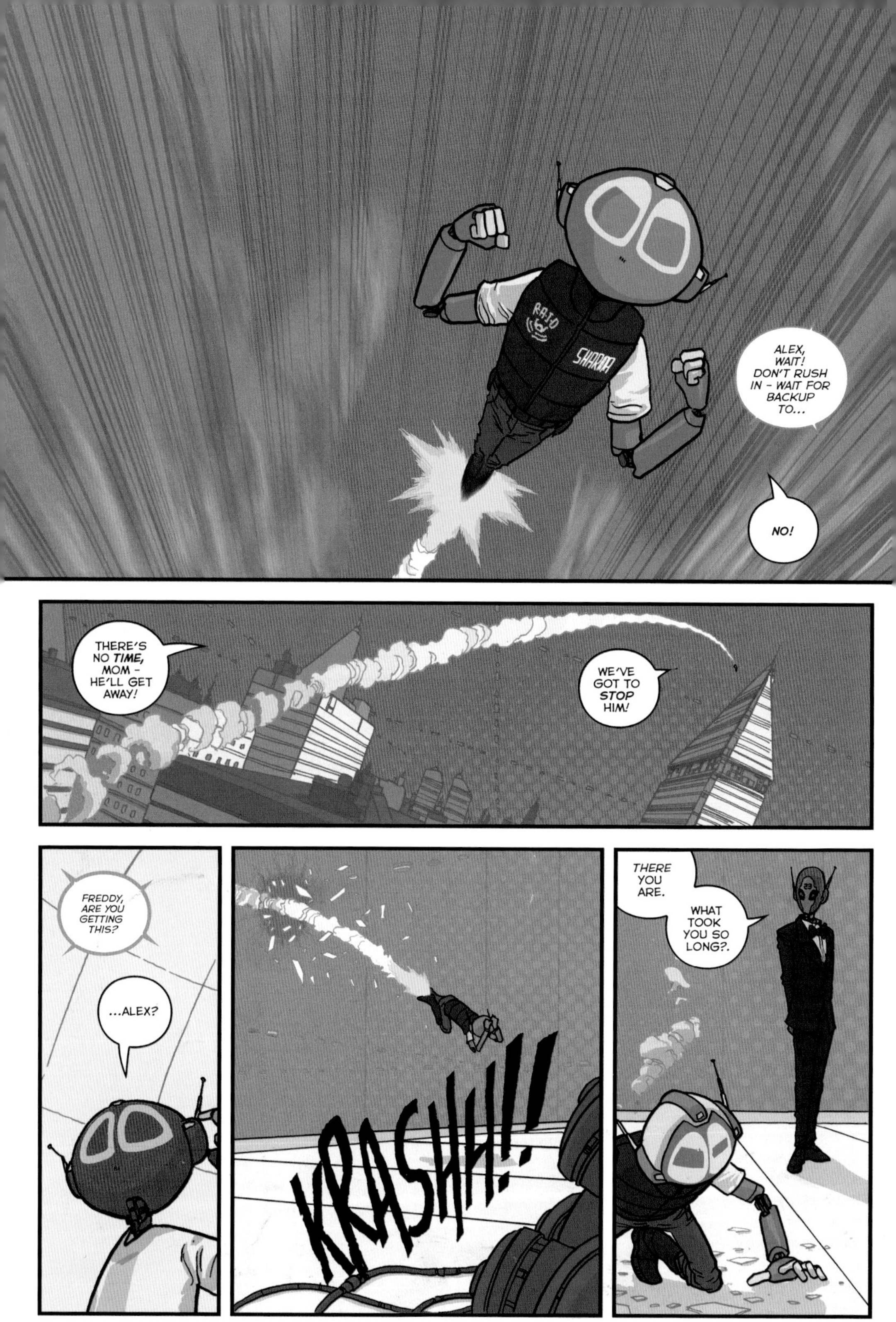
ALEX, WAIT! DON'T RUSH IN - WAIT FOR BACKUP TO...
NO!
THERE'S NO TIME, MOM - HE'LL GET AWAY!
WE'VE GOT TO STOP HIM!
FREDDY, ARE YOU GETTING THIS?
...ALEX?
KRASHH!!
THERE YOU ARE.
WHAT TOOK YOU SO LONG?.

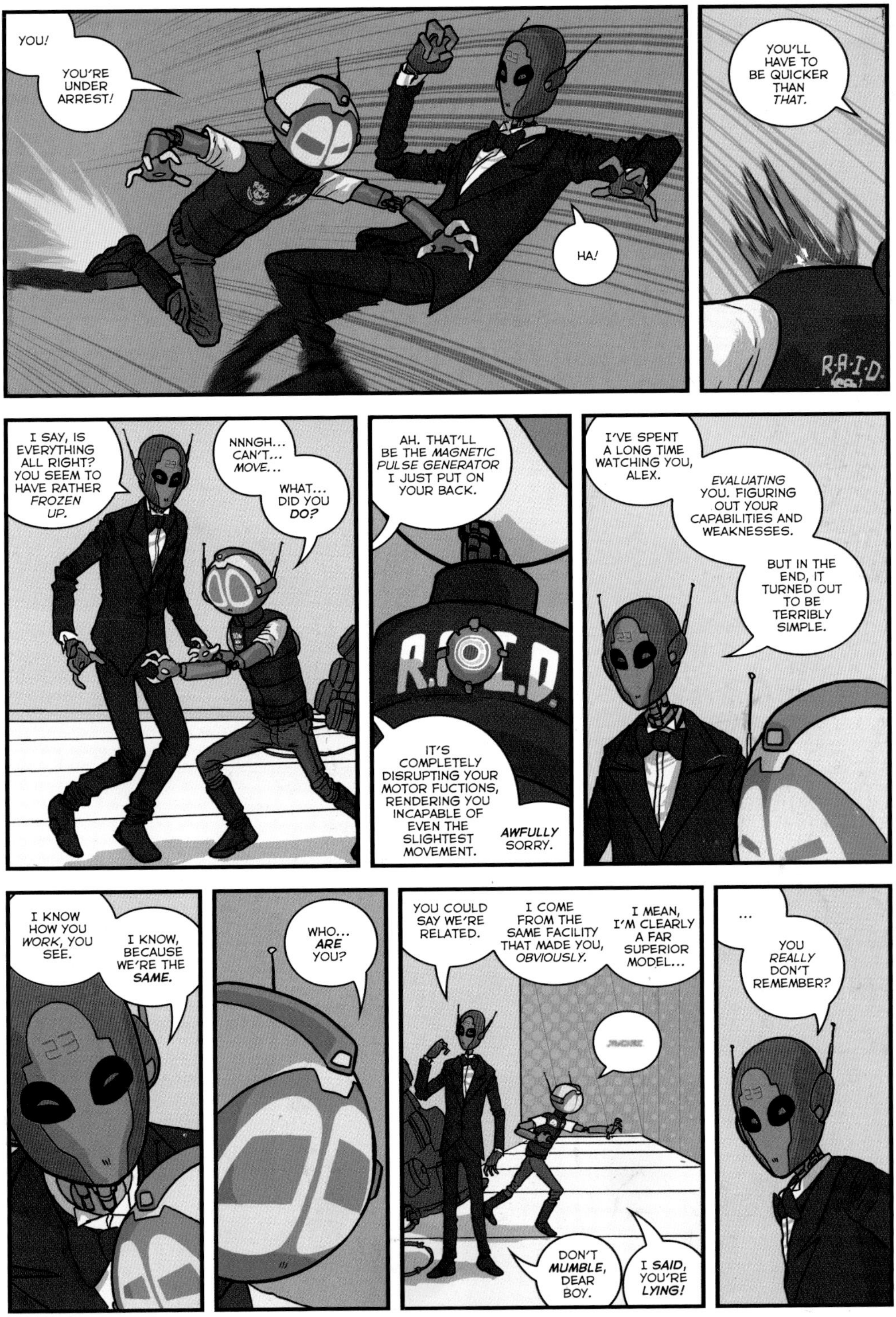
YOU!
YOU'RE UNDER ARREST!
HA!
YOU'LL HAVE TO BE QUICKER THAN *THAT.*
R.A.I.D.
I SAY, IS EVERYTHING ALL RIGHT? YOU SEEM TO HAVE RATHER *FROZEN* UP.
NNNGH... CAN'T... *MOVE...*
WHAT... DID YOU ***DO?***
AH. THAT'LL BE THE *MAGNETIC PULSE GENERATOR* I JUST PUT ON YOUR BACK.
IT'S COMPLETELY DISRUPTING YOUR MOTOR FUCTIONS, RENDERING YOU INCAPABLE OF EVEN THE SLIGHTEST MOVEMENT.
AWFULLY SORRY.
I'VE SPENT A LONG TIME WATCHING YOU, ALEX.
EVALUATING YOU. FIGURING OUT YOUR CAPABILITIES AND WEAKNESSES.
BUT IN THE END, IT TURNED OUT TO BE TERRIBLY SIMPLE.
I KNOW HOW YOU *WORK*, YOU SEE.
I KNOW, BECAUSE WE'RE THE ***SAME.***
WHO... ***ARE*** YOU?
YOU COULD SAY WE'RE RELATED.
I COME FROM THE SAME FACILITY THAT MADE YOU, *OBVIOUSLY.*
I MEAN, I'M CLEARLY A FAR SUPERIOR MODEL...
DON'T ***MUMBLE***, DEAR BOY.
I ***SAID,*** YOU'RE ***LYING!***
...
YOU *REALLY* DON'T REMEMBER?

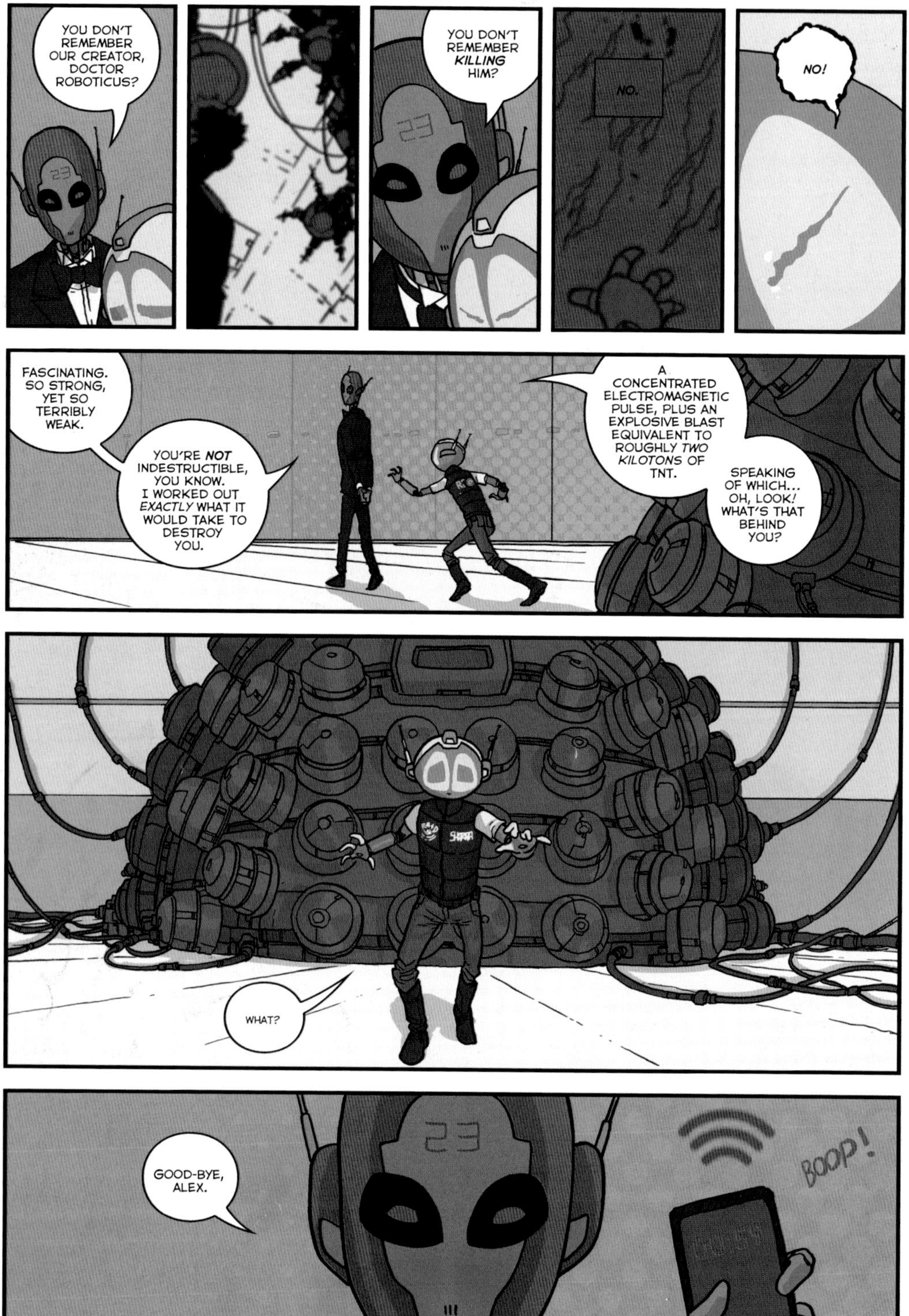
YOU DON'T REMEMBER OUR CREATOR, DOCTOR ROBOTICUS?
YOU DON'T REMEMBER *KILLING* HIM?
NO.
NO!
FASCINATING. SO STRONG, YET SO TERRIBLY WEAK.
YOU'RE ***NOT*** INDESTRUCTIBLE, YOU KNOW. I WORKED OUT *EXACTLY* WHAT IT WOULD TAKE TO DESTROY YOU.
A CONCENTRATED ELECTROMAGNETIC PULSE, PLUS AN EXPLOSIVE BLAST EQUIVALENT TO ROUGHLY *TWO KILOTONS* OF TNT.
SPEAKING OF WHICH... OH, LOOK*!* WHAT'S THAT BEHIND YOU?
WHAT?
GOOD-BYE, ALEX.
BOOP!

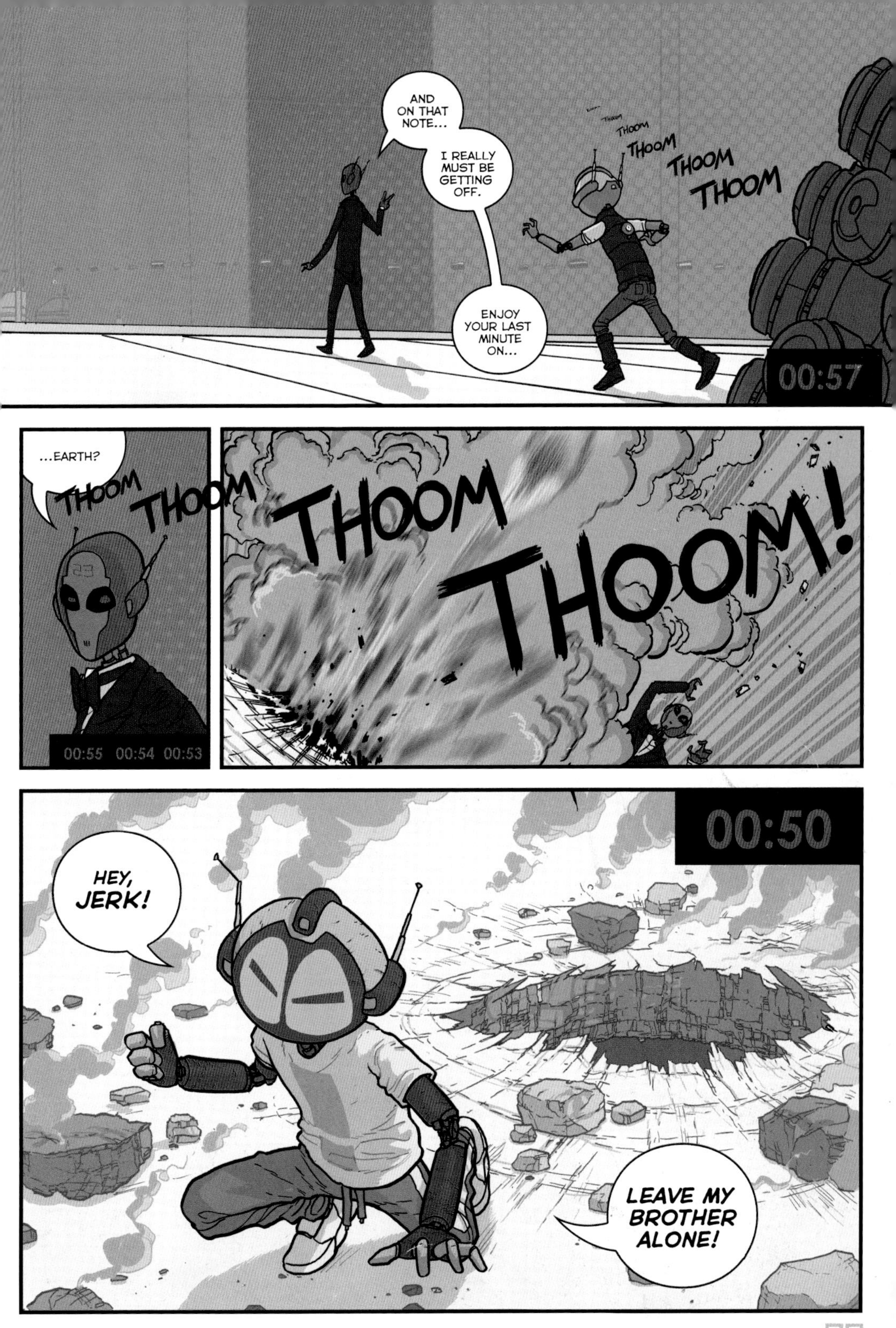

AND ON THAT NOTE...
I REALLY MUST BE GETTING OFF.
ENJOY YOUR LAST MINUTE ON...
THOOM
THOOM
THOOM
THOOM
THOOM
00:57
...EARTH?
THOOM
THOOM
00:55 00:54 00:53
THOOM
THOOM!
00:50
HEY, JERK!
LEAVE MY BROTHER ALONE!

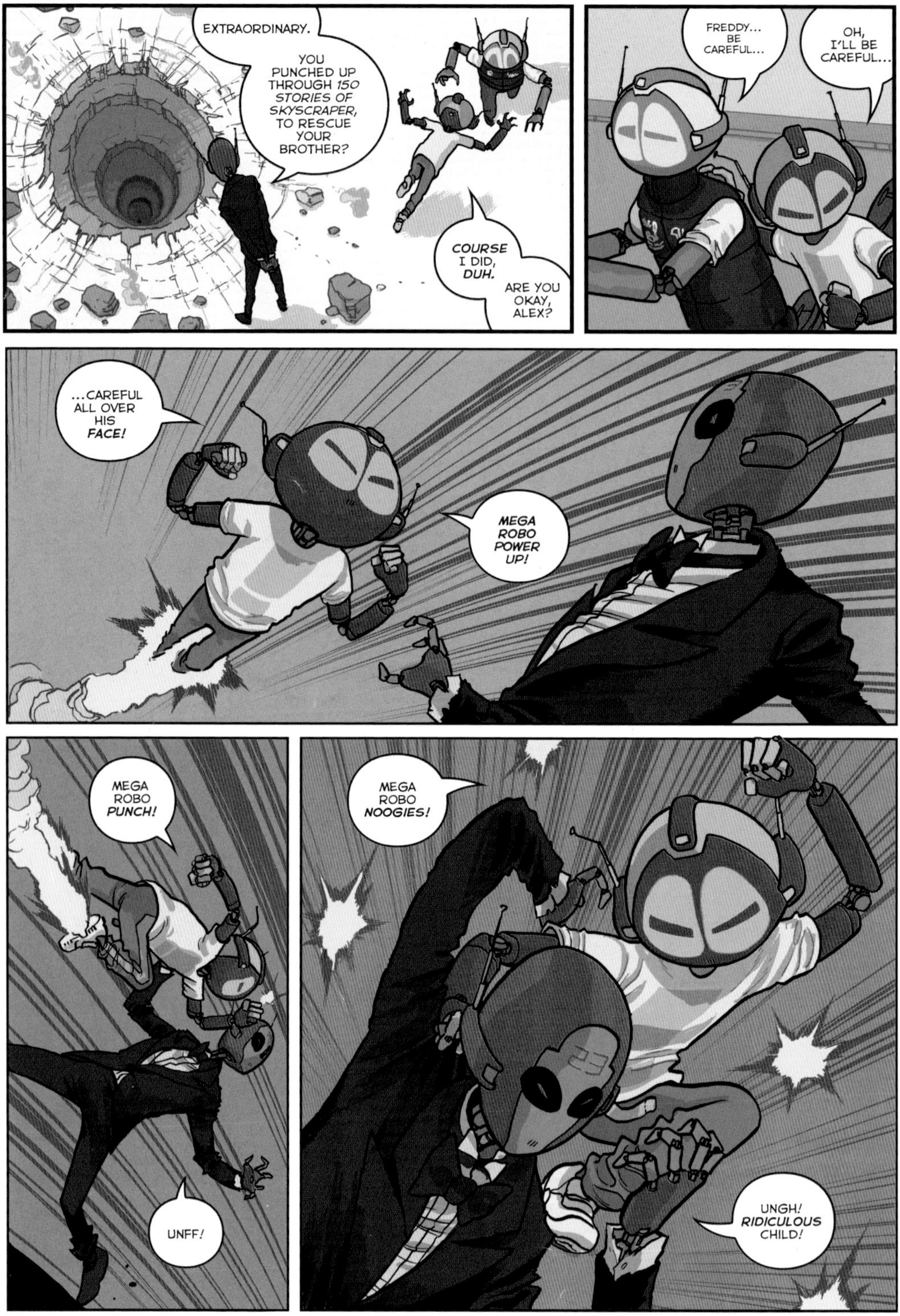
EXTRAORDINARY.
YOU PUNCHED UP THROUGH *150* *STORIES OF SKYSCRAPER*, TO RESCUE YOUR BROTHER?
COURSE I DID, *DUH.*
ARE YOU OKAY, ALEX?
FREDDY... BE CAREFUL...
OH, I'LL BE CAREFUL...
...CAREFUL ALL OVER HIS *FACE!*
MEGA ROBO POWER UP!
MEGA ROBO *PUNCH!*
UNFF!
MEGA ROBO *NOOGIES!*
UNGH! *RIDICULOUS* CHILD!

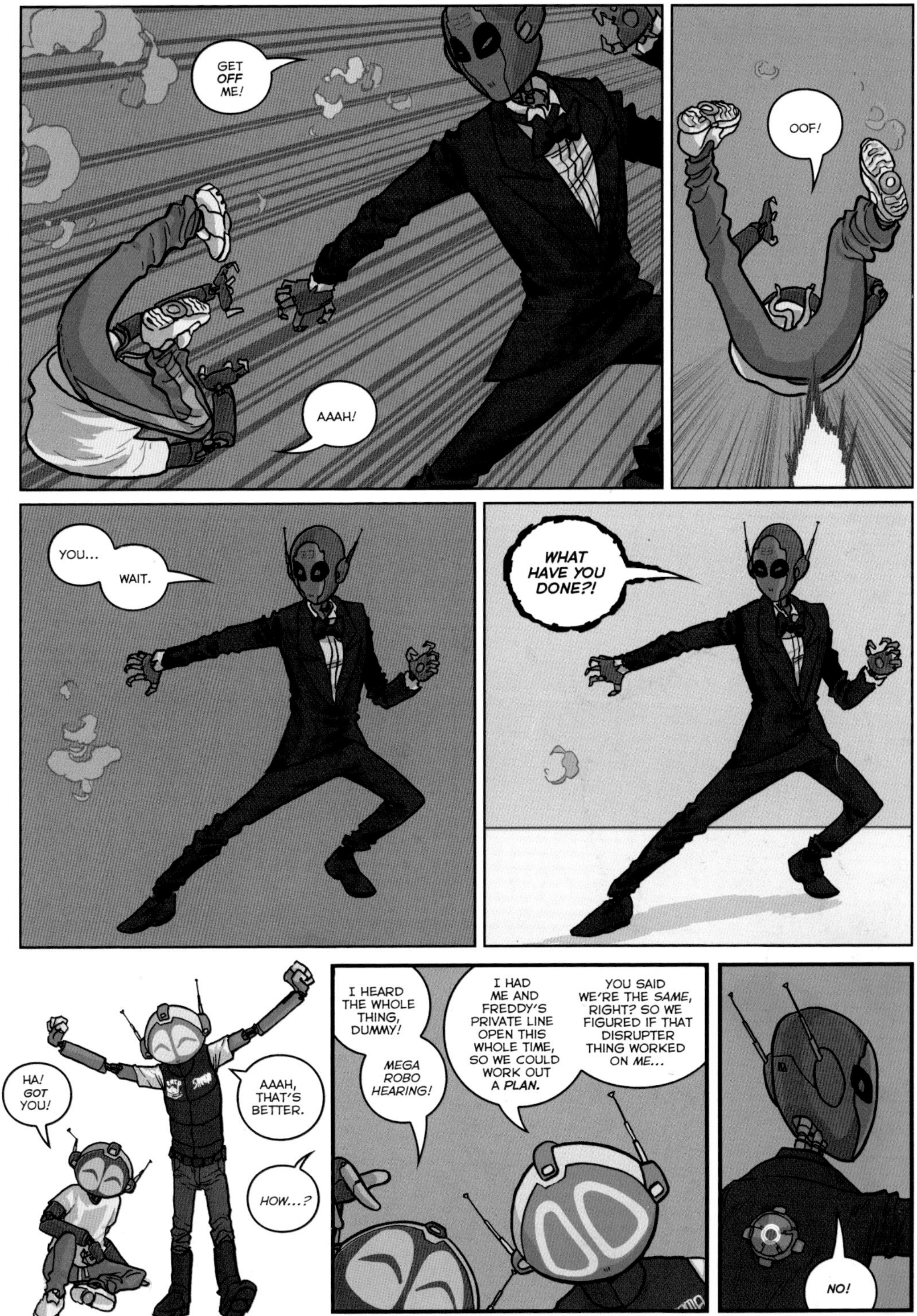
GET OFF ME!
AAAH!
OOF!
YOU... WAIT.
WHAT HAVE YOU DONE?!
HA! GOT YOU!
AAAH, THAT'S BETTER.
HOW...?
I HEARD THE WHOLE THING, DUMMY!
MEGA ROBO HEARING!
I HAD ME AND FREDDY'S PRIVATE LINE OPEN THIS WHOLE TIME, SO WE COULD WORK OUT A PLAN.
YOU SAID WE'RE THE SAME, RIGHT? SO WE FIGURED IF THAT DISRUPTER THING WORKED ON ME...
NO!

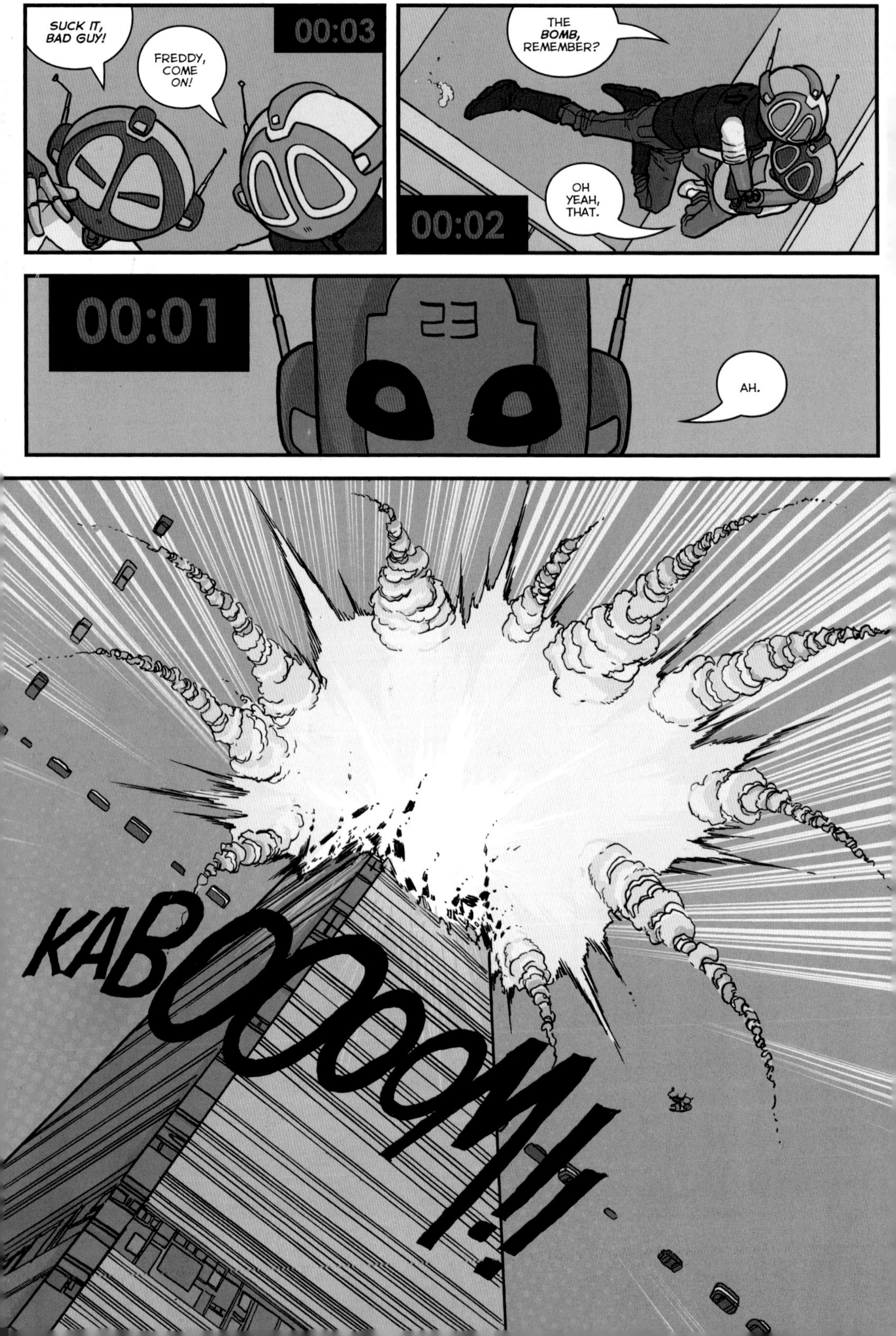
SUCK IT, BAD GUY!
FREDDY, COME ON!
00:03
THE BOMB, REMEMBER?
OH YEAH, THAT.
00:02
00:01
23
AH.
KABOOOOM!!!

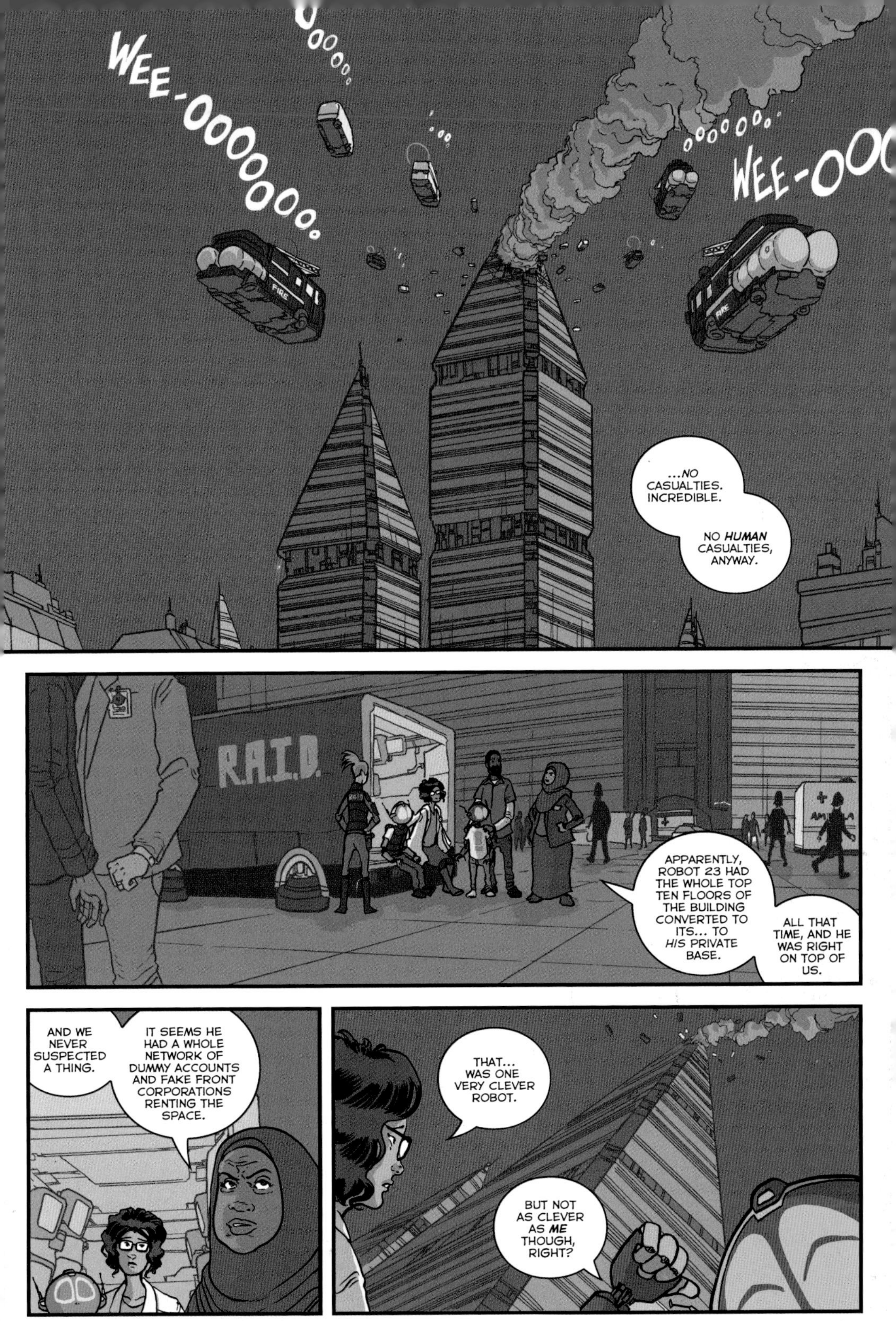
WEE-OOOOOOOOo
WEE-OOO
...NO CASUALTIES. INCREDIBLE.
NO HUMAN CASUALTIES, ANYWAY.
R.A.I.D.
APPARENTLY, ROBOT 23 HAD THE WHOLE TOP TEN FLOORS OF THE BUILDING CONVERTED TO ITS... TO HIS PRIVATE BASE.
ALL THAT TIME, AND HE WAS RIGHT ON TOP OF US.
AND WE NEVER SUSPECTED A THING.
IT SEEMS HE HAD A WHOLE NETWORK OF DUMMY ACCOUNTS AND FAKE FRONT CORPORATIONS RENTING THE SPACE.
THAT... WAS ONE VERY CLEVER ROBOT.
BUT NOT AS CLEVER AS ME THOUGH, RIGHT?

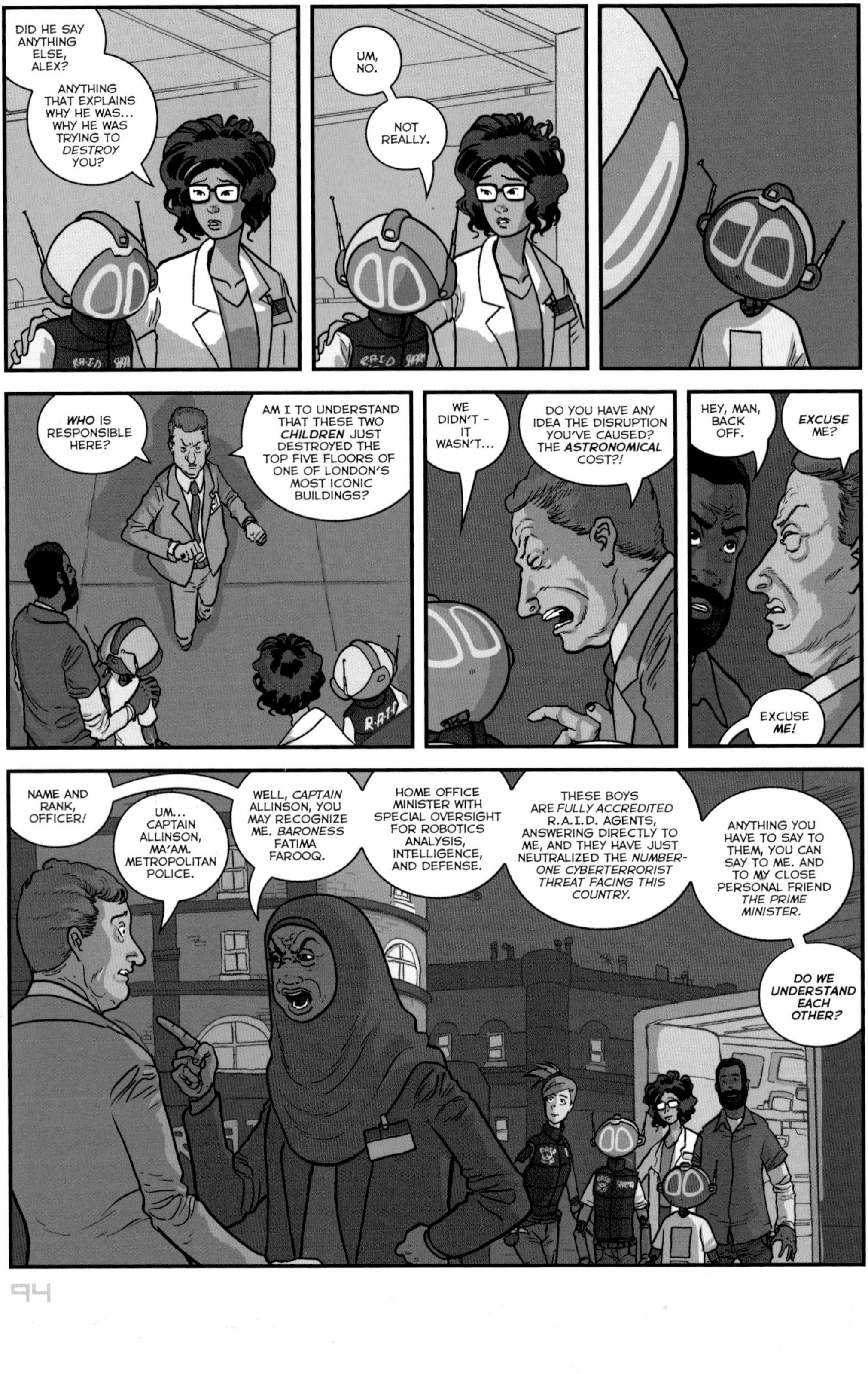
DID HE SAY ANYTHING ELSE, ALEX?
ANYTHING THAT EXPLAINS WHY HE WAS... WHY HE WAS TRYING TO *DESTROY* YOU?
UM, NO.
NOT REALLY.
WHO IS RESPONSIBLE HERE?
AM I TO UNDERSTAND THAT THESE TWO ***CHILDREN*** JUST DESTROYED THE TOP FIVE FLOORS OF ONE OF LONDON'S MOST ICONIC BUILDINGS?
WE DIDN'T - IT WASN'T...
DO YOU HAVE ANY IDEA THE DISRUPTION YOU'VE CAUSED? THE ***ASTRONOMICAL*** COST?!
HEY, MAN, BACK OFF.
EXCUSE ME?
EXCUSE ***ME!***
NAME AND RANK, OFFICER!
UM... CAPTAIN ALLINSON, MA'AM. METROPOLITAN POLICE.
WELL, *CAPTAIN* ALLINSON, YOU MAY RECOGNIZE ME. *BARONESS* FATIMA FAROOQ.
HOME OFFICE MINISTER WITH SPECIAL OVERSIGHT FOR ROBOTICS ANALYSIS, INTELLIGENCE, AND DEFENSE.
THESE BOYS ARE *FULLY ACCREDITED* R.A.I.D. AGENTS, ANSWERING DIRECTLY TO ME, AND THEY HAVE JUST NEUTRALIZED THE *NUMBER-ONE CYBERTERRORIST THREAT FACING THIS COUNTRY.*
ANYTHING YOU HAVE TO SAY TO THEM, YOU CAN SAY TO ME. AND TO *MY* CLOSE PERSONAL FRIEND *THE PRIME MINISTER.*
DO WE UNDERSTAND EACH OTHER?

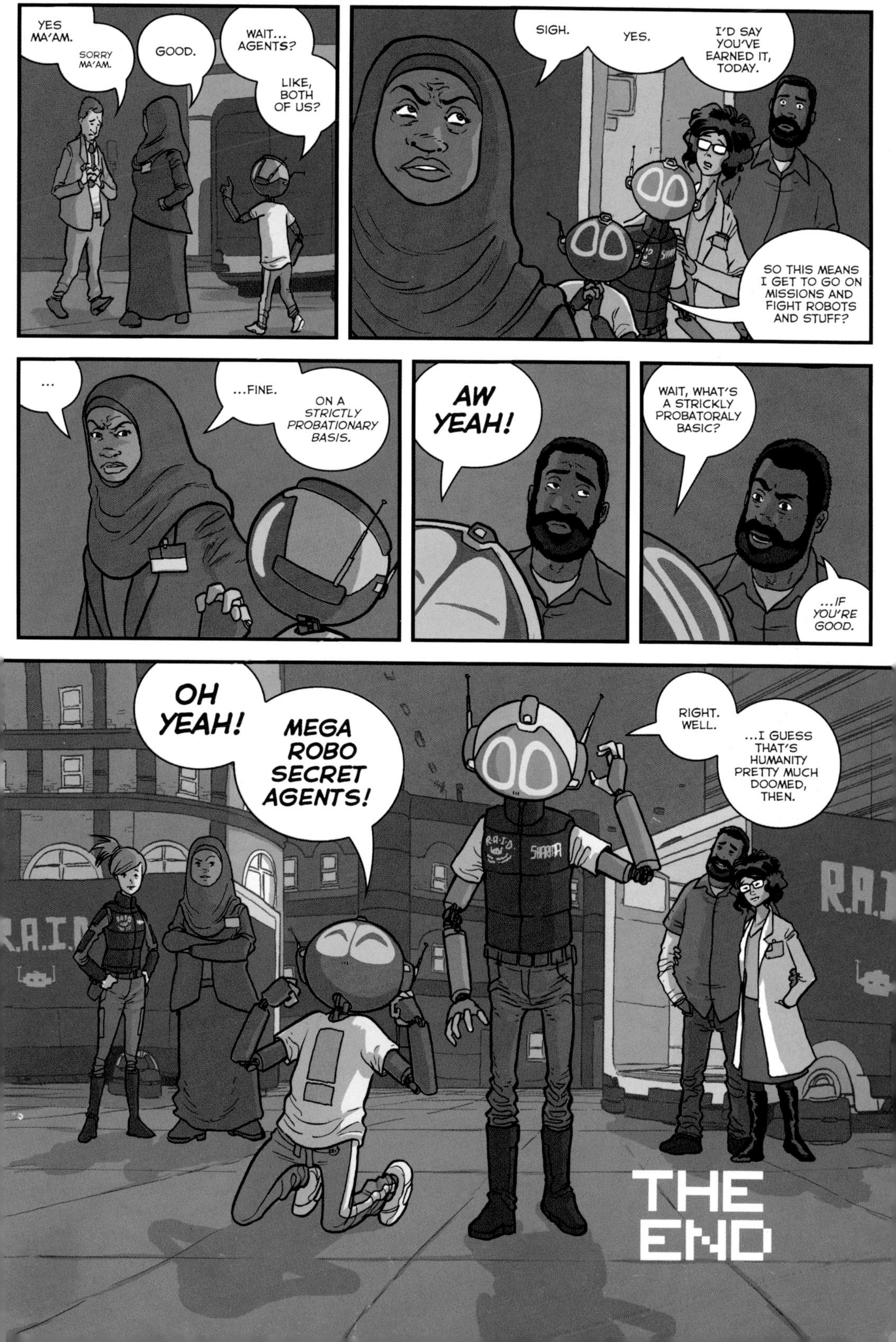
YES MA'AM.
SORRY MA'AM.
GOOD.
WAIT... AGENTS?
LIKE, BOTH OF US?
SIGH.
YES.
I'D SAY YOU'VE EARNED IT, TODAY.
SO THIS MEANS I GET TO GO ON MISSIONS AND FIGHT ROBOTS AND STUFF?
...
...FINE.
ON A STRICTLY PROBATIONARY BASIS.
AW YEAH!
WAIT, WHAT'S A STRICKLY PROBATORALY BASIC?
...IF YOU'RE GOOD.
OH YEAH!
MEGA ROBO SECRET AGENTS!
RIGHT. WELL.
...I GUESS THAT'S HUMANITY PRETTY MUCH DOOMED, THEN.
THE END

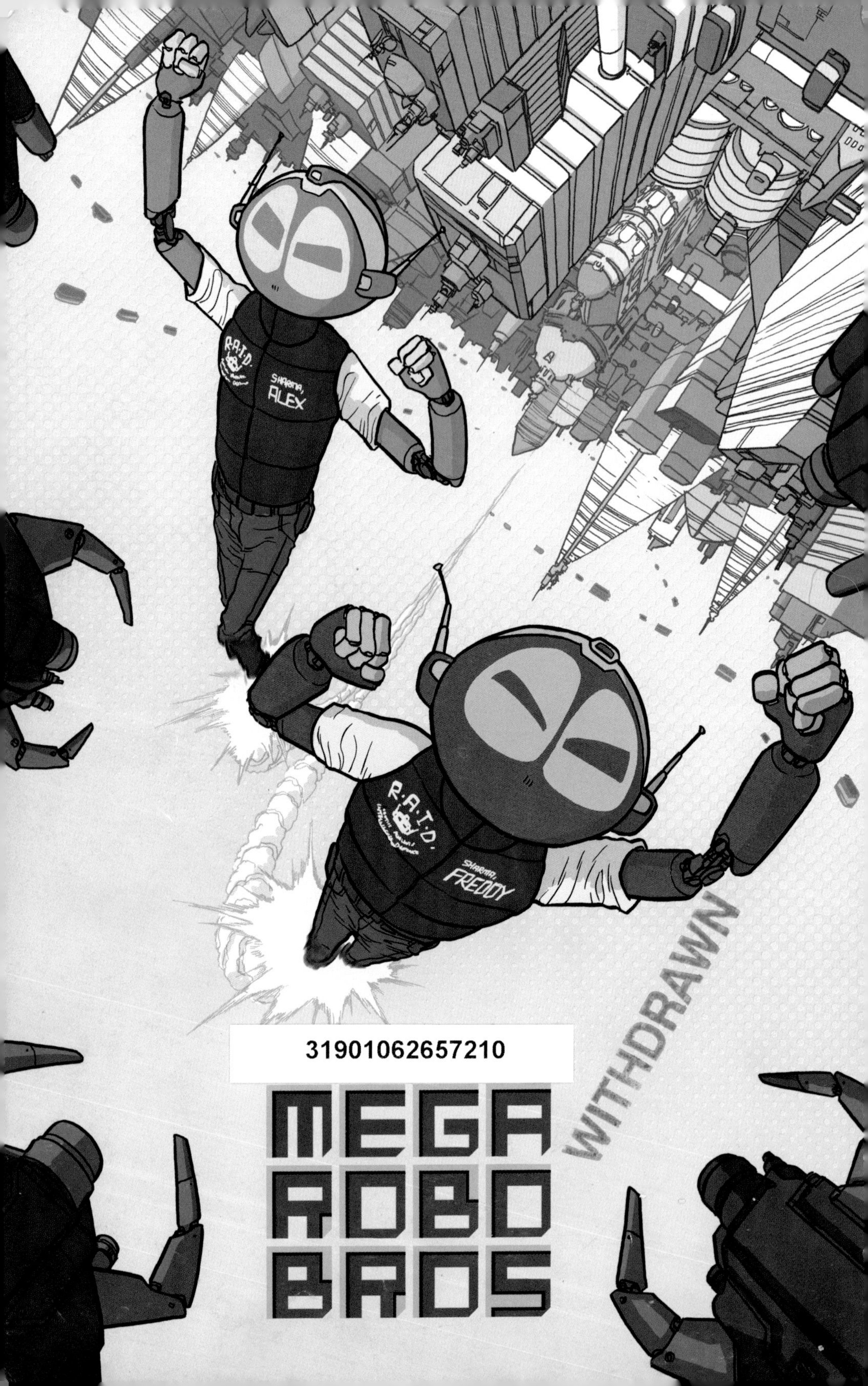
R.A.I.D.
SHARMA, ALEX
R.A.I.D.
SHARMA, FREDDY
MEGA
ROBO
BROS